"I'm in love with you, Kyla."

She turned her back on him. "Stop saying that. Please."

He moved behind her. She felt him there even before he placed his hands on her shoulders. His warmth crept over her back the way the sun glides over the beach at dawn.

"What are you afraid of, Kyla? Are you afraid of what you're feeling?"

"I'm not feeling anything."

"You're feeling something." He moved her hair aside and trailed his finger from one side of her nape to the other. "You kissed me back."

"It didn't mean anything."

"Didn't it?"

"Only that I hadn't been kissed in a long time."

"And it felt good?"

"Yes . . . no . . . please. I can't talk about this with you."

"It felt good to me, Kyla. So damn good. And right."

Dear Reader,

When two people fall in love, the world is suddenly new and exciting, and it's that same excitement we bring to you in Silhouette Intimate Moments. These are stories with scope, with grandeur. These characters lead the lives we all dream of, and everything they do reflects the wonder of being in love.

Longer and more sensuous than most romances, Silhouette Intimate Moments novels take you away from everyday life and let you share the magic of love. Adventure, glamour, drama, even suspense—these are the passwords that let you into a world where love has a power beyond the ordinary, where the best authors in the field today create stories of love and commitment that will stay with you always.

In coming months look for novels by your favorite authors: Maura Seger, Parris Afton Bonds, Elizabeth Lowell and Erin St. Claire, to name just a few. And whenever you buy books, look for all the Silhouette Intimate Moments, love stories *for* today's women *by* today's women.

Leslie J. Wainger
Senior Editor
Silhouette Books

Above and Beyond

Erin St. Claire

Silhouette Intimate Moments

Published by Silhouette Books New York

America's Publisher of Contemporary Romance

SILHOUETTE BOOKS
300 E. 42nd St., New York, N.Y. 10017

ISBN: 0-373-07133-7

First Silhouette Books printing March 1986

America's Publisher of Contemporary Romance

Printed in the U.S.A.

ERIN ST. CLAIRE

has pursued several careers, but there is no occupation she enjoys more than writing. When asked why she writes romances, she replies, "I believe in happy endings, and I love a love story!" Erin St. Claire is a pseudonym for Sandra Brown, who also writes as Rachel Ryan.

Chapter 1

Y ou're doing fine, Kyla. Take quick, light breaths. That's right. Good, good. How do you feel?''

"Tired."

"I know, but hang in there. Go with the pains now and push. That's it. A little harder."

The young woman on the delivery table ground her teeth while the labor pain held her in its fierce grip. When it subsided, she forced her body to relax. Her face, though flushed and mottled, was radiant. "Can you see him yet?"

No sooner were the words out of her mouth than another pain seized her. She pushed with all her might.

"Now I can," the doctor said. "Give me one more push...there...here we are. All right!" he exclaimed when the new life slipped into his waiting hands.

"What is it?"

"A boy. Beautiful. Heavy son of a gun, too."

"And he's got great lungs," the obstetric nurse said, beaming down on Kyla.

"A boy," she murmured, pleased. She let the blessed lethargy steal over her and sank back onto the table. "Let me see him. Is he all right?"

"He's perfect," the doctor reassured her as he held up the squirming, crying baby boy where his mother could see him.

Tears stung Kyla's eyes when she saw her son for the first time. "Aaron. That's what we're naming him. Aaron Powers Stroud." For a moment she was allowed the privilege of holding him on her chest. Emotion welled inside her.

"He's a boy his daddy can be proud of," the nurse said. She lifted the baby from Kyla's weak arms, wrapped him in a soft blanket and carried him across the room to be weighed. The doctor was attending Kyla, though it had been an easy, routine birth.

"How soon before you can notify your husband?" the doctor asked.

"My parents are standing by outside. Dad's promised to send Richard a telegram."

"He's nine pounds three ounces," the nurse called out from across the room.

The obstetrician peeled off his gloves and took Kyla's limp hand. "I'll go out now and break the news so he can get that telegram on its way. Where did you say Richard was stationed?"

"Cairo," Kyla replied absently. She was watching Aaron kick angrily as he was footprinted. He was beautiful. Richard would be so proud of him.

Considering that Aaron had been born at dusk, she spent a reasonably peaceful night. They brought him to her twice during the night, though her milk hadn't started and he wasn't hungry yet. The pleasure of holding his warm little body against hers was immense. They communicated on a level that was unlike any other she had experienced.

She studied him, turning over his tiny hands and examining his palms when she could pry open the fingers he stubbornly kept clenched in a fist. Each toe, each fine strand of hair on his head, his ears, were investigated and found to be perfect.

"Your daddy and I love you very much," she whispered drowsily as she relinquished him to a nurse.

Hospital sounds—squeaky laundry carts, rattling breakfast trays, clanking equipment dollies—roused her early. She was in the middle of a huge yawn and a luxuriant stretch when her parents entered her private room.

"Good morning," she said happily. "I'm surprised you're here instead of at the nursery window with your noses pressed against the glass. But then they don't open the curtain—" She broke off when she noted their haggard expressions. "Is something wrong?"

Clif and Meg Powers glanced at each other. Meg gripped the handle of her purse so tightly that her knuckles turned white. Clif looked as though he'd just swallowed bad-tasting medicine.

"Mom? Dad? What's happened? Oh, my God! The baby? Aaron? There's something wrong with Aaron?" Kyla threw off the covers with flailing arms and pumping legs, unmindful of the pinching soreness between her thighs, intent only on racing down the hospital corridor to the nursery.

Meg Powers rushed to her daughter's bedside and restrained her. "No. The baby's fine. He's fine. I promise."

Kyla's eyes wildly searched those of her parents. "Then what's wrong?" She was on the verge of panic and her voice was shrill. Her parents rarely got ruffled. For them to be so obviously upset was cause for alarm.

"Sweetheart," Clif Powers said softly, laying a hand on her arm, "there's some distressing news this morning." He silently consulted his wife once more before saying, "The American embassy in Cairo was bombed early this morning."

A violent shudder shimmied up through Kyla's stomach and chest. Her mouth went dry. Her eyes forgot how to blink. Her heart thudded to a halt before sluggishly beginning to beat again. Then, gradually gaining momentum as she assimilated what her father had said, it accelerated to a frightening pace.

"Richard?" she asked on a hoarse croak.

"We don't know."

"Tell me!"

"We don't know," her father insisted. "Everything is in chaos, just like the time this happened in Beirut. There's been no official word."

"Turn on the television."

"Kyla, I don't think you should—"

Heedless of her father's warning, she snatched the remote control from the bedside table and switched on the television set that was mounted on the wall opposite the bed.

"...extent of the destruction at this point is undetermined. The President is calling this terrorist bombing an outrage, an insult to the peacekeeping nations of the world. Prime Minister—"

She changed channels, frantically punching the buttons on the remote control with trembling fingers.

"...costly, though it will probably be hours, even days before the death toll is officially released. Marine units have been mobilized and, along with Egyptian troops, are clearing the rubble looking for survivors."

The camera work on the videotape was substandard and testified to the pandemonium surrounding the ruins of what had been the building that housed the American embassy. The shots were jerky and out of focus, random and unedited. "Taking credit for this abomination is a terrorist group calling itself—"

Kyla changed channels again. It was more of the same. When the video camera swept the area and she saw the bodies that had already been recovered neatly lined up on the ground, she threw down the remote control device and covered her face with her hands.

"Richard, Richard!"

"Darling, don't give up hope. They think there are survivors." But Meg's soothing words fell on deaf ears. She clutched her weeping daughter's body hard against hers.

"It happened at dawn Cairo time," Clif said. "We were notified just as we were getting up this morning. There's nothing we can do at this point but wait. Sooner or later, we're bound to get word of Richard."

It came three days later, delivered by a Marine officer who rang the doorbell of the Powers's house. Kyla realized the moment she saw the official car pull up to the curb that subconsciously she had been waiting for it. She waved off her father and went to answer the door alone.

"Mrs. Stroud?"

"Yes."

"I'm Captain Hawkins and it is my duty to inform you . . ."

"But, darling, that's wonderful!" Kyla had exclaimed. "Why are you so downcast? I thought you'd be jubilant."

"Well, hell, Kyla, I don't want to go off to Egypt while you're pregnant," Richard had said.

She touched his hair. "I'll admit I don't like it for that reason. But this is an honor. Not every Marine is selected for guard duty at an embassy. They chose you because you're the best. I'm very proud."

"But I don't have to do it. I could apply—"

"This is a chance of a lifetime, Richard. Do you think I could live with myself if you turned down this honor on account of me?"

"But nothing's more important than you and the baby."

"And we'll always be here." She hugged him. "This will be your last tour and it's a fabulous opportunity that will only come around once. Now you're going and that's final."

"I can't leave you alone."

"I'll live with Mom and Dad while you're away. This is their first grandbaby and they'll drive me crazy calling and checking on me. I might just as well make it easy on us all and move in with them."

He framed her face between his hands. "You're terrific, you know that?"

"Does that mean I don't have to worry about you with those mysterious eastern women?"

He had pretended to ponder it. "Do you know how to belly dance?"

She had socked him in the tummy. "That would be a sight to see, with the belly I'm going to have soon."

"Kyla." His voice was tender as he threaded his fingers through her hair. "Are you positive you want me to do this?"

"Positive."

That conversation, which had taken place seven months earlier, played through Kyla's mind as she stared at the flag-draped casket. The soulful notes of taps were snatched from the lone trumpet by an unkind winter wind and scattered over the cemetery. The pallbearers, all Marines, stood rigidly at attention, resplendent in their dress uniforms.

Richard was being interred beside his parents, who had died within a year of each other before Kyla ever met him. "I was all alone in the world before I met you," he had told her once.

"So was I."

"You have your parents," he had reminded her, perplexed.

"But I've never belonged to anyone, really *belonged*, the way I do to you."

Because they had loved each other so much, he had then understood.

His body had been shipped home in a sealed casket that she had been advised not to open. She didn't have to ask why. All that was left of the building in Cairo was a dusty pile of twisted stone and steel. Since the bomb had exploded early in the morning, most of the diplomatic corps and clerks had yet to arrive for work. Those who, like Richard and the other military personnel, had had apartments in the attached building, had been the victims.

A friend of Clif Powers had offered to fly the family to Kansas for the burial. Kyla could only be away from Aaron for several hours at a time because of his feeding schedule.

She flinched when she was handed the American flag, which had been removed from the coffin and ceremonially folded. The casket looked naked without it. Irrationally she wondered if Richard were cold.

Oh God! she thought, her mind silently screaming. *I have to leave him here.* How would she be able to? How could she turn and walk away and leave that fresh grave like an obscene, open wound in the ground? How could she get into that private plane and be whisked back to Texas as though she were deserting Richard in this stark, barren landscape that she suddenly hated with a passion?

The wind whistled with a keening sound.

She would and she could because she had no choice. This part of Richard was dead. But a living part of him was waiting for her at home. Aaron.

As the minister recited the closing prayer, Kyla offered one of her own. "I'll keep you alive, Richard. I swear it. You'll always be alive in my heart. I love you. I love you. You'll always be alive for Aaron and me because I'll keep you alive."

He was cocooned inside a cotton ball. Once in a while the world would intrude on his cloudlike confinement and these were unwelcome interruptions. All sounds were clamorous. The slightest movement was like an earthquake to his system. Light from any source was painful. He wanted no part of anything outside the peacefulness of oblivion.

But the intrusions became more frequent. Compelled by a force he didn't understand, finding handholds and footholds in sound and feeling, clinging precariously to every sensation that hinted he was still alive, he slowly climbed upward, out of that safe white mist to greet the terrifying unknown.

He was lying on his back. He was breathing. His heart was beating. He wasn't certain of anything else.

"Can you hear me?"

He tried to turn his head in the direction of the soft voice, but splinters of pain crisscrossed inside his skull like ricocheting bullets.

"Are you awake? Can you answer me? Are you in pain?"

It took some doing, but he managed to coax his tongue to breach his lips. He tried to wet them, but the inside of his mouth was as dry and furry as wool. His face felt odd and he didn't think he could move his head even if the pain hadn't been severe. Tentatively he tried to raise his right hand.

"No, no, just lie still. You have an IV in this arm."

He struggled valiantly and finally managed to pry his eyes open to slits. His lashes, forming a screen across his field of vision, were magnified. He could almost count them individually. Finally they lifted a trifle more. An image wavered in front of him like a hovering angel. A white uniform. A woman. A cap. A nurse?

"Hello. How do you feel?"

Stupid question, lady.

"Where . . ." He didn't recognize the croaking sound as his own voice.

"You're in a military hospital in West Germany."

West Germany? West Germany? He must have been drunker than he thought last night. This was a helluva dream.

"We've been worried about you. You've been in a coma for three weeks."

A coma? For three weeks? Impossible. Last night he'd gone out with that colonel's daughter and they'd hit every night spot in Cairo. Why the hell was this dream angel telling him he'd been in a coma in where? ... West Germany?

He tried to take in more of his surroundings. The room looked strange. His vision was blurred. Something—

"Don't become distressed if your vision is fuzzy. Your left eye is bandaged," the nurse said kindly. "Lie still now while I go get the doctor. He'll want to know that you're awake."

He didn't hear her leave. One instant she was there, the next she had vanished. Maybe he had imagined her. Dreams can be bizarre.

The walls seemed to sway sickeningly. The ceiling swelled and then receded. It was never still. The light from the single lamp hurt his eyes ... eye.

She had said his left eye was bandaged. Why? Disregarding her caution, he raised his right hand again. It was a Herculean effort. The tape holding the IV needles in place pulled against the hairs on his arm. It seemed to take forever for his hand to reach his head and when it did, he knew the first stirrings of panic.

My whole damn head is covered with bandages! He raised his head off the pillow as far as he could, which was only an inch or two, and glanced down at his body.

The scream that echoed through the hall seconds later came straight out of the bowels of Hell and set the nurse and doctor flying down the corridor and into the room.

"I'll hold him down while you give him a shot," the doctor barked. "He'll tear up everything we've done so far if he keeps thrashing that way."

The patient felt the sting of a needle in his right thigh and cried out in indignation and frustration over his inability to speak, to move, to fight.

Then darkness closed in around him again. Soothing hands lowered him back to the pillow. By the time he reached it, velvet oblivion had claimed him again.

He drifted in and out for days...weeks? He had no point of reference with which to measure time. He began to know when IV bottles were changed, when his blood pressure was being taken, when the tubes and catheters entering or exiting his body were monitored. Once he recognized the nurse. Once he recognized the doctor's voice. But they moved around him like ghosts, solicitous specters in a soft misty dream.

Gradually he began to stay awake for longer periods of time. He came to know the room, to know the machines that blipped and beeped out his vital signs. He was increasingly aware of his physical condition. And he knew it was serious.

He was awake when the doctor came through the door, studying a chart in a metal file. "Well, hello," the doctor said when he saw his patient staring up at him. He went through a routine checkup, then leaned against the side of the bed. "Are you aware that you're in a hospital and pretty banged up?"

"Was...I...in an accident?"

"No, Sergeant Rule. The American embassy in Cairo was bombed over a month ago. You were one of the few who survived the blast. After you were dug out of the rubble you were flown here. When you're well enough, you'll be shipped home."

"What's...wrong with me?"

A flicker of a smile touched the doctor's mouth. "It would be easier to say what's right." He rubbed his chin. "Want it straight?"

An almost imperceptible nod encouraged him to proceed in a blunt, no-nonsense manner. "The left side of your body was crushed by a falling concrete wall. Nearly every damn bone you've got on that side was broken, if not mangled. We've set what we could. The rest," he paused to draw in a deep breath, "well that will take some doing by the specialists back home. You're in for a long haul, my friend. I would say eight months at least, though twice that long would be a more accurate guess. Several operations. Months of physical therapy."

The misery reflected on the bandaged face was almost too poignant to witness, even for the doctor who had earned his stripes on the battlefields of Vietnam.

"Will I . . . be . . . ?"

"Your prognosis at this point is anybody's guess. A lot of it will be up to you. Sheer gut determination. How badly do you want to walk again?"

"I want to run," the Marine said grimly.

The doctor came close to laughing. "Good. But for right now, your job is to get stronger so we can begin patching you up."

The doctor patted him lightly on the right shoulder and turned to go. "Doc?" The medical man turned at the hoarse sound. "My eye?"

The doctor looked down at his patient sympathetically. "I'm sorry, Sergeant Rule. We couldn't save it."

The doctor's stride was brisk and businesslike as he strode from the room, and belied the tight lump in his throat. The most eloquent sign of despair he'd ever seen was that single tear trickling down a gaunt, darkly bewhiskered cheek.

George Rule was allowed to see his son the next day. He came to the bedside and clasped Trevor's right hand. Slowly he lowered himself into a nearby chair. Trevor never remembered seeing his father cry, not even when his mother had died several years earlier. Now, the attorney from Philadelphia, who struck terror in the heart of any lying witness, wept bitterly.

"I must look worse than I thought," Trevor said with a trace of wry humor. "Shocked?"

The elder Rule pulled himself together. He'd been cautioned by the medical staff to appear optimistic. "No, I'm not shocked. I beat you here by several hours and saw you when you first arrived. It might not feel like it, but you've come a long way since then."

"Then I must have been bad because I feel like hell now."

"They would only let me see you once a day while you were in the coma. Then since you came out of it, they wouldn't let me see you at all. You're going to be fine, son, fine. I've already been talking to doctors in the States, orthopedic surgeons who—"

"Do something for me, Dad."

"Anything, anything."

The last time Trevor had seen his father they hadn't been on very good terms. If Trevor hadn't been so preoccupied with other thoughts now, he would have noted his father's drastic change of attitude toward him.

"Check the casualty list. See if Sergeant Richard Stroud made it."

"Son, you shouldn't be worrying—"

"Will you do it?" Trevor groaned, already physically taxed by his father's visit.

"Yes, of course I will," George rushed to say when he saw his son's anxiety. "Stroud, you say?"

"Yes. Richard Stroud."

"Friend of yours?"

"Yes. And I hope to God he didn't die. If he died, it's my fault."

"How could it be your fault, Trevor?"

"Because the last thing I remember is falling asleep in his bunk."

"Psst! Stroud? You awake, buddy?"

"I am now," came the grumbled reply. "Jeez, Smooch, it's three o'clock. Are you drunk?"

"How 'bout a drink?"

Richard Stroud sat up in his bunk and shook off sleep. "Must have been a helluva weekend pass."

"'s wonderful. Ever had an orgasm?"

Stroud laughed. "You're drunk all right. Here, let me help you with your pants."

"An orgasm, an orgasm. I think I had three las' night. Or was it four?"

"Four? That's a record even for you, isn't it?"

A wobbly finger was pointed at the end of Stroud's nose. "Now shee, Schtroud. You're always thinkin' the worscht of me. I was talking about the *drink*. An Orgasm. Has vodka and liqueur and... Are my pants off yet?"

"They will be if you'll lift your feet up."

"Oops!" Trevor Rule fell over onto Stroud's bunk, dragging the other man with him. "Do you know Becky?" he asked with a goosey smile.

"I thought her name was Brenda," Stroud said, disentangling their limbs.

"Oh, yeah. Come to think of it, I think it is Brenda, I think. Great legs." He winked lewdly as Stroud helped him with his shirt. "Strong thighs. Know what I mean?"

Stroud chuckled and shook his head. "Yeah, I know what you mean. And I don't think Colonel Daniels would appreciate you talking about his daughter's strong thighs."

"I think I love her." Trevor said the words with the seriousness only a drunk can conjure. The avowal was punctuated with a moist belch.

"Sure you do. Last week you loved the brunette secretary on the third floor. And the week before that it was the blond AP reporter. Now come on, Smooch, let's get you to your own bunk."

He put his arms under Trevor's and tried to heave him up, but the other man was deadweight and only grinned up at him sappily. "I've got a better idea," Stroud said when Trevor couldn't be budged. "Why don't you just stay in my bunk tonight?"

For an answer, Trevor fell backward onto the pillow. Stroud felt his way across the dark room to Trevor's bunk. He settled down to go back to sleep.

"Nighty-night."

He raised his head to see Trevor waggling his fingers at him like a dimwit. Laughing, Stroud said, "Nighty-night."

Before either of them woke up, the terrorists struck.

Trevor's recovery was harder than he anticipated—and he had anticipated that it would be a living hell.

He was in the hospital in West Germany for another month before he was transported home. The expert doctors who examined him went away grimly shaking their heads. The left side of his body was a mess.

"Fix it," Trevor said tersely. "Do what you can. I'll do the rest. But you can bank on this. I'll walk out of here."

He had had nurses read him newspaper accounts of the embassy bombing. He went through stages of disbelief, then despair, then anger. The anger was healthy. It gave him the strength he needed to fight the pain, to overcome the trauma of one operation after another, to withstand the grueling hours of physical therapy.

Once his medical discharge was official, he let his Marine haircut grow out long. He had told the nurse who came in to shave him every morning to leave his mustache. He refused to be fitted with a prosthesis for his eye.

"I think it looks ... dashing," was the opinion of one nurse. There were several clustered around his bed as a doctor fitted him with a black eye patch. Half the nursing staff was in love with him. His extensive injuries hadn't detracted from his brawny build. Greatly admired and discussed at the nurses' station were his ruggedly hand-some face, long limbs, wide chest and narrow hips.

"It goes with your wavy black hair."

"When you leave here, you'll have to fight the women off with a stick."

"With my cane, you mean," Trevor remarked, study-ing the eye patch in the hand mirror someone had passed to him.

"Don't give up yet," the doctor said encouragingly. "We've only just started."

He knew of seasonal changes only by the landscape through his hospital room window. The days bled into each other. He kept track of time by keeping a calendar on his bedside table and jotting down at least one entry on it each day.

One afternoon an orderly, who occasionally came in to play poker with him after his shift, dumped a duffel bag onto the chair near the bed.

"What's that?"

"All the stuff they could salvage from your room in Cairo," the orderly told him. "Your dad thought you might want to sift through it and see if there was anything worth saving."

There wasn't. But one thing caught his attention. "Hand me that metal box please."

It was an unremarkable green square box with a hinged top. The combination lock had only one number. Mirac-ulously he remembered it. He turned the lock and, when it came open, raised the lid.

"What's all that?" The orderly was peering at the con-tents over Trevor's shoulder. "Looks like a pile of let-ters."

Trevor felt a constriction in his chest. It squeezed his throat as well, so much that he could barely say, "That's exactly what it is."

He hadn't remembered them till now, but suddenly he recalled that afternoon with stark clarity.

"Hey, Smooch?"

"Hiya, Stroud. What can I do for you?"

"You know that metal box you keep your poker stakes in?"

"What about it?"

"Would you mind if I put these in there for safekeeping?" Embarrassed, Stroud held up a stack of letters, bound with a rubber band.

"Hmm. Are those from that wife who keeps you as chaste as a monk?"

"Yeah," he admitted bashfully.

"I didn't think she could write."

"Huh?"

"I didn't know angels did such mundane things," Trevor teased, poking his friend in the ribs.

"Not you, too, please. The guys are ribbing me about saving her letters, but I like to read them several times."

"Mushy?" Trevor's green eyes twinkled mischievously.

"Not really. Just personal. What about the box?"

"Okay, sure, lock them away. All you have to do to open it is turn the lock to four."

"Four? Thanks, Smooch."

He caught Stroud's arm as he turned away. "Sure they're not mushy?"

Stroud grinned. "Well, a little mushy."

They had gone out for a beer and that was the last Trevor had thought of Stroud's letters from his wife. Until now.

He slammed the lid down, feeling as guilty as if he had watched them making love through their bedroom window. "Throw the rest of that junk away," he said irritably.

"You keepin' the box with the letters?" the orderly asked.

"Yeah, I'm keeping it."

He didn't know why he did. It probably had something to do with his guilt over being alive when Stroud had died while sleeping in his bunk. He told himself a million times through that afternoon's hand and arm exercises that he wasn't going to violate a dead man's privacy by reading letters from his wife.

But when night fell, when the hall was emptied of visitors, when the last of the medication had been dispensed, when the nurses had taken up their posts at their station, Trevor lifted the box from the bedside table and set it on his chest.

He was lonely. It was dark. He had slept alone for more nights than he cared to count. It had come as a tremendous relief to him to feel his body respond every time the orderly sneaked him the monthly issues of *Playboy* and *Penthouse*. That part of him wasn't impaired.

He needed a woman.

It wasn't that he couldn't have one. He knew that if he gave any of several nurses a certain look, they would have been more than willing to accommodate him.

But he had had about all the melodrama in his life that he could handle. Hospital gossip being what it was, it would be foolhardy to become romantically entangled, especially when what he wanted and needed had little or nothing to do with romance.

Yet he yearned for a woman's touch. A woman's voice. There was no satisfaction to be derived from looking through the magazines on this night like so many others. Those women, with their voluptuous bodies and abundant hair and affected smiles were as two-dimensional as the slick pages they were printed on.

The composer of the letters was real.

The lid to the metal box opened without a sound, but the paper rustled when he touched the letters. He yanked his hand back. Then, cursing himself for a fool, he picked up the letter on the top of the stack.

There were twenty-seven in all. He sorted them and put them in chronological order. When all the busywork—designed to delay the commission of what he supposed was a grievous sin—was finished, he opened the first envelope, took out the plain pastel sheet, and began to read.

Chapter 2

Sept. 7
My darling Richard,
It's only been weeks, but it seems like years since
you left. Missing you has become a sickness. Instead of getting better each day, I grow worse. My
imagination plays cruel tricks. I often think I see
you, especially in a crowd. My heart begins to beat
fast with excitement. Then I go through the
wrenching realization that someone only reminded me of you....

Sept. 15
Dearest Richard,
I dreamed about you last night and woke up
crying....

Sept. 16
My darling,
Forgive me yesterday's letter. I was blue....

Oct. 2

Dearest Richard,

I felt the baby move today! Oh, darling, I can't tell you what a thrilling experience that was. At first it was only a fluttering. I held my breath, standing very still. Then he (I know it's a boy) moved again, much stronger. I laughed. I cried. Mom and Dad came running. They couldn't feel the movements because they are slight, but somehow I know you could. If you were here, touching me, I know you could. I love you. So much.

Oct. 25

...and your excursion to the pyramids sounds wonderful. I'm jealous. Mom and I went to NorthPark yesterday and did some shopping. If anything, the traffic in Dallas is getting worse. I was so tired by the time we got home, I could barely climb the stairs and Dad brought me supper on a tray. But we had a productive day. I won't have to buy clothes for the baby until he's six!

We all laughed over your story about the consul's wife. Does she really dress that way? And about your friend Smooch, STAY AWAY FROM HIM! He doesn't sound like a very good influence on a married man with a pregnant wife....

Thanksgiving Day

...and I want you here so badly. I went to a movie with Babs last night. I should have know better. It was sexy, steamy actually. And now I want you! I'm climbing the walls. For shame! Nice pregnant ladies aren't supposed to feel like sex kittens, are they? But it's cold and rainy and I think, given the chance, I could even lure you away from the football games on television today.

Dec. 21

My love,

I got your letter yesterday and laughed out loud. So you want me to stay away from Babs? You've got a deal if you'll end your friendship with Smooch. He sounds like the kind of man I detest. Thinks he's God's gift to women, doesn't he? Even though you say he's as handsome as the devil, I know I wouldn't like him....

Dec. 24

My dearest,

The days are short, but they seem endless. My spirits are down. I wish I could have slept through Christmas. Everywhere I look people are celebrating, smiling, sharing the season with those they love. I feel like an alien in a world made up of couples only. Where are you? I can tell Mom and Dad are worried about me because I've been so depressed. They've done their best to cheer me, but I miss you so terribly that nothing they do works. The packages you sent are under the tree. Dad splurged and got a Noble fir this year, my favorite. I hope you received your presents in time. I would trade all the presents I've ever gotten and will get on future Christmases for one of your kisses. One of those long, slow kisses that fulfills and tantalizes. Oh, Richard, I love you. Merry Christmas, darling.

Jan. 11

...but I'm much better now that the holidays are over and we've passed the halfway point of your year away.

It grows increasingly uncomfortable to sleep. The baby is going to be a fullback, you'll be glad to know. Or maybe a placekicker. But in any event, in about twenty-two years the Cowboys will be recruiting him for sure! By the way, what do you think of Aaron as a name? If it's a boy, of course. Which it had better be since I've come up empty on girls' names so far.

You would go wild for my breasts. They're huge! Unfortunately the rest of me matches them. I didn't realize the baby would make such a drastic change in them. Even the nipples have grown larger. I'm preparing them to breast-feed. (That naughty Babs says she wishes she had that good an excuse. She's so bad!) I wish you were here to help out on the project. (Come to think of it, I'm pretty bad myself.)

But I can't think of anything more wonderful than nursing our baby... Aaron....

Jan. 25

...and it was the most horrible dream I've ever had. I woke up sweating. I won't eat any more chili before the baby comes!

Was Smooch along on that weekend trip to Alexandria you wrote me about? You didn't mention him and I think that was an intentional oversight. If you have done something indiscreet, if you have a real lech for a belly dancer, don't confess it to me. I feel like a water buffalo and cried yesterday because I was so fat...at the same time I was stuffing down a banana split that Babs assured me would cheer me up. (Three scoops of chocolate almond!) Sometimes I despair that I'll never see you again, Richard. Will you ever hold me? Will I ever feel you inside me again? Sometimes I think you aren't real, that you're someone wonderful that I dreamed up. I need you, darling. I need to know that you love me. As I love you... with all my heart....

"You're being released next week?"

Trevor turned away from the window. "Yeah. Finally."

"That's great, son," George Rule said earnestly. "You look as good as new."

"Not quite."

There was no bitterness in Trevor's tone. Over the past thirteen months, he had come to realize how fortunate he'd been. His strolls through the wards of the hospital had convinced him of that. He could have been confined to a wheelchair for the rest of his life, like so many he saw in physical therapy.

He could walk, with a slight limp, but he could walk. He had even gotten accustomed to the eye patch, so that he wasn't bumping into furniture any longer. It was true what was said about the body's ability to compensate for the loss of one of its members. He could barely remember what it was like to have both eyes.

"They want me to come back every week on an outpatient basis for physical therapy, but I said no," he told his father. "I think this is as good as I'll get. I can do the exercises myself."

"What do you plan to do now?" George Rule asked his son hesitantly.

Trevor's choice of career had been a bone of contention since his graduation from Harvard. His joining the Marines had been an act of rebellion against his father, who had wanted Trevor to become a lawyer like himself and had refused to listen to his son's own plans.

"What I always planned to do, Dad. Be a builder."

"I see." Rule's disappointment was apparent, but he squelched it. He had almost lost his son. Trevor's close brush with death had scared the indomitable George Rule. He didn't want to lose Trevor in another way now. He had no doubt that he would if he tried to direct Trevor's future. "Where? How do you plan to start?"

"Texas."

"Texas!" It might just as well have been another planet.

Trevor laughed. "You've heard of the building boom in the Sunbelt states. That's where the action is now. There's still land waiting to be developed. I've chosen a small town near Dallas. Chandler. It's a booming community and I intend to capitalize on its growth."

"You'll need a bankroll."

"I've got back pay from the Marines coming."

"That's hardly enough to go into business."

Trevor looked at his father steadily. "How much would a law degree from Harvard have cost you, Dad?"

George Rule nodded. "You've got it." He stuck out his hand and Trevor gripped it firmly and shook it.

"Thanks."

For the first time in Trevor's memory, he was embraced by his father and hugged tight.

Later that night, after he had packed his things, Trevor stretched out on the hospital bed for the last time. But he was too excited to sleep. He had been given a second chance at life. His first shot at it hadn't amounted to much. But this new one, which would start tomorrow, would. No more angry wasted years. Now he had a mission.

He reached for the green metal box. It was never far from his hand. The letters were worn at the creases, frayed around the edges. He knew all twenty-seven letters by heart. But he derived pleasure from looking at the swirls and curves of her feminine handwriting. He selected one, and it wasn't a random choice.

...end your friendship with Smooch. He sounds like the kind of man I detest. Thinks he's God's gift to women, doesn't he? Even though you say he's as handsome as the devil, I know I wouldn't like him....

Trevor folded the letter carefully and replaced it in its envelope. He didn't go to sleep for a long time.

She was beautiful.

He had seen her many times in the past few weeks. But

never this close. Never for this long. It was a luxury to be able to study her.

In a thousand years he would never be able to describe the color of her hair. "Blond" wasn't sufficient because of those burnished streaks threaded through it. But she wasn't a true redhead. "Strawberry blond" connoted sweetness to the point of insipidity. And there was nothing insipid about Kyla Stroud. She radiated energy and light like a sunbeam.

That indescribable hair was pulled back into a casual ponytail. The ends of it were curly, as were the strands that had escaped it to frame her face.

And what a face. Heart-shaped. With a dainty chin. Brows that arched over wide-set eyes. A smooth, high, intelligent forehead. A complexion that made his mouth water for a taste. Cheeks naturally tinted the color of ripe peaches.

She had on casual tan slacks, a striped cotton shirt with the sleeves rolled up to her elbows and a cardigan tied around her neck. Her figure was neat and trim. Perfectly proportioned.

She was ... well ... perfect.

He liked the way she talked to the child, as though he was understanding every word she said. And perhaps he was, because when she smiled, so did the robust toddler. They seemed impervious to the heavy foot traffic in the mall, unaffected by the Saturday afternoon crowd that was patronizing the shops and food stands.

It was at one of those concessions that she had bought the ice-cream cone. With miraculous agility she had held the ice-cream cone in one hand while she pushed the baby stroller through the crowd to a bench. She had assisted the little boy, though he hadn't needed much encouragement to climb out.

Now, they were seated on a bench and the child was destroying the ice-cream cone while his mother alternately laughed with delight and admonished him for making such a pig of himself. Her right hand governed the cone, while her left deftly wielded a napkin.

When the cone and napkin had both been mutilated to a soggy mess, she spoke sternly to the child, then left the bench to throw the refuse away in the nearest trash can.

The instant her back was turned, the toddler slid off the bench and hit the floor of the mall running. As fast as his short, sturdy legs could carry him, he headed for the sparkling fountain that gushed toward the skylit ceiling. Surrounding the fountain was a pool about two feet deep.

Reflexively Trevor pushed himself away from the wall where he had been indolently propped on one shoulder while he watched them. He risked taking his eyes off the child for a few seconds to see Kyla turn away from the trash can and notice that the boy was gone. Even from that distance he read in her expression the instantaneous panic only a mother whose child is missing can register.

Without thinking, Trevor began weaving his way through the crowd toward the fountain. The boy was now climbing onto the low wall surrounding it and reaching toward the bubbling water.

"Oh, God," Trevor murmured as he pushed aside a man with a pipe. He increased the length of his stride and picked up his pace. But he wasn't fast enough. He watched the child go over the wall and into the water.

Several bystanders noticed, but Trevor was the first to reach the fountain. He swung his right leg over the wall, stepped into the pool, caught the boy under the arms and scooped him out of the water.

"Aaron!" Kyla was frantically pushing her way through the crowd.

Aaron, sputtering water, looked curiously at the man holding him. With apparent approval of his rescuer, the boy smiled, revealing two neat rows of baby teeth, and said something that could have been "water."

Sloshing water, Trevor stepped out of the fountain. The bystanders fanned out to give him room.

"Is he all right?"

"What happened?"

"Where's his mother?"

"Wasn't anybody watching him?"

"Some parents just let their kids run wild."

"Excuse me, excuse me." Kyla finally elbowed her way through the gathering onlookers. "Aaron, Aaron!" She lifted her son out of Trevor's arms and clutched him to her chest, squeezing hard, regardless of his wet clothes. "Oh, my baby. Are you okay? You scared Mommy. Oh, God."

The moment Aaron sensed his mother's distress, his adventure turned into a trauma. His lower lip began to tremble, his eyes filled with tears and his face crumpled. Opening his mouth wide, he began to wail.

"He's hurt! Is he hurt?" Kyla said frantically.

"Come on, let's move over here. Please, folks, let us through. He's okay, just scared."

Kyla was vaguely aware of a large man beside her. She felt his hand between her shoulder blades, propelling her through the crowd toward an out-of-the-way bench. She was so busy examining Aaron for possible injuries that the man went unnoticed until she was seated on the bench. Finally, hugging a crying Aaron to her, she looked up at him.

It took a long time for her eyes to reach his face, so her first impression of him was that he was very tall. She wasn't quite prepared for the curving mustache, much less the black patch over his left eye, and caught her gasp just in time. "Thank you."

The large man sat down next to her. "I think he's all right. Your reaction frightened him."

She whipped her head around, showing him that her chin wasn't only dainty. It could be stubborn when she was challenged. When she saw that he wasn't being critical, she smiled with chagrin. "I guess you're right. I overreacted."

Aaron's crying was beginning to subside. She held him away from her and wiped the tears off his ruddy, round cheeks. "You scared me half to death, Aaron Stroud," she scolded. Then looking at the man again, she said, "One minute he was there, the next he wasn't."

She had brown eyes. Velvety, dark-brown eyes that he felt himself sinking into.

"He moved like greased lightning." When she tilted her head, obviously puzzled, he explained. "I had been watching him eat his ice-cream cone."

"Oh." It didn't occur to her to ask why they had attracted his attention in the first place. She was wondering what had happened to his eye. It was a shame he had lost it because the one that looked back at her was green, deeply green, beautifully green, surrounded by spiky black lashes.

It gazed back at her like a steady emerald flame. Self-conscious at having been caught staring, she looked away. It was then that she noticed his wet jeans and boots. "You went into the fountain?"

He laughed, glancing down at his legs. His jeans were wet from his knees down. He rolled his foot back on the heel of his wet boot. "I guess I did. I don't remember it. I was thinking about Aaron."

"How did you know his name?"

Trevor's heart did a somersault. "Uh, I heard you call him that when you reached for him."

She nodded. "I'm sorry you got wet."

"It'll dry."

"But those look like expensive boots."

"They're not as valuable as Aaron." He chucked the boy under the chin. Aaron had the sleeve of his mother's cardigan in his mouth, gnawing away. Mechanically, she lifted it away from him and smoothed it back down over her chest.

"Oh, my gosh!" she exclaimed. As though to reinforce what she'd just realized—that they were both soaking wet—Aaron sneezed.

"You're wet," Trevor said.

He was staring down at her front in a way that made Kyla feel hot rather than chilled. She surged to her feet. "Thank you again. Goodbye." Holding Aaron in front of her like a shield, she rushed toward the nearest exit.

"Wait!"

"Why?"

"Aren't you forgetting something?"

"What?"

"Your purse for one thing. And Aaron's stroller. They're still over there by the ice-cream stand."

Feeling like a colossal fool, she shook her head, laughing shakily. "I'm still—"

"Upset. I can imagine. Let me get them for you."

"You've done enough."

"No problem."

He was walking away from her before she could offer another protest. Surreptitiously she glanced down at her chest to see if she was indecently exposing herself and was only slightly relieved to see that her exposure wouldn't get her arrested.

Hastily she glanced back up at the man's retreating figure. It was then that she noticed his limp. It was almost undetectable, but he definitely favored his left side. He must have been in a terrible accident to have lost his eye and partially crippled his entire left side.

But even the limp didn't hamper the lithe way he moved. For such a large man, he was graceful and had the oiled gait of an athlete. And the build. Broad shoulders and narrow hips. His hair was midnight-black, wavy and long enough to cover the tops of his ears and curl over his collar. Kyla noticed that the women he passed took a second look. None seemed put off by the eye patch. In fact, it contributed to his appeal, which was rakish and a tad disreputable.

Yet, masculine as he was, he seemed indifferent to slinging the strap of her purse over his shoulder and pushing the baby stroller through the mall back toward where she stood waiting with Aaron.

"Thank you again," she said, avoiding Aaron's swinging fist, which was aimed for her earring. She reached for her purse. Trevor slid the strap down his arm, up hers, and patted it into place on her shoulder.

She's so dainty, he thought.

He's so tall, she thought.

She leaned down and tried to seat Aaron in the stroller, but he was having none of it. His stout little body went as stiff as a board and she couldn't forcibly bend his legs. He began to protest strenuously.

"He's getting tired," she said by way of explanation, embarrassed that her child was behaving in such an undisciplined way. They were attracting attention again, and those passersby new on the scene were staring curiously at the sodden child, damp mother and the man with the wet jeans.

"Why don't you carry Aaron and let me push the stroller out to your car?"

She straightened, lifting Aaron with her. "I can't let you do that. I've inconvenienced you enough."

He smiled. His teeth were very straight and very white behind his very sexy mustache. "It's no inconvenience."

"Well . . ." she hedged.

The man made Kyla nervous. Why, she couldn't exactly say. He had behaved with enough courtesy to earn him a Boy Scout badge. He hadn't looked at her suggestively. More than likely he thought she had a husband out playing golf or at home working in the yard.

Still, *she* was aware that *he* was aware of her wet blouse, and even though he couldn't actually *see* anything the suggestion was there, and that made her jittery.

"Come on. Let's go before Aaron becomes more than the two of us can handle."

The boy was becoming heavier in her arms with every passing second and his fractiousness was increasing. He was squirming discontentedly, because he was no doubt as uncomfortable as she in his wet clothes. "All right," she said, pushing back a wayward strand of hair that had met with the flying fist she had tried to dodge. "I would appreciate that."

"Out this way?" Trevor asked, nodding toward the exit.

She looked uneasy. "No, actually, I'm parked on the other side of Penney's."

He could have asked why, if she was parked on the other side of Penney's, she had headed toward this exit as though the devil were after her just a few minutes ago, but in true gentlemanly fashion he said nothing and, after waiting for her to precede him, steered the empty stroller toward the department store at the other end of the mall.

"My name is Trevor, by the way. Trevor Rule." Holding his breath, he watched her face for signs of recognition and when none were forthcoming, he felt a tightness in his chest relax.

"I'm Kyla Stroud."

"Pleased to meet you." He cocked his head toward Aaron, who had stopped crying now that he was in motion again. "And Aaron, of course."

Smiles like his should be outlawed, Kyla thought. It was hazardous to the female population. His appeal crossed generational barriers. She saw a gaggle of teens openly flirt with him as they walked past. Plenty of grandmothers turned their heads. It didn't matter whether a woman was accompanied by another man or not, they all noticed Trevor Rule.

He wasn't classically handsome. There was nothing pretty about his face. It was lined. Twin grooves extended from the edges of his nostrils down to bracket his mouth and wide mustache. Kyla wondered how they could be so deeply engraved there. Pain from his debilitating accident? He couldn't be any older than his early thirties. Not much older than Richard would be.

Richard. At the thought of him that familiar pang shot through her. If he were alive, he would be walking by her side. She wouldn't need the assistance of a stranger. The first anniversary of his death had passed.

According to all the books on the subject, that was a landmark and she should be getting over the loss by now. But not a day went by that she didn't think of Richard, usually at a moment when she least expected it. Like now. And she was glad. She had vowed to keep her husband alive both for her sake and for Aaron's. Nursing memories of Richard day by day kept him a vital part of her life.

"How old is Aaron?" Trevor asked suddenly.

"Just over fifteen months."

"He's hefty, isn't he? I don't know much about babies."

"Yes, he's hefty," Kyla said, laughing and shifting him from one arm to the other. "But his daddy was muscular."

"Was?"

Why had she left that gate open? She hadn't intended to. "He died," she said without elaboration.

"I'm sorry."

And he meant it. Or did he?

Trevor had waited for this day for months. After he left the hospital, he had marked time, waiting until the time was right. He was anxious to get his business started, but even with his father's unabashed string-pulling, there had been a million and one tedious details to see to. The hours he had spent cooped up in offices seemed endless to a man who had months of his life to catch up on. There had also been hours spent outdoors shirtless, so he would lose his sickly hospital pallor.

During it all, he had imagined his first meeting with Kyla a hundred times, asking himself where it would happen, what she would look like, what he would say.

He hadn't set out to meet her that day. But it was happening! He was living it. And having seen her, he honestly couldn't say whether he regretted sleeping in Richard Stroud's bunk that fateful night or not. Out of sheer selfishness, he was extremely glad to be alive at the moment.

"I'm afraid we still have quite a walk," Kyla said apologetically as he held the door open for her.

"I don't mind."

The parking lot was a good indicator of the crowd inside the mall. Motorists just arriving were fighting over parking spaces as they became available.

"Are you from around here, Mr. Rule?" Kyla asked conversationally as they entered the melee.

"Call me Trevor. No, I'm not. I moved here about a month ago."

"What brought you to Chandler?"

You.

"Greed."

Startled by his answer, she looked up at him. "Pardon?"

A strand of hair blew across her lips. His heart skipped a beat, just thinking about moving aside that strand of spun gold and kissing her lips. She had the most kissable mouth he'd ever seen. "I'm a builder," he said a trifle too loudly after clearing his throat. "I want to be a part of the expansion going on around here."

Maybe he should have bought a few nights with a woman before meeting Kyla. Maybe he should have cultivated some casual relationships based solely on sex. Maybe he shouldn't have subjected himself to abstention.

"Oh, I see. Well, that's my car." She pointed out a pale blue station wagon.

"Petal Pushers?" he asked, reading the stenciled logo on the side panel.

"My friend and I have a flower shop."

Fifty-two ninety-eight Ballard Parkway. He knew exactly where it was, the colors in the striped awnings over the paned windows, and what the hours of operation were. "A flower shop, hey? Sounds interesting."

He waited while she secured Aaron in his car seat and helped her put the collapsible stroller into the back seat. "I can't thank you enough, Mr. uh, Trevor. You've been awfully kind."

"Don't thank me. I enjoyed it. Everything but seeing Aaron go over that wall into the water."

Kyla shuddered. "I don't even want to think about that." She looked at him for a long moment. There seemed to be no graceful way to leave. How did she say thank you and goodbye to a stranger who had saved her child's life? "Well, goodbye," she said, feeling awkward and having absolutely nothing to do with her hands.

"Goodbye."

She slid behind the steering wheel and closed the door. He stepped back, waved and walked away. Kyla turned the key. The car made a hateful grinding sound, but the engine didn't catch. She pumped the gas pedal and tried again. Wrrra, wrrra, wrrra. Again and again. But the car didn't start. She muttered something her mother would be horrified to hear coming from her daughter's mouth. Or, more likely, her mother didn't even know that word.

"Problem?" Trevor Rule had spoken through the window on the driver's side. His hands were braced on his bent knees.

She rolled down the window. "It doesn't want to start."

"Sounds like your battery has gone dead."

Stubbornly she tried again, several times. Finally admitting defeat, she twisted the key off and flopped back against the seat. Aaron was fussing in his car seat, flailing all four limbs against the confinement. This was turning out to be a heck of a Saturday.

"Can I help?" Trevor asked after a moment.

"I'll just go back into the mall and call my dad. He'll come pick us up and send someone out to look at the car."

"I have a better idea. Why don't I drive the two of you home?"

She stared at him mutely, then looked away. A prickle of fear chased up her spine. She didn't know this man. He could be anybody. How did she know he hadn't rigged her car not to start, then befriended her in the mall and . . .

Stop it, Kyla. That's crazy. He couldn't have orchestrated Aaron's fall into the fountain. Still, she had better sense than to get into a car and go anywhere with a total stranger.

"No thank you, Mr. Rule, I'll manage."

The refusal came out sounding brusquer than she had intended, but she couldn't let herself feel charitable toward a possible abductor. She reversed the energy-draining process she had gone through only minutes before, unbuckling Aaron and lifting him out of the car, picking up her purse, rolling up the window and locking the car door. She struck out in the direction from which they had just come.

"I don't want to detain you, Mr. Rule," she said as he fell into step beside her.

"It will be no trouble for me to take you anywhere you want to go."

"No thanks."

"Are you sure? It would be much—"

"No thank you!"

"Is it this damn thing?" He flung his hand up toward his left eye. "I know it automatically makes me suspect, but I swear I'm not someone you need to be frightened of."

Kyla came to a sudden halt and turned to face him. *Oh, Lord*. Now he probably thought she had a prejudice against handicapped citizens. "I'm not afraid of you."

The tension in his face was gradually replaced by an engaging grin. "Well, you should be. You can't trust strangers these days.'' They laughed softly. Unmindful of the traffic they were blocking, he took a step closer and looked down at her earnestly. ''I'm only trying to help by offering you a ride.''

She felt like an idiot. Any man who would ruin a four-hundred-dollar pair of boots to fish a little boy out of a fountain wouldn't be inclined to kidnap, kill or maim. ''All right,'' she conceded softly.

''Good.''

The patience of the driver waiting to pull out of the space finally gave out and he honked his horn. They started walking.

''Where's your car?''

Trevor indicated the direction with a hitch of his chin. ''About an acre and a half from here,'' he said, laughing. ''Why don't you let me carry Aaron?''

With only a trace of reluctance, Kyla handed her son over to him. Aaron smacked him on the cheek with the palm of his chubby hand. He seemed to be not at all wary of the tall, dark, handsome man with the patch over his left eye, the charm of a medicine show barker and a smile that could do an iceberg serious damage.

Chapter 3

He apologized for driving her in a pickup truck.

"I didn't know I'd be driving you this afternoon, or I would have left the truck at home and brought my car."

He unlocked and opened the door with his right hand while still holding Aaron in his left arm. As soon as Kyla was situated in the cab of the truck, he passed Aaron to her, setting him in her lap.

Trevor's arm brushed against her breasts. She pretended not to notice. So did he. At least he closed the door quickly. They pretended it hadn't happened, but she knew he must be thinking about that fleeting touch just as she was.

"It's warm in here," he remarked as he slid behind the steering wheel and started the motor. "The sun's been shining in."

"It feels good. We're still damp."

She could have bitten her tongue for mentioning that. He glanced down at her chest, swiftly and guiltily. She was glad that Aaron still provided her with a shield.

They fell into an awkward silence as he negotiated the traffic through the parking lot. Once he looked toward her and smiled apologetically for the delay. She smiled back and wondered if the tepid grin looked as sickly as it felt. Why couldn't she think of anything to say?

When he pulled up to the exit ramp, he turned his head. She could feel him looking at her, but she concentrated on smoothing down Aaron's soft brown hair.

Why was he staring at her like that? And maybe she should have asked that he please turn on the air conditioner. It was becoming uncomfortably warm inside the truck. Or was it her own temperature that was rising?

"I have to ask you something," he said softly.

Her heart lurched.

Are you game?

What should we do with the kid?

Are you protected?

Your place or mine?

The possibilities marched through her head. She dreaded hearing any of them. Up until now he had been so nice. She should have known it wouldn't be that easy. No man picks up a woman, get her into his car, does her a favor and expects nothing in return.

Keeping her eyes trained on the cowlick on the crown of Aaron's head she said, "What?"

"Which way?"

A nervous laugh of relief escaped her lips on a gust of breath. "Oh, I'm sorry. To the right."

He smiled disarmingly and followed the directions she now supplied without being prompted. *He must think I'm a real ninny,* Kyla thought. He's just a nice man who is playing the good Samaritan to a widow with a baby. Nothing more.

He might have suited the role better if he hadn't been quite so handsome, quite so...manly. His hands for instance. Large, strong, tan. When he reached for the dial on the radio she saw that his nails were bluntly trimmed. The back of his hand and knuckles were sprinkled with dark hair, sun-bleached on the tips.

He moved his right foot from accelerator to brake. Kyla noticed the supple contraction and stretching of long thigh muscles.

His lap, too, attracted her attention.

"Hot?"

"What?"

"Are you hot?"

Her face was flaming. Her insides were afire. Had he caught her staring at . . . that? "Yes, a little." He adjusted the thermostat and cool air began to whisper through the cab. But from that moment, she kept her eyes away from him.

Clif and Meg Powers had lived in the same house since Kyla was born. When they purchased it, it had been in a fashionable part of town. But the town's industrial expansion and its increased importance as a commuter's alternative to living in Dallas had changed their neighborhood. It was no longer fashionable.

The houses, once attractive and well maintained, now belonged to owners who didn't take much pride in them. Like frumpy matrons who had resigned themselves to middle age, the houses looked unkempt, the yards ungroomed.

The only exception on the block was the Powers's property. The deep front porch was bordered by a white wrought-iron railing, which Clif had painstakingly repainted the previous summer. The shrubbery had been pruned to make room for new growth. Flowers bloomed in well-tended beds.

As Trevor's truck turned onto the street, a sprinkler was vigorously watering one half of the yard. The grass on the other side of the center sidewalk leading up to the front porch was glistening in the late afternoon sunlight, having already been watered.

"That's it," Kyla said, pointing out the house for him.

Trevor's foot was already on the brake. He knew which house she lived in. In the past month he'd driven by it often enough to know what days their garbage was collected.

Kyla hadn't noticed his familiarity with the neighborhood because she was inwardly groaning. A familiar car was parked in the driveway. Babs. As if making explanations to her parents wasn't going to be difficult enough, she would have Babs and her vivid imagination to contend with. Maybe she could just hop out and thank Trevor without further ado. Maybe he would drive off before anyone saw him.

No such luck.

Trever had no sooner pulled the pickup to a stop at the curb than the front door opened and her father came out. He looked at the truck curiously as he bent down to turn off the water faucet and cut off the sprinkler. He looked even more curious when he recognized Kyla and Aaron sitting on the far side of the cab.

"That's my dad," Kyla said, as Clif Powers came ambling down the front walk. For reasons she couldn't explain she felt nervous and shy.

Trevor pushed open his door. "Hi," he said with a friendly air as he stepped out of the truck. "I've got some passengers who say they belong here." Clif Powers appeared dumbstruck.

Kyla already had her door open by the time Trevor came around to her side. "Better hand Aaron to me. It's a long step down for you." Reluctantly she let him lift Aaron off her lap.

As though he'd been doing it for years, he caught Aaron under the bottom and anchored the boy against his chest. With his free hand, he helped Kyla down. He kept his hand beneath her elbow as they rounded the truck to face her puzzled father.

"Hi, Dad."

"Where's your car? Is something wrong?"

"No, nothing's wrong, but it wasn't the most uneventful trip to the mall I've ever had," she said ruefully. She wondered how she could take her son out of Trevor's arms without creating an awkward situation. She didn't want to risk touching him again. Which was ridiculous because he was perfectly harmless.

"What's going on? Clif? Kyla?"

The voice belonged to Meg Powers, who was just then pushing her way through the front screen door. Her pleasant face wore an expression of concern. Behind her was Babs. Kyla didn't even want to contemplate what Bab's speculative expression conveyed.

Meg rushed down the front steps and took the sidewalk at a trot. Her eyes were moving back and forth between Kyla and the tall, dark-haired stranger who was holding her grandson.

"Mom, Dad, this is Mr. Rule. Trevor Rule."

"Sir, ma'am," Trevor responded politely and shifted Aaron to his left arm to shake hands with Clif Powers.

"And that's my friend and business partner, Babs Logan," Kyla added.

"Hello, Ms. Logan."

Babs's eyes danced over Trevor appreciatively. "Hi. Where did she find you?"

Babs wasn't acquainted with tact. She didn't know how to exercise restraint. She blurted out precisely what the Powerses were thinking, but didn't have the gumption or lack of manners to ask.

"He sort of found us," Kyla said.

"Where's your car?" Clif repeated.

"Still at the mall."

"I think the battery has run down, sir," Trevor added politely for Clif's benefit.

"Mr. Rule offered us a ride home."

"How chivalrous," Babs said. Her eyes were still busy with their inspection of Trevor. "What did Mrs. Rule think about that?"

Kyla was going to kill her! As soon as she had an opportunity, she was going to kill her with her bare hands!

Trevor only smiled as he bent down to set Aaron on the ground. Normally Aaron would have taken off at a run. But as soon as his feet made contact with the sidewalk, he began to whine. His chubby hands clutched at Trevor's damp pant legs. Bending down again, Trevor lifted him back into his arms and patted his bottom. Contentedly Aaron snuggled against him.

"I'm sorry," Kyla murmured, embarrassed that her son had formed such an attachment so quickly. "I'll take him now so you can get on your way."

"It's all right," Trevor assured her with a soft smile.

For an instant, as their gazes locked, it was as though they were alone. They momentarily forgot that they had an avid audience of three.

"The baby's clothes are wet," Meg ventured meekly.

"Oh, yes," Kyla said, shaking herself out of the brief trance. "He fell into the fountain."

The Powerses were immediately alarmed. Babs was merely more curious. "Was this before or after the battery ran down?" she asked, amused.

"Before. Trevor reached in and pulled him out. Don't worry, Mom, Aaron was okay. Just wet."

"How did it happen?"

"I was feeding him an ice cream." Kyla gave them a condensed rundown of the sequence of events. "When I looked around, Aaron was gone, but a crowd had encircled the fountain. Mr. Rule was standing there with a dripping Aaron in his arms."

"You jumped in the fountain and fished Aaron out?" Babs asked Trevor, nodding toward the denim that was obviously still damp below the knees.

"Yeah."

"Hmm," Babs purred, looking at Kyla in a knowing way that made Kyla want to slap her.

Clif and Meg were busy thanking Trevor for his quick action and commending him for his kindness to Kyla and Aaron. None of them saw the mouthed conversation going on between the two friends.

"He's yummy."

"Shut up."

"Your blouse is wet."

Kyla immediately ducked her head and saw that indeed the damp material of her shirt was still clinging to her breasts and outlining the lacy brassiere.

Her eyes swung up in time to catch Trevor looking at her. His gaze had followed hers down. It immediately sprang back up to her face. All this happened just as Meg, who had been expounding on how quickly a toddler could get out of sight and into mischief, concluded with, "Why don't you come in and have a cup of coffee with us, Mr. Rule?"

"No!"

Kyla's cheeks turned a warm pink when she realized she had voiced aloud the word that had shot through her mind. She wet her lips. "I mean, we've kept Mr. Rule too long as it is." She reached for Aaron and virtually yanked the boy out of Trevor's arms. "Thank you again. You've been very helpful, and I appreciate the ride home." Now please leave! she finished silently.

"It was my pleasure." He pinched Aaron's chin. "Bye, Scout. Nice to meet you," he said, nodding his head toward the others. With a lean-hipped saunter, only slightly hindered by his limp, he turned and walked back to his truck. With a final wave, he drove off.

Self-consciously, Kyla faced her parents and Babs, who were staring at her expectantly. "I've got to get Aaron out of these wet clothes." She wedged past them, but they trooped after her and were surrounding her by the time she reached the wide, spacious entrance hall.

"Tell us!" Babs demanded.

She had been Kyla's best friend since grade school. Her mother had died when they were in junior high. Since then her father often worked double shifts at a manufacturing plant in Dallas. Through the secondary school years, Babs had spent as much time under the Powerses' roof as she had under her own. She considered herself part of the family and so did they.

"Tell you what?"

"About him! What gives?"

"Nothing." Kyla headed for the kitchen, ostensibly to get Aaron a drink of juice. She placed him in his high chair and opened the refrigerator. Her parents and Babs crowded around her.

"Did he really jump into the fountain to rescue Aaron?" Meg asked, moving aside only when Kyla reached around her for a glass.

"Don't make it sound so heroic, Mom. He didn't dive into shark-infested waters. It's a shallow fountain, and Aaron couldn't have been in the water for more than a few seconds."

She couldn't believe she was making light of the incident now. Only an hour ago, she was thinking that Aaron could have drowned had it not been for Trevor Rule's quick reflexes.

"What about the car?" her father asked. "How did he know about the car?"

"Well, he, uh, had walked out with me."

"All the way to your car?"

"Yes. Because Aaron was crying and I was still shaken."

"He volunteered to do that?" Babs asked.

"Yes," Kyla said tightly.

"Hmm."

"Will you stop saying, 'Hmm'? You're not making a diagnosis. And I wish all three of you would stop looking at me like I've got the lowdown on a juicy piece of gossip. He's just a man, all right? A male person who was kind enough to offer his help. Honestly," she said with exasperation, "you're acting like hungry cats who've trapped the last mouse in town."

"He didn't have to drive you home," Meg said.

"He was being nice."

"He limps. Wonder what happened to him," Clif mused.

"It's none of our business. We'll never see him again. And, Dad, you'd better call someone at the garage and have my car taken care of. Do you need any help with supper, Mom?"

They recognized her tone. It was the clipped, terse one she had started using several months ago to let them know that she was officially out of mourning for Richard. With that brusque inflection she had indicated to them that they didn't need to walk on eggshells around her anymore or speak in hushed tones as though they were still at the funeral. It clearly stated that she would brook no more coddling. They knew by that tone when to back off, and now was the time.

"No, dear, thank you," Meg said, declining her offer. "You take Aaron upstairs and change him. We're only having sandwiches and I can manage. Are you staying, Babs?"

"Not tonight, thanks. I have a date."

Kyla left the kitchen and carried Aaron upstairs. Babs followed her. "I thought you had a date," Kyla said crossly as she carried Aaron into the spare bedroom that had been converted into a nursery for him.

"I've got time."

"Anybody I know? Or is this a new one?"

"Won't work, Ky," Babs said, plopping down in the rocking chair and crossing her legs Indian fashion.

"What won't work?" Kyla asked nonchalantly as she unsnapped Aaron's suspenders and took his shorts off.

"Trying to avoid the subject of your tall, dark and handsome hunk."

"He's not *my* . . . anything."

"Do you think he's married?"

"How should I know? Besides what difference does it make?"

"You mean you'd get involved with a married man?"

"Babs!" Kyla exclaimed, whirling around. "I'm not getting 'involved' with anybody. He offered me a ride home, for Pete's sake. What kind of day did we have at the shop?"

"Fair to middling. I don't think he's married," Babs went on doggedly. "He wasn't wearing a wedding band."

"That doesn't mean anything."

"I know. But he didn't have that married *look*, you know?"

"No. I don't know. I didn't look at him that closely."

"Well *I* did. All six feet three or so inches of him. And speaking of inches, did you notice the way he filled out the front of those jeans?"

"Stop it!" Babs had touched a nerve and Kyla kept her back to her friend because she didn't want her to see the telltale stain on her cheeks. "You're terrible."

"What did you think of the eye patch?"

"I didn't think anything of it."

Babs shivered. "I think it's wildly sexy. With that positively wicked mustache it makes him look like a highwayman or something."

"Wildly, wicked? You've been reading too many historical romances."

"And that single blue eye."

"It's green." The moment the words left her mouth, she knew she had incriminated herself. Hoping that Babs had missed the slip, she cautiously glanced over her shoulder.

Babs's smile was angelic, but there was pure devilry in her eyes. "Thought you said you didn't look at him that closely," she taunted.

"Will you go home?" Kyla pulled Aaron, now naked, into her arms. "I'm going to give Aaron a bath because he's going to bed as soon as he's had his dinner. You've got a date. And . . .'' She drew in a deep breath. "I don't want to talk about Mr. Rule anymore. I don't even want to think about him."

"Bet he's thinking about you," Babs said, unfolding her legs and coming to her feet. She wasn't perturbed by Kyla's crankiness.

"Don't be ridiculous. Why should he give me a second thought?"

"Because he seemed damned reluctant to leave. If you hadn't acted like you'd just sat on a tack when your mother offered him a cup of coffee, I'll bet he would have accepted her invitation as an excuse to stay. *And* he noticed your wet blouse just like I did."

"He did not!" Kyla cried indignantly.

"Oh, yes, he did. Bye."

Before Kyla could offer another protest Babs was on her way downstairs. Through dinner the Powerses were just as curious about the man who had "rescued"—as Meg seemed determined to call it—Kyla and Aaron. Their questions weren't as explicit as Babs's, nor as sexually oriented, but they were just as pointed.

When she could stand their subtle quizzing no longer, Kyla stood up and said, "I wish I had just called a cab. I didn't know one man could cause such a commotion. We'll never see him again. Now good night!"

She carried Aaron upstairs and put him to bed. In her own bedroom, she tried to read, but she kept thinking about Trevor Rule. "No wonder, with everybody talking about him all evening," she grumbled, slamming her book closed.

"No matter what Babs says, he wasn't looking at my wet blouse," she averred as she pulled it off. "He wasn't!" she muttered again as she took off her brassiere.

But the thought that he *might* have been kept her awake for a long time.

"I don't believe it," Babs said suddenly, making the front-porch swing rock erratically as she sat up from her lounging position.

"Don't believe what?" Kyla asked around a yawn. She was stretched out in one of the chairs on the porch. Her head was resting on the back and her eyes were closed. It was a warm, sunny Sunday afternoon and she was feeling lazy and luxuriously indolent.

"It's *him*."

Kyla opened one eye and saw whom Babs was referring to, then her other eye popped open as well. Trevor Rule was braking a car in front of her house.

"What'd I tell you?" Babs said. "He's come back for another look."

"If you say anything to embarrass me, I'll murder you," Kyla threatened her friend. She smiled wanly at Trevor as he made his way up the sidewalk to the front porch.

"Hi."

"Hi," the women chorused.

He gave Babs a cursory glance before his gaze homed in on Kyla. She became shyly aware of her shorts and bare feet. Her sandals had been kicked aside, but to retrieve them now would have called more attention to how casually and comfortably she was dressed.

"I was worried about your car, but I see you got it back all right." He indicated the station wagon parked in the driveway.

"Yes. Dad called the garage he patronizes. He met the mechanic on the mall parking lot and they charged my battery. The car started, but I'll probably have to get a new battery."

"That would be a good idea. Did you go with him?"

"No."

"How did he locate it in the sea of cars that was out there yesterday?"

She laughed. "It was the only one with Petal Pushers painted on the side."

His rich laughter echoed softly off the porch's covering. "Well I'm glad you got it back okay."

"Me, too."

Nervously Kyla hooked a strand of hair behind her ear, wondering if it looked like it had been styled with an eggbeater.

Trevor's own nervous reaction to the cessation of conversation was to slide his hands into the back pockets of his jeans, stretching the cloth tight across his narrow hips. Kyla wished she couldn't remember what Babs had said about his build. But she did remember and it left her mind wide open for unladylike speculation.

For her own part, Babs could have throttled Kyla for acting like such a simp. She took matters into her own hands. "Won't you sit down, Trevor? Would you like something to drink?"

"Uh, no," he said, swiftly removing his hands from his pockets. "In fact, I came by hoping I could talk Kyla and Aaron into going for an ice cream with me. I know he likes ice cream."

Kyla opened her mouth to refuse his invitation, but Babs piped up, "Now isn't that a shame? Aaron's taking his nap." Then her blue eyes opened wide with sudden inspiration. "But *you* could go, Kyla."

Flustered, Kyla stammered, "I don't—"

"Am I interrupting anything?" Trevor looked at Babs inquiringly.

"Oh, don't worry about me," Babs said laughing. "I don't live here, but I'm not company who has to be entertained. Kyla and I are old friends. Why, her folks practically raised me. We've been working on our tans this afternoon. You see, there's this part of their roof just outside Kyla's bedroom where we can sunbathe in total privacy." She winked audaciously. "If you get my meaning."

He did. He wasn't stupid. And when it came to playing these kinds of word games, he could make even the flirtatious Babs look like an amateur. Hell, he had invented some of the games. He could have leaned down, included them both in a suggestive smile and glibly delivered a dozen witty, leading innuendos on the subject of nude sunbathing. But the smile on Kyla's face was so strained that he didn't pursue the subject.

"But it got too hot," Babs went on. "So we came in and showered and now we're just relaxing here in the shade. In fact, I was about to drop off to sleep, so there's no reason for Kyla not to go."

Trevor met her gaze and smiled. "Would you like to?"

"No, I—"

"Kyla, who's . . . Oh, Mr. Rule," her father said from behind the screen door. He pushed it open and came out in stocking feet, wearing only his old-fashioned undershirt over his trousers.

"Hello, sir." Trevor shook his hand politely. "I hope I didn't disturb a nap."

"No, no," Clif lied. "I wasn't finished with the Sunday paper yet. I think I'll bring it out here on the porch."

"Trevor came by to take Kyla out for an ice cream. Wasn't that nice of him?" Babs made the announcement with a broad smile, as though some monumental decision had been reached and signed into law.

"Yes, it was," Clif agreed.

"But I don't think I'd better go because Aaron—"

"He'll be fine. He and your mother are still asleep. I just checked on him. Go on. It would do you good to get away for a spell."

Kyla couldn't remember when she had last been allowed to complete a sentence. She could have gladly strangled all three of them, her father for being so accommodating, Blabbermouth Babs, and Trevor Rule for putting her in this compromising position in the first place. "All right, I'll just go in and change." She bounded out of her chair and headed for the front door.

"You don't need to change." Babs spoke with the authority of a drill sergeant. She knew what Kyla would do.

She would go upstairs and wake up Aaron and use him as an excuse not to go.

Well she wasn't going to get by with that trick. She was a widow, granted. But she was a young, vibrant widow, and Babs intended to see that Kyla didn't retreat any further into her shell.

Trevor Rule was the first man brave enough to pursue Kyla despite the cold shoulder she had given him. Whether Kyla wanted her to or not, Babs was making it her business to see that he didn't get discouraged, take his losses and go away. Her inflection softened as she asked, "Does she need to change, Trevor? You're not going anyplace where she would need to dress up, are you?"

"Hardly. Kyla?"

There was such a compelling tone to the way he spoke her name that she couldn't find a polite means of turning him down. "I guess I could go," she said, nervously tugging on the hem of her shorts. "If we're not gone too long." She returned to her chair and put on her sandals. After shooting Babs a venomous look, she came to her feet again. "I guess I'm ready."

Trevor placed his hand under her elbow and they left the porch. "Don't rush back. Take your time," Clif called after them. "We'll watch the baby."

"Have fun," Babs said, waving gaily.

Mortified, Kyla slid into the front seat. She fought a compulsion to hide her face behind her hand as Trevor got in and started the car. As soon as they turned the corner at the end of the block, he surprised her by pulling the car to the curb. He put the automatic gear into "Park" and, laying his right arm on the back of the front seat, turned to face her.

"Look, I know they embarrassed you back there, but I don't want you to be. Okay?"

There was a hint of a smile at the corners of his mouth. She ducked her head and let go of a short, small laugh. "I was embarrassed."

"I know. I'm sorry."

"It was nothing you did. They acted like they wanted to hog-tie you before you ran away."

"I take it you haven't dated much since your husband's death."

"I haven't dated at all. And I don't want to."

Trevor took the news like a surprise right hook under his chin. He turned forward and contemplated the hood of the car through the windshield. On the one hand he was thrilled to know that she hadn't been seeing other men. On the other hand, she was spelling out the ground rules right off the bat and seemed in no rush to alter them. But she was in his car, right? He had gotten this far, right?

Kyla was thinking that perhaps she had been blunt to the point of rudeness and was just on the verge of offering an apology when he turned his head and said, "Not even to go for ice cream?" He took her spontaneous laugh as consent and engaged the gears of the car again. "Besides, eating ice cream is kind of like drinking."

"How's that?"

"It's no fun if you do it alone."

He drove through Chandler's streets, which should have been familiar to her, but which he seemed to know more about than she did. "I bought this tract of land."

"That's where the post office used to be before it moved into that new shopping center."

"That's what I hear. Anyway, I'm building a small office complex on this lot. Very nice. There'll be a central courtyard with plants and fountains. I hope it'll attract the professionals—doctors, lawyers—you know."

"I've bid on that piece of land but I don't think I'll get it," he said of other property as they cruised past. "There'll be a new supermarket over there."

"But it's a cow pasture!"

He laughed. "Give it a year. I understand there will be a movie theater complex, too."

He seemed to have inside information on what was going on in a town she had lived in all her life. What's more he seemed to be one of the movers and shakers who were making it all happen.

"Maybe Babs and I should consider moving Petal Pushers to a new location."

"No, you're fine where you are."

She looked at him quickly. "How do you know where we are?"

"I drove past your shop today before I picked you up," he said easily after a slight pause. "I was curious about any store called Petal Pushers. How long have you been in business?"

"Almost a year. Six months after Richard died . . . that was my husband." Idly she pleated the hem of her shorts between her fingers. "Anyway, when Babs and I were growing up, we loved the movie *My Fair Lady* and had always said we were going to work in a flower shop like Eliza Doolittle wanted to. So, when I found myself at loose ends, Babs started hounding me about it. She was unhappy with her job at the time. My parents thought it was a good idea. I needed something to do with my life and an investment for Aaron's future. So . . ." she said, drawing out the word, "we pooled our resources and before I knew it, I was co-owner of a flower shop."

"And has it been good for you?"

"So far, very good. The other florist in town has dated ideas and no imagination. We're closing in on him," she said with a mischievous smile that Trevor would have given heaven and earth at that moment to taste. He had been aware of every pleat she had pressed into the cotton shorts against her smooth, lotion-creamy, flower-scented, suntanned thigh.

To his supreme irritation he had to devote his attention to his driving. He had driven off the main highway into a lane that hadn't yet been paved. It was rough.

"Do you know about an ice-cream parlor I don't?" Kyla asked.

He smiled broadly and winked. "Maybe I'm just carrying you off into the woods." Her smile faltered and he laughed. Reaching over, he patted her knee. "Relax." *I'm touching her knee. My skin against hers. God! But don't press your luck. Remove your hand. Now, Rule, now.* "I'm building this house on spec. Some of the carpenters are working today for overtime wages and I want to make sure I'm getting my money's worth out of them. Do you mind stopping for a few minutes?"

No, she didn't mind. But "relax"? Impossible. Not when she could still feel the imprint of his hand burning into the skin of her bare knee.

Chapter 4

The lane wound through a forest of pine, oak and pecan. At the end of it stood a house currently under construction. Even at this stage of completion Kyla could see that the structure would be contemporary and impressive. The lot sloped through the woods to a shallow creek.

"This is beautiful, Trevor," she exclaimed, not even noticing how easily his name had come to her lips.

But he noticed and smiled at her as he brought the car to a stop. "Do you like it?"

"The lot is beautiful."

"Come on, let me show you around."

"I don't think I should get out." She was self-conscious of her skimpy outfit and the curious workmen, who, without exception, had suspended their labors when the car drove into the clearing.

"I'm the boss around here," Trevor said, shoving open his door. "If I say you should get out, you should get out."

The sun spread heat over her bare legs. A warm breeze caressed them. But she wasn't nearly as conscious of the

elements as she was of the stares directed toward her as
Trevor prodded her forward over the rough ground and
around piles of building materials toward the house. They
picked their way carefully. After one dark frown from
Trevor, the building activity was resumed. Hammers rang
out. A buzz saw shrilled. A drill whirred.

"Careful of nails," he cautioned. One of his hands was
curled around her elbow. The other was riding the small of
her back. When they had cleared most of the obstacles, he
regretfully removed his hands. "The front door will be
here. I was thinking of something with etched glass."

"How lovely."

"You'll step into an entry with a tall ceiling. Sky-
lighted."

"I like skylights."

"Yeah?" One of her letters had told him so.

*...and went in. It was just the kind of house I've al-
ways dreamed about. Contemporary. It was surrounded by
trees and had a skylight.*

"I saw a house like this once and loved it."

"Watch your step." Taking her hand chivalrously,
Trevor led her down to the next level. "This is the living
room. Very informal. A fireplace on that wall. The dining
room is through there. Kitchen is that way." He pointed
out the floor plan and Kyla tried to imagine what it would
be like when the walls were up. Concentrating on the house
kept her mind off how small her hand felt in his.

"Can you step through here?"

"Sure," she said, grateful for the opportunity to remove her hand from his.

But it didn't turn out that way, because he kept her hand
firmly tucked into his as they squeezed through a maze of
two-by-fours. "This is the master bedroom. Of course,
before too long you won't be able to walk through the
walls. You'll have to use the hallways."

"It seems a shame to enclose it."

The rooms were so open and airy, you could get the feeling that you lived outside.

"Exactly what I thought. Nearly every hallway has one wall of floor-to-ceiling windows so you won't get that closed-in feeling."

Dappled sunlight angled in through the overhead beams to shadow and highlight his face. The light found each iridescent streak in his black hair. His dark mustache spread wide over a lower lip so sensual that it bordered on being pouty.

Kyla withdrew her hand from his and just barely resisted the urge to wring it with her other. Casual as his touch had seemed, she didn't think it was casual at all. It just wasn't possible for a man to have a face and body like Trevor Rule's and not be a lady-killer. She could well imagine any number of female hearts dangling from his belt like trophies. The sooner he knew she wasn't in the chase, the better.

"What goes there?" she asked, putting space between them.

"Another fireplace."

"You're kidding!"

"No, why?"

She had always pictured her dream house as having a fireplace in the master bedroom, but something cautioned her about telling that to Trevor. "Nothing. I think having a fireplace in here sounds wonderful."

"And romantic."

She glanced away. "I suppose so."

"Mr. Rule?" One of the carpenters had joined them, but up until that instant had gone unnoticed. "Excuse me, but as long as you're here, could I ask you a question? It's about that breakfast nook."

"Sure. We'll be right with you." They retraced their footsteps through the framework of the house into the area of the kitchen.

"Over here in this informal dining area, you said you wanted a window. Which wall did you want the window on?" the carpenter asked.

Crossing his arms over his chest, Trevor pivoted on his boot heels to face Kyla. "Since you seem to have an instinct for these things, which wall should we put the window on?"

"I don't know anything about building."

"I'm merely asking for your opinion."

"Well," she said hesitantly, "let's see. That's south, right? And that's east?"

"Yep," the carpenter confirmed.

She contemplated the layout for a moment then said, "Why not both?" At their puzzled expressions she rushed on, "Could they meet in the corner? Maybe have one of those angled roofs that are made of glass? Then it would be like eating outdoors surrounded by trees."

The carpenter was scratching his head skeptically. "I've seen those prefab sunrooms. I reckon one might work."

Trevor, sold on the idea, clapped the carpenter on the back. "Consult with the architect tomorrow and let me know. I love the idea." He turned to Kyla. "Thanks!"

She felt her cheeks growing warm beneath his praise. "I'm sure the architect won't be too happy with me for spoiling his house plans."

"The architect has to worry about pleasing me."

They stepped out into the open again and began making their way to the parked car. "I think the house is going to be spectacular," Kyla said honestly. "I wonder who'll end up living in it."

"Never can tell. Maybe you and Aaron."

She stumbled over a discarded sack of concrete mix. Trevor's arm shot out, encircled her waist and secured her against his chest before she could blink.

"Careful there. Are you all right?"

She was fine except for a sudden breathlessness, a tingling sensation along her exposed skin and a curling warmth in her middle. She had forgotten how wonderful it felt to be held in a man's arms. The scents associated with masculinity—shaving soap, cologne, sweat—filled her head. She had missed those distinctive smells. He was hard and lean and strong. His breath was warm as it fanned against her cheek when he bent over her solicitously.

"I'm f-fine," she stammered and pushed herself away.

"Sure?"

"Yes. Clumsy, that's all."

The near fall had caused a strap on her sandal to become loose. She bent down to readjust it and when she did, one of the workers whistled. She sprang back up and whipped her head around. All of them were bent industriously over their tasks. And all of them looked too innocent not to be guilty.

She glanced up at Trevor, who smiled sheepishly and said with a shrug, "So they've got terrific taste. Ready?"

By all means she was ready to get away from there. She had gone on this outing to appease Babs and her father. It shouldn't have lasted longer than half an hour. How long did it take to drive to the ice-cream parlor and buy two cones?

But they had driven all over town before coming here. She had no business being on a work site with him, offering him her opinions on the house he was building. What had she been thinking of?

"You'd better take me home," she said as soon as he guided the car into the bumpy lane. "Aaron will be waking up soon."

"I promised you an ice cream."

"That doesn't matter."

"It does to me."

And that, it seemed, was that. At least if the rigid way he held his jaw was any indication. Kyla got a glimpse of another Trevor Rule then. He might be affable enough to jump into a fountain and lift a little boy out. He might be good-natured enough to push a baby stroller through a crowded mall on a Saturday afternoon. He might be kind enough to see that a stranded woman got home safely. But he also had a purely male stubborn streak. That sheer male dominance was slightly intimidating and vaguely unsettling to the woman sitting next to him in the air-conditioned car.

The car was another contradiction. She would have expected him to drive something powerful, mean, low, sleek and probably imported. Instead he was driving an all-American, conservative, middle-class family car with a full-size back seat that would accommodate Aaron's car seat.

Good Lord! What had made her think that?

"What's your favorite?"

She jumped, startled by his sudden question and her last thought. "My favorite what?"

"Ice cream. Mine's chocolate almond."

"Mine, too!"

He grinned at her. "Seriously?"

"When it comes to my chocolate almond ice cream, I'm dead serious."

On this first summery Sunday afternoon of the season, the ice-cream parlor was packed with people. Trevor seated Kyla on a high stool near the windows, then patiently stood in line. She had asked for a single dip; he brought her a double. "I'll never eat all this," she said, licking at the sinfully rich ice cream.

"Give it your best shot. Let's go outside to the gazebo. You're cold."

The air-conditioning in the ice-cream store had been turned up high and Kyla had goose bumps on her bare arms and legs. She didn't know whether to be impressed by his attentiveness or disconcerted that he was so aware of her body as to notice her chills.

As they went through the door on their way outside, a family of five came in. A little girl about six said, "Daddy, what's that thing on that man's eye?"

The mortified parents hustled the children inside and in frantic whispers admonished them not to stare.

"I'm sorry," Trevor mumbled.

Kyla was at a loss for words. She was embarrassed for him and for the parents. She certainly didn't blame the children who were naturally curious and didn't mean to be cruel.

"Does it bother you to be seen with me?" His voice was self-defensively harsh.

"No," she cried, turning to face him.

"I know the patch puts some people off."

"And attracts others." He looked at her in surprise. She explained. "Babs said it makes you look like a highwayman."

He shook his head, laughing. "A highwayman, huh?" Then his smile faded. "One who frightens children."

"Aaron wasn't frightened," she pointed out quietly.

"No, he wasn't, was he?" His tense posture began to relax. "I'm sorry if you were embarrassed by what the little girl said."

"I wasn't. It's just that I know situations like that must be awkward for you."

"I'm getting used to them." He licked at his cone, then ran his tongue along his upper lip beneath his mustache. Kyla couldn't help but wonder what that felt like. Silky or scratchy? "Sometimes I even forget what I look like to other people. Like today. I pulled on a pair of shorts, then changed my mind and put on these jeans."

"Why?"

He laughed. "If you think this damn thing is scary, you ought to see my left leg. I didn't want to repulse you."

"Don't be silly. Wear shorts around me anytime you want to."

His smile became reflective as he gazed deeply into her eyes. "I'll remember that," he said in a low, stirring voice.

Damn! Did he think she was hinting that they would be seeing each other again? To alter the course of the conversation she asked, "Were you in an accident?"

"Sort of."

Another blunder. Obviously talking about the cause of his disabilities made him uncomfortable and that topic was closed. She searched for something they could talk about and came up empty. What did they have in common but a hectic half hour at a shopping mall?

Trevor didn't seem to notice their lack of common ground as he led her into a latticed gazebo that provided shade from the new summer sun. They sat down on the bench ringing it and fell to eating their ice-cream cones.

"Better?" he asked after a long silence, nodding down toward her arm. "Your goose bumps are gone."

"Much better." If she broke out in goose bumps now it would be because his thigh was resting very near hers on the bench. Occasionally she could feel the brush of soft denim against her leg.

"You're wearing another pair of boots," she remarked. Her teeth crunched into her sugar cone.

He glanced down at his feet, which were indeed shod with another pair of lizard boots. Having grown up in Texas, Kyla knew they hadn't come cheap. "I've never owned a pair of cowboy boots until recently. Now I'm convinced I may never wear anything else."

The ice-cream parlor was situated in a row of shops and boutiques. The developer of the shopping center, who, as Trevor had told Kyla earlier, was one of the cleverest around, had created a parklike setting in the open-air mall. Willow trees bowed toward a man-made, rock-lined brook as though paying homage to the waterfowl that swam there. Halved whiskey barrels overflowed with blooming flowers. It was a pastoral place for sitting in the grass, wading in the water, walking hand in hand with someone special.

Kyla noticed that another couple had come to stand near the gazebo. Obviously the two young people were so absorbed with each other that they didn't see Trevor and herself sitting in the shadows of the interior. Speaking in soft whispers, his arms around her waist, hers locked behind his head, their middles nudging playfully, they nuzzled in the universal manner of all lovers.

"You obviously didn't grow up in this part of the country." Kyla cleared her throat uneasily, wondering if Trevor had seen the other couple. When he took a long time responding to her leading statement, she glanced up at him. He was staring at the young man and woman through the slats of the gazebo.

Feeling her eyes on him, he swiveled his head around guiltily. "Uh, no. Philadelphia. I went to school in the Northeast."

The man's hand was now strumming on the woman's arm, sliding the backs of his fingers from her elbow to her shoulder. Then he loosely closed his hand around her neck.

"That's why you don't have an accent," Kyla said.

The young man kissed the woman lightly, a soft pecking kiss.

"I guess so."

The woman angled her head back and said something that made her lover laugh softly.

"Do you have a family?" Kyla's voice was light and breathy, as though it was her neck that hungry male lips were nibbling.

"Family?" Trevor repeated dully. "Oh, family. Yes, my dad. He's a lawyer."

The man's mouth nudged aside the woman's collar and disappeared between the folds of fabric. Reflexively Trevor raked his mustache with the tip of his tongue.

"That's all? Just your dad?"

The woman made a soft sound and moved one of her hands to the man's chest. Her thumb languidly stroked the vicinity of his nipple.

Squirming on the bench, Trevor coughed. "That's all. My mother died several years ago. No brothers or sisters."

The lovers kissed. In earnest this time. There was a tilting of heads. A caressing of tongues. Arms and legs moved simultaneously to bring two yearning bodies together. Thighs adjusted themselves to interlock. Groans of pleasure and murmurs of arousal were carried on the whimsical wind that danced in and out and around the gazebo.

The muscled thigh that was now pressed tightly against Kyla's on the bench, bunched and went hard. "Lick it."

At the raspy command, Kyla's eyes flew up to meet a fierce green stare. "What?"

"Lick it. Quick. Before it drips." Lips parted, eyes glazed, she stared back at him mutely. "Your ice cream."

That roused her and she immediately jumped back. "Oh!" The melting ice cream was running over her fingers.

Trevor stood up abruptly, a pained expression on his face. "Are you finished with it?"

She glanced down at the remains of the ice-cream cone and was amazed to find that she had squeezed it to a pulp. As though it were a murder weapon she'd been caught holding, she practically threw it at him. "Yes, I'm done."

No matter how hard her mind willed, her heart would not slow down. Her mouth was dry. Lord, what she would give for one good deep breath. Oxygen, that's what she needed to ward off this vertigo that had first hit her when he mentioned her and Aaron's living in the house he was building.

Trevor carried their trash to the receptacle near the doorway of the gazebo. Kyla stood, though her knees were wobbly, and followed him. He was stunned by how lovely she looked framed in the opening.

Sunlight struck her hair and set it aflame as it swirled around her face. Her parted lips were red and moist. She squinted against the sun, and long curly lashes crinkled around velvety brown eyes.

"Trevor? Is something wrong?"

"No," he replied huskily. "I was just thinking about you sunbathing on the roof." Color, hot and vivid, rose out of Kyla's halter and spread up over her throat and onto her cheeks. She said nothing. But his face seemed to have magnetized her eyes. She couldn't look away. "That must be a sight worth seeing."

She swallowed. "Yes. Babs has a terrific figure."

He waited an interminable amount of time before he said softly, "I wasn't thinking about Babs."

When they pulled up in front of the house, Kyla knew there was a pair of eyes at each window. She wished she could bolt from the car and race for the front door, but she knew that a gentleman like Trevor wouldn't allow that. He came around to her side and held the door for her, offering her his hand as she climbed out. She pretended not to see it. She couldn't bring herself to touch him.

On the porch, she faced him awkwardly. She hadn't been able to meet his gaze since he had mentioned what she looked like sunbathing. "Thank you, Trevor. I had a nice time."

How insipid can you get, Kyla? He probably can't wait to get away, she was thinking.

I had to go and get horny and make that comment about her sunbathing. That probably ruined everything, he was thinking.

"So did I." The new boots suddenly felt too tight for his feet and he shifted from one to the other. "Well, goodbye, Kyla."

"Goodbye."

She turned toward the front door and nearly collided with her mother, who was stumbling over her own feet in her haste to get to the porch. "Oh, my goodness," Meg said, flustered. "Mr. Rule, how nice to see you again."

Her surprise over catching them together was as phony as a three-dollar bill. Trevor knew it and Kyla knew he knew it, and she wanted to sink into a deep hole and never have to come out again.

"Hello, Mrs. Powers," he said.

"I just made some sandwiches and lemonade. We thought we'd eat in the backyard on the picnic table. Why don't you join us?"

Tempted, Trevor glanced at Kyla. Her smile was strained. No, better not, he thought. He'd pushed just about as far as he could for one day. If he hadn't said what he had about the sunbathing.... But he had. Well, damn it, she had looked good enough to eat standing there in the sunshine, and he had had to endure watching while she made eating a damned ice-cream cone look like an erotic exercise. Oh, hell, the damage was already done.

Hating the necessity of it, he declined Meg's invitation. "That sounds great, but I've got some work waiting for me."

Meg's anxious smile collapsed. "What a shame. Well, another time."

"I'd be delighted." He smiled at them both, then loped down the front porch steps and down the sidewalk to his car. As soon as he had driven out of sight, the front door disgorged Babs and Clif.

"Well, how was it?" Babs asked. "Did he ask you out?"

"Will you see him again?"

"Did he ask permission to call?"

"Oh, for heaven's sake!" Kyla exclaimed cantankerously. "I wish all of you would grow up and leave me alone." She stormed past them and went through the front door in a huff.

But who was she mad at? Trevor? Her well-meaning parents? Babs? Or herself?

Because she was just the slightest bit sorry Trevor hadn't accepted her mother's invitation.

"No, no, Aaron," Kyla repeated for the hundredth time. "Don't touch the flowers."

They were in the back room of Petal Pushers. Meg, who sat with Aaron when Kyla worked, had needed to go to the dentist. Clif hadn't returned from an errand in time, so she had dropped Aaron off at the flower shop saying she wouldn't be long.

Kyla was keeping an eye on him while she did the month's accounting. When they had divided the labor of running the shop, Babs had volunteered to keep it open and actually deal with the customers if Kyla would do all the ordering, billing and accounting. Babs loved people but was a disaster at figures. The bookkeeping tasks kept Kyla's hours flexible, which was essential since she had a child to care for.

As she ran another tape through the adding machine, Kyla was vaguely aware of the tinkling sound of the bell over their front door. She didn't pay any attention to it until Babs called out, "Oh, Kyla?"

"Hmm?" she responded absently, jotting down the sum of her tally.

"You have a customer."

"A cus—"

The question died on her lips as Trevor Rule stepped through the swinging louvered door that separated the shop proper from its back room.

"Hi."

Babs was standing behind him, grinning like a Cheshire cat. "I thought you might want to deal with this customer personally."

Kyla's eyes threatened her friend with annihilation. Sunday evening had been torture. They had eaten supper in the backyard on the picnic table under the trees. The old table's paint was blistered and peeling because it had been in the backyard for as long as Kyla could remember. She and Babs used to drape it with blankets and play "tent" under it.

"Aren't you going to tell us *anything*?" Babs had asked around a mouthful of Meg's famous baked beans.

"There's nothing to tell," Kyla had said. "And would the three of you stop staring at me? My nose is not going to start growing like Pinocchio's."

"You can lie by omission," Babs intoned. "I don't think it's very sporting of you to keep us in the dark."

Kyla laid her fork on her plate, stared down at it while she slowly counted to ten, then raised her head. "All right. He drove me into the woods, parked, tore off all my clothes and we made wild, passionate love in the back seat of his car. We were both like wild beasts, consumed by spontaneous lust and licentiousness."

Kyla was the only one smiling when she finished her tale. "That's not very funny," Meg said stiffly. "For months we've been telling you you're too young and pretty to seal yourself off from life. We've encouraged you to start seeing men. Mr. Rule is the first one you haven't run from. We're only excited for you."

Kyla sighed wearily. "That's my point, Mom. There's nothing to be excited about. I had a husband. His name was Richard Stroud. He'll remain my husband until I die. I'll never fall in love again, never love anyone but Richard, and am not looking for someone to love that way again."

"Love, love, love," Babs cried in exasperation. "Do you always have to bring *love* into it? Why not just go out for kicks? Have some fun. You don't have to love a guy to enjoy him."

"Maybe you don't, but I do. And you know damn good and well, Babs, that men don't take out women 'for kicks' without expecting them to jump into bed with them for a payoff. I'm sorry, Mom, Dad," she said to them when their faces paled, "but that's the way it is these days. Now, I don't want to hear another word about Trevor Rule or any other man. I'm not in the market for one. Is that clear?"

They had honored her request and changed the subject, though she could tell that Trevor Rule was far from being a dead issue. All day Monday her parents had leaped toward the telephone each time it rang. It was the same at work with Babs. Kyla was relieved that none of the callers had been the one they obviously expected.

Relieved, but a trifle disappointed, too. He could have at least *tried* to reach her and given her the satisfaction of saying she didn't want to see him again. Despite her best intentions, her thoughts often strayed back to him.

Now, seeing him filling the doorway to the back room made her insides turn to mush. A dull roaring sound, not unlike the ocean, was rushing through her head.

"Hello, Trevor."

Some smart advertising executive should hire him to model jeans, she thought. He wore them so well. His chest and upper arms filled out the cotton shirt to perfection. His hair was agreeably mussed by the wind. The patch over his eye gave him the dangerous air of a mercenary, a man who lived just beyond the pale, a man to be wary of. Extremely wary of.

Belying his macho image, Trevor crouched down to speak to Aaron, who was standing in front of the large refrigerated cabinet that stored the flowers they used in their arrangements. "Hiya, Scout." The boy was happily slapping his hands against the cold glass. Trevor patted him on the bottom and Aaron gurgled a happy sound by way of greeting. He flashed their unexpected visitor a slobbery, toothy grin.

"I've got work to do. Excuse me," Babs said and disappeared.

For no good reason Kyla stood up behind her desk. Then, when Trevor also stood up, she sat back down. If she could have found it within herself to see the humor in their seesawing, she would have laughed.

"You look nice," he said.

She glanced down at her simple dress. It was the color of champagne, a color she knew she wore well. But it was nothing special and she wondered why he had even commented on it. Then she remembered that he'd never seen her dressed up. "Thank you." Was she supposed to tell him he looked nice, too? But he didn't look nice. He looked . . . sexy. She certainly wasn't going to tell him that because she had an idea he already knew.

"It smells good in here."

She forced her hands, which were gripping her ballpoint pen, to relax. "That's one of the benefits of working in a flower shop. It always smells good."

"I thought it might be you. Your perfume."

The ballpoint pen was strangled again. She tore her eyes away from Trevor's face and happened to catch sight of Aaron. "No, Aaron." She came out of her chair and rounded the desk hurriedly in an attempt to save the carnations. They were standing in a bucket of water, waiting to be used in an arrangement that had been ordered that morning. Kneeling down, she turned her meddlesome son away from the allure of the flowers and tried to distract him with his toys. "Here, play with Pooh Bear."

When she stood up again, she found herself as close to Trevor as his shadow. She stepped back quickly. "He's into everything." A nervous hand fluttered up to the gold chain around her neck, which seemed to have captured Trevor's interest. Count Dracula had never studied a neck so intently.

"Do you always keep Aaron here while you're working?"

"No." She explained about her mother's dental appointment. At that moment she couldn't have said whether she wished her mother would return and save her from being alone with Trevor. (Babs certainly was no help.) Or whether she would rather her mother never know about his visit to the shop.

But why was she herself making such a big deal of it? He was just another customer. "Can I help you with anything?"

"Oh, yeah," he said, jerking his attention back to the business at hand. "I need to order a corsage."

"I see."

Several thoughts tumbled through her head. Uppermost was whom the corsage was for. Then: If that's all he wanted, why hadn't he placed the order with Babs out front? Then: Oh Lord, maybe he hadn't wanted to see her at all. Had Babs ushered him back here to see her when all he had intended to do was give Petal Pushers his business?

"I'll, uh, let's see, yes, here's an order pad." She yanked up the tablet and held her pen over it. She filled in his name at the top. "What did you have in mind?"

"I'm not sure. What do you suggest?" He moved up behind her as she bent over the desk. She felt his legs brush against her skirt and madly thought about a French movie Babs had dragged her to a few months ago. She closed her eyes for a moment until the pornographic image was banished.

Drawing a ragged breath, she asked, "What's the occasion?"

"A banquet. Semiformal."

What banquet? Where? Whom was the corsage for? "A banquet. All right."

"I like orchids," he said.

"Orchids?"

"Yeah. Those big, fluffy ones. White ones."

You'll never guess what I found in a keepsake box the other day. That first orchid corsage you gave me for the Chi Omega spring dance. Remember? That's when I fell in love both with you and Bow Bells.

Kyla looked at Trevor with surprise. "Bow Bells?"

"Pardon?"

"Bow Bells. That's what you described. It's a cattleya hybrid." When he said nothing, she elaborated. "They're very pretty. They have large white ruffled petals and a deep golden throat." He was watching her lips as they formed each word. Kyla wondered how, in only a matter of seconds, "throat" had become the most provocative word in the English language.

"That's exactly what I had in mind."

"I . . . I have to order them from Dallas. When did you need the corsage?" Why was he looking at her as though he were about to make her his lunch and why was she allowing it?

"Saturday night." He took a step closer.

"No problem," she said briskly, alarmed by how quiet it had become in the shrinking room and how close they were standing. She could delineate each hair in his thick mustache.

She bent back over the desk. "One flower or two?"

"Two."

"They're expensive."

"That's okay. Don't scrimp on it."

"What time do you want to pick it up?"

"Do you deliver?"

"Yes."

"Then please deliver it Saturday afternoon."

"The address?"

"Two twenty-three East Stratton."

The ballpoint pen fell from fingers suddenly gone boneless. It rolled across the desk and dropped off the edge. Kyla turned around and gazed up into the dark, handsome face bending over hers. "That's my address."

"Will you go to the banquet with me?"

Speechless, she stared at him and began shaking her head even before she found her voice. "No, no I can't."

"It wouldn't be a date," he said in a rush. "It's a banquet for bankers and other potential lenders. A group of us developers have put together a videotape presentation on business opportunities in the community.''

"What does that have to do with me?"

"You've lived here all your life. I'm still a stranger in town. I'd like having you there to introduce me around."

If Kyla was ever certain of one thing, it was that Trevor Rule didn't need anyone to introduce him around. One smile like the one he was bestowing on her now and people, especially women, would flock to him. His grin was of the stuff that sold everything from toothpaste to brandy. When sex appeal had been doled out, Trevor Rule had gone through the line at least twice. He had charisma. He was the kind of man who attracted men and women alike. Everyone would want to be his friend.

"No, Trevor, I'm sorry, but I can't."

If he had posed no threat, then maybe she would have accepted. But he was too attractive. All she needed to do to start rumors flying was to be seen in the company of the newest eligible bachelor in Chandler. By Sunday morning her mother's friends would be talking wedding.

He made a small regretful sound and rubbed the back of his neck. "I never thought I'd have to resort to this to get a date with a beautiful woman, but I'm desperate."

"Resort to what?"

He looked at her cajolingly from beneath his brows. The green eye was twinkling. "You owe me a favor."

"Do either of you claim this little hoodlum?"

As one, they turned toward the door to see a vexed Babs holding Aaron in her arms. He had three drooping carnations clutched in one tight, moist fist. He had left a trail of wilted flowers from the back room into the shop. The stems had dripped water onto the floor. Aaron was waving at them with another battered blossom.

"Oh gosh, Babs, I'm sorry." Kyla rushed forward and took Aaron out of Bab's arms.

"That's all right. He only destroyed about ten dollars worth of carnations, not to mention the vase he was stuffing his Pooh Bear into. You must have been awfully busy in here.'' Her blue eyes were teasing as they bounced between Trevor and Kyla.

"We were, uh...Mr. Rule was ordering a, uh, some flowers.''

Babs gave them both a knowing glance before smiling benignly and leaving them alone again.

"Well?'' Trevor said. "About Saturday night.''

"I don't know.'' Kyla and Aaron were battling over possession of the carnations because she was afraid he was going to eat them and she didn't know if they were poisonous or not. When he finally lost that skirmish, he reached for her earring.

How could she wrestle with him and make a decision like this? She should coolly refuse Trevor's invitation, no matter how charmingly it had been extended. She had never written up an order for flowers she was to receive before. And that much charm coming from a man she hardly knew was disturbing.

But, she did owe him a favor, and if he considered this a business occasion...

"It wouldn't be a date?'' she asked tentatively.

"No.''

"Because I wouldn't want you to get the wrong idea.''

"I understand.''

"I mean, I'm a widow and I don't date.''

"You've already told me that.''

She had, hadn't she? So why was she babbling on about it? If she made too much out of it, he would think she was protesting too much. "All right, I'll go.''

"Great. I'll see you Saturday about seven. And don't forget the corsage.''

"You still want me to make it?''

"Sure. Goodbye, Aaron.'' He cuffed the boy under the chin. "See you Saturday night, Kyla.''

Seconds after he had gone through the swinging door, Babs pushed it open. "'See you Saturday night, Kyla.' Is that what he said?"

"Yes. I'm going to a banquet with him."

"That's wonderful," Babs said, clapping her hands together. "What'll you wear?"

"I won't wear anything." When Babs's mouth formed a small *o*, Kyla sighed resignedly. "I mean, it doesn't matter what I wear because it's not really a date."

"Oh sure."

"It's not. It's a business affair and he asked me to go with him to introduce him around."

"Uh—huh."

"He did!"

"Uh-huh."

"It's not a date."

"Uh-huh."

"He said so himself. It's not a date."

Chapter 5

It certainly felt like a date.

Kyla didn't remember being this jittery getting dressed for her first car date, her senior prom or her wedding. She didn't want to think about her wedding or Richard. But *not* thinking about them only implied that this "date" with Trevor Rule meant something, which she vowed repeatedly that it didn't.

Still, she was clumsy as she tried to apply her makeup. Nothing went right. She had to do one eyelid three times. Aaron, who seemed to have grown an extra pair of hands, was into everything. Her mother and father kept popping into her room, apprising her of the time, the current weather conditions, asking questions, offering assistance and generally making pests of themselves.

Thankfully, Babs had a "heavy date," so Kyla was spared her interference. Babs had insisted that Kyla buy a new dress for the occasion when all the while Kyla had insisted that it wasn't an "occasion."

Kyla's eventual capitulation only resulted in another argument, over which dress she should buy. Babs had gone on the shopping expedition without invitation.

"I like this yellow dress," Kyla said. Babs had mimed gagging herself by poking her index finger into her open mouth. "Very eloquent," Kyla had said sarcastically.

Placing her hands on her shapely hips, Babs asked, "Would you rather look like Mata Hari or Little Mary Sunshine?"

"I'd rather look like me."

"Try on the black one again."

"It's too...too..."

"Exactly," Babs had said, shoving the garment at Kyla impatiently. "It's terrific and it *is* you. Right?" she demanded of the intimidated sales clerk who was cowering against the dressing room wall.

"Right."

Kyla had left the store with the black dress, knowing instinctively that she was making a mistake. The yellow would have been much more suited to her. The black dress was too sophisticated. Trevor would think...God knows what he would think.

Her previous worries were compounded as she zipped up the back of the cocktail dress and caught her reflection in the mirror. The silk clung and swirled just where it was required to. Black complemented her complexion, especially since she had already enhanced it with pastel blushers and frosted eye shadows, and lip gloss the color of peach sorbet. Her hair was soft and shiny and had about it a look of artful disarray. She had left it to curl softly on her shoulders, sweeping one side back and holding it above her ear with a decorative comb. At the base of her throat lay a single strand of pearls. Pearl studs adorned her ears.

Hearing the doorbell downstairs, she reached for the orchid corsage and hastily pinned it to her dress. She pricked herself with the pins and was glad that Aaron, who parroted everything these days, wasn't in the room to hear her soft curses.

The corsage had brought on another argument between herself and Babs as recently as that afternoon. "It's four-thirty and you haven't made that corsage Trevor ordered."

"I'm not going to," Kyla had replied.

"The hell you're not. I've already sent him a bill."

"You what?"

"He's a customer, Kyla. He ordered a corsage and I billed him for it. Now we owe him an orchid corsage."

Casting her smiling friend a stormy look, Kyla made up the corsage.

"Won't do," Babs said, surpervising over Kyla's shoulder. "He asked for two flowers."

"How do you know?"

"I overheard. And he said not to scrimp either, so put some more of that lacy stuff behind it."

"Did you eavesdrop on the entire conversation?"

"Sure. At least I think I did. Did either of you say anything you're ashamed of?"

"Of course not," Kyla said heatedly.

"Then why are you getting so bent out of shape?"

Now, as Kyla made one last inspection of herself in the mirror, she had to admit that it all went together well: the black silk dress, the pearls, the hothouse flowers.

And that was just what she felt like, a hothouse flower who had been cultured and protected and was about to be thrust into the elements for the first time.

Such qualms were juvenile. She knew they were. But knowing they were juvenile and shaking them off were two different things. She had been married. She was a mother. But she felt like an old-world, convent-bred ingenue about to meet her first man.

"This is ridiculous," she told herself in exasperation as she yanked up the small black beaded evening bag and switched out the light. "This isn't even a date." She repeated that to herself, in cadence to her trepid footsteps down the stairs.

Trevor was standing in the entrance hall holding Aaron in his arms. He was bouncing the boy up and down as he conversed with Meg and Clif.

"...should be finished in about two weeks." He swung his dark head around when he realized that something on the staircase had captured the Powerses' attention.

Only an act of will kept Kyla's feet from faltering on the next step as Trevor looked up at her. She forced herself to descend calmly. Unfortunately she had no such control over her heartbeat.

"Hello, Trevor."

"Hi."

Aaron was plucking at Trevor's mustache, but he seemed not to notice. His gaze was fixed on Kyla. She was having just as hard a time keeping her eyes off him. He was gorgeous.

His suit was charcoal-gray, so dark that it almost looked black. The crisp white shirt only intensified the color of his hair and the depth of his tan. The correct silver and black striped tie would have looked ordinary on any other man, but Kyla realized then that Trevor was by no means ordinary. He was never going to be. Perhaps his distinction lay in the ever-present eye patch, which was so familiar now, so much a part of his face, that she didn't see it as something apart.

"The orchids are beautiful."

"Yes," she said breathlessly. She touched the corsage lightly, self-consciously, where it reposed on her breast. "Thank you. Do you like them?"

"Do you?"

"Very much."

"Good."

Think of something else to say, you idiot, she ordered herself.

Aaron came to her rescue. He chose that moment to take one of those unpredictable dives that toddlers often take from one pair of arms to another. Without warning, he lunged toward her and she barely had time to get her arms up before he landed against her with a solid thud.

But Trevor, whose relaxed arms tensed around the child immediately, hadn't quite let go of Aaron yet. So his right arm became trapped between Aaron and Kyla's breasts. As she gradually got a better grip on Aaron, Trevor withdrew his arm. There ensued a few moments of awkwardness, which everyone tried to cover with loud chatter.

"Here, give me the baby," Meg said.

"You two had better be going or you'll be late," Clif said.

"Are you ready?" Trevor asked.

"Yes. I think I have everything. Good night, Aaron."

"We'll get Aaron to bed, so there's no rush about coming home early," Meg said.

"Drive carefully. You've got plenty of time," Clif called to them as they went down the walk.

Kyla was grinding her teeth. Anyone would think this was her first date. She wouldn't have been surprised if Clif had posed them in the hall while Meg went searching for the camera.

Trevor stepped around her to open the car door. He didn't touch her and she was grateful. All too well she was remembering the feel of his hard arm moving across her breasts. It had left a tide of heat in its wake.

Once he was behind the wheel, he said, "I know this isn't a date, but am I allowed to tell you how pretty you look?"

His attempt at humor put her at ease somewhat and she glanced over at him. "Yes, and thank you."

"You're welcome."

He reached for the dials of the radio and turned to an easy-listening music station. His suit coat sleeve slid up. His shirt cuff was starched and stiff and had been skewered with a cuff link that had a smooth square of ebony fixed in a trim gold setting.

He had impeccable taste.

"I haven't talked to you since Tuesday. How was your week?"

"Busy," she said, silently thanking him for opening up an avenue of conversation. She seemed to have lost all talent for making small talk. Trevor hadn't, though, and before she knew it they had arrived at their destination.

The Chandler Country Club was only two years old. The landscaping was still immature, but the modern building of native stone couldn't be faulted. Sprinklers out on the dark golf greens were swishing as Trevor escorted her up the footpath that connected the parking lot to the front door.

She had almost, *almost*, gotten accustomed to having his hand wrapped around her elbow. But she wasn't prepared for him to slow his stride, lean down close to her and come near to pressing his face against her neck before standing straight again.

"This time I know that fragrance isn't flowers. It's you. And you smell wonderful."

"Thank you."

The words had been difficult to speak for the constriction in her throat. He overwhelmed her. He was so tall, so purely masculine. Around her, he had never acted like anything but a gentleman. Nonetheless she felt threatened by him. Not afraid, just threatened.

Every time he smiled down at her, as he was doing now, she remembered the discussions she and Babs used to have about kissing and how it would feel to kiss a man with a mustache.

Trevor's dark mustache was thick, but well groomed. It virtually obliterated his upper lip, while emphasizing the shape of the lower. It curved over the corners of his mouth as though caressing it. His teeth shone beneath it, startlingly white. The overall effect was disturbingly sensual.

Kyla tried convincing herself that her interest in it was purely casual, a holdover from youthful curiosity. But her powers of persuasion seemed to be taking the night off.

The cocktail party preceding the banquet had already started by the time they entered the room overlooking the golf course and swimming pool. The laughter-spiked din almost drowned out the music being provided by the combo playing a popular hit from a dais in the corner.

"Would you like something to drink?" Trevor had to bend down and place his lips close to her ear to be heard over the racket.

She turned, stretched up and spoke directly into his ear. "Club soda and lime, please." He nodded, smiled and elbowed his way through the crowd toward the bar, leaving behind him the scent of his cologne. Kyla liked it very much. It was clean and brisk, with an air of citrus. She couldn't help but notice how well the tailored coat fit his broad shoulders and— "Why, Kyla Stroud! I told Herbie it was you. It's so good to see you out, dear."

"Hello, Mrs. Baker, Mr. Baker."

"How are your folks?"

"They're fine, thanks."

"And your little boy?"

"Aaron's a typical toddler." She laughed softly. "Almost more than I can keep up with."

"Kyla, your drink." She turned and accepted the glass of soda from Trevor. The surprised expressions on the older couple's faces were just what she had expected and dreaded.

"Thank you, Trevor. I'd like you to meet Mr. and Mrs. Herb Baker. Mrs. Baker taught me seventh grade English grammar and literature. Mr. Baker has an insurance company. Trevor Rule," she said, presenting Trevor to them.

"Rule, Rule," Mr. Baker repeated as he pumped Trevor's hand. "Sure, Rule Enterprises! I've seen your signs everywhere. Contractor, aren't you?"

"Yes, sir. I've just formed my own company."

"Couldn't have picked a better place to start," Baker said. "Chandler used to be a sleepy little town. Nothing but a cotton gin here for decades. We're gradually changing all that. You joined the Chamber of Commerce last week, didn't you?"

"Yes, sir, I did."

"Glad to hear it. I'm on the membership committee."

While this conversation had been going on, Mrs. Baker's eyes had been busily bouncing between the two of them. She couldn't have been more obviously greedy for information if she had had a radar detector growing out of her forehead. "Did the two of you know each other *before*?"

Before exactly what, Kyla was never to know because Trevor intervened. "Please excuse us. Someone across the room is waiting to meet Kyla. Mrs. Baker, Mr. Baker."

Trevor nodded politely; Kyla smiled vapidly and let him usher her away. "I know that makes you uncomfortable."

"What?"

"Being seen with me."

"It's not that. It's what everyone is thinking that bothers me," she admitted.

"What do you think they're thinking?"

"You know, things like, 'It's about time the little widow got out in circulation again.' Or, 'It's too soon for her to be out in circulation again.' My parents acted like they had to foist off the eldest daughter before they could marry off the other six."

Trevor laughed. "It wasn't as bad as all that."

"Wasn't it?"

"No. You're far more self-conscious about that than I am."

"I wouldn't have blamed you if you had turned and run."

"But I didn't. I'm still here."

He spoke with such intensity, that Kyla's uneasiness was far from relieved. To avoid looking at him, she gazed out over the crowded room. "Now I feel like people I've known all my life have become spies and gossips."

"You can waste a lot of time and energy worrying about what people are thinking and saying behind your back."

She sighed. "I know. But this can't be much fun for you either. Don't you get the feeling that you're a window dressing and everyone's staring at you?"

He drew a serious face. "Don't worry about me. What people think doesn't really bother me. I don't want *you* to be uncomfortable. That's the only reason I mind it."

"We know this isn't actually a date. I just wish everyone else did."

"Short of announcing it over the microphone, what can I do to let them know this is not a date?"

For starters he could remove his hand from the small of her back. Because they had reached the other side of the room after maneuvering through the crowd—and his hand was still there, a firm, warm pressure against the arch of her back.

Then they could dispel more rumors by engaging other people in conversation. As it was, with the two of them silhouetted against the sunset beyond the plate glass windows, with Trevor's face bending close to hers in serious conversation, they must surely be giving everyone the impression that what they were saying was private and personal. It *felt* private and personal.

She moved, ostensibly to take a sip of her drink. Actually it was to put a few safe inches between them. Trevor sipped at his own drink, a pale whiskey.

"Would it make you feel better if I told you that you look sensational?" he asked.

She traced the rim of her glass with her finger. "No, I don't think so."

"Okay. Then maybe I'd better not mention that your dress is a real knockout."

Her eyes slid up to his face and caught his teasing smile. Her own stiff, plastic, party-manners smile became genuine. "Thank you for not mentioning that."

"Maybe we should migrate toward the dining room," he said. "Some are already moving in that direction to locate their table."

On their way into the dining room they were joined by a young banker and his wife. Lynn and Ted Haskell were new to town and therefore didn't know Kyla and her past. Trevor introduced her merely as his "friend." She enjoyed their lively conversation through the filet mignon dinner.

Trevor was attentive to her every need, always making certain she had salt, pepper, butter, fresh bread, water, coffee. She found herself basking in his attention. Mealtimes with Aaron were more like battles. Attack and retreat. Sometimes when she finished, she couldn't remember having eaten because she had snatched bites between mopping up spilled milk and wiping Aaron's dodging mouth.

"Didn't you like the food?" Trevor asked as the waiter whisked away her embarrassingly empty plate.

She blushed at his teasing and laughed self-deprecatingly. "I loved it, mainly because I got to eat it in peace. Having dinner with Aaron isn't quite so relaxing. It was all I could do to keep myself from cutting your meat for you. If I start patting your napkin back into your lap, try not to notice."

He blinked, startled. Then a slow grin spread across his rugged face. Leaning closer he said, "Kyla, if you start patting my lap for any reason, I'm going to find it damn near to impossible not to notice."

She could easily have died at that moment. In fact she even prayed for a sudden death. Her cheeks were scalding. Her fingertips and toes were throbbing with an influx of blood. Never had she been so embarrassed.

"I . . . I meant—"

"I know what you meant." Trevor, sensing her mortification, squeezed her hand. "More coffee?"

She made no more verbal blunders and they settled back in their hard chairs for the program. After the videotape presentation, the speakers droned on endlessly, extolling the attributes of Chandler in particular and north central Texas in general.

"Bored?" Trevor whispered, leaning close.

She had unsuccessfully tried to hide a delicate yawn with her hand. "No. It's all very interesting."

"You're a terrible liar," he growled close to her ear. She laughed, ducking her head. "Do you want to leave?"

"No!" she exclaimed, knowing this evening was important to him. He was here to see and be seen.

"We can sneak out."

"No. I'm fine. Really."

"Sure?"

She nodded her head.

"Positive?"

She nodded again.

"You're lovely, Kyla."

Her head snapped up and she met his gaze, which was compelling and hot. "I just threw that in to see if you were paying attention."

Slowly he pulled away and sat back in his chair. Kyla swallowed hard and removed her gaze from his. She glanced around anxiously, wondering if anyone had noticed their whispered exchange. She caught sight of Mrs. Baker's expectant face and looked away quickly.

Her eyes landed on the banker and his wife. Lynn's hand was lying on Ted's thigh. He was idly stroking the back of her hand. Kyla smiled at such a sweet display of marital intimacy. The subconscious kind. The kind that came automatically. Those demonstrations that said so much, but that wouldn't even be remembered later.

Richard and I used to do things like that all the time.

Mentally she sprang erect. That was the first time she had thought of Richard in hours. Guilt pierced her to the core. What was wrong with her?

She concentrated on him, on his face, his smile, his funny laugh, until the final speaker concluded his speech. Trevor and she said their good-nights and were among the first to leave. They barely made it to the car before it began to rain.

Once under way Trevor asked, "Would you like to go somewhere for dessert?"

"Remember the cherry cheesecake?"

"Oh, yeah." After a pause he said, "Coffee?"

"I don't think so."

"A drink?"

"No thank you, Trevor. I should be getting home."

"Right."

He sounded disappointed. Surely she was mistaken. He must be as glad as she that this evening was almost over.

They said little, which only made the tapping of the rain on the roof of the car and the rhythmic clacking of the windshield wipers seem louder.

Apparently he wasn't accustomed to driving with both hands on the wheel because he kept his right one in constant motion while he steered the car with his left. At first he fiddled with the radio, turning the volume up, then seconds later turning it back down.

He reached for the thermostat. "Comfortable?"

"Yes, fine."

His hand was withdrawn, but was no less restless. With that fidgeting right hand he worked loose the knot of his necktie. He raked back his hair. He adjusted the volume on the radio one more time. Finally he let that hand rest.

On the seat.

Halfway between them.

From the corner of her eye, Kyla watched that hand as though it posed some grave threat.

What if it inched toward her? Would she say something?

What if it reached out and grabbed her? Would she scream?

What if it reached for her own? Would she allow her hand to be held?

What if it caressed her thigh? Would she slap it away?

Her heart was thudding and she felt her palms grow slick with moisture. Never had the house where she lived safely with her parents and baby been such a welcome sight.

The hand didn't do anything but turn off the key in the ignition after the car had rolled to a slow stop. "Sit tight," he said, when she reached for the door handle. "I have an umbrella." Turning, he stretched his arm over the seat and reached behind him for the umbrella. His coat gaped open and Kyla saw the hard muscles of his chest straining against his shirt.

He got out and popped the umbrella open. He was holding it over his head when he opened her door and reached inside to take her hand and lift her out.

How it happened, she was never quite sure. Maybe they were crowding beneath the umbrella in an effort not to get wet. But somehow, *somehow*, when she stood up on the sidewalk, she was very close to him. So close that their clothes were brushing against each other.

Instinctively, her head tilted back. His face loomed close. He was holding the umbrella with his left hand. With his right, he loosely enfolded her neck.

She felt the tickling brush of his mustache first, then his lips, warm and firm, rubbing against hers.

Oh, God, that feels good.

She pulled back quickly and lowered her head. He removed his hand from her neck. She could still feel the imprint of each finger, though he had barely touched her and his clasp could hardly be classified as such.

The rain pecked against the silk umbrella and rolled down its slick surface to drip off the edge. Beneath that meager shelter they stood still and silent . . . and close.

"I'm sorry," Trevor said after a long moment. "No kisses allowed on the first date?"

"This isn't a date."

"Oh, yeah. Damn. I keep forgetting that."

He turned them toward the front door. Carefully they made their way up the walkway, made treacherous by the rainfall. No outside light had been left on to aid them in reaching the safety of the porch.

Trevor swung the umbrella down and shook it hard.

"Thank you for the evening, Trevor," Kyla said, edging toward the door.

"I know we said this wasn't a date." The umbrella was dropped onto the porch. It made a lazy spin on the axis of its handle before coming to rest.

"Yes. That's what we said."

"Right. We agreed that it wasn't a date, only—"

"What?"

"I'm not pushing. I don't want you to think I'm pushing."

"I don't."

"But . . ." He took a step toward her. Another. "Say this *was* a date."

"Yes?"

"Would you—"

"Would I what?"

His hands came up to frame her face tenderly. Her eyes slid closed. His lips met hers again. But they stayed this time. And pressed. And angled until hers parted. The tip of his tongue dared to penetrate, to make fleeting contact with hers, to sweep her mouth once, to sink deeply. Then it withdrew. He lifted his mouth away from hers. His hands fell to his sides.

"Good night, Kyla."

"Good night."

How the words found their way out of her mouth, she couldn't fathom. After watching him retrieve his umbrella and walk to his car, she automatically unlocked the front door and let herself in.

She drifted upstairs, telling herself every step of the way that since it hadn't really been a date, that hadn't really been a kiss either.

But her alter ego was saying, "Oh, it was a kiss all right. It was a dilly of a kiss. Babs, at her wildest, couldn't have imagined such a kiss. If you looked up the word 'kiss' in the dictionary, a description of what you just experienced beneath Trevor's mouth would be the definition."

She unpinned the orchid corsage and laid it on the dresser. She carelessly dropped her pearls amidst her perfume decanters, when normally she would have stored them in their velvet box. The black silk dress was left heedlessly lying on a chair with her underclothes piled atop it.

She floated toward the bed, naked—for the first time in a long time.

When she reached to turn out the lamp on the bedside table, she noticed Richard's picture.

Then she burst into tears.

Chapter 6

You're a damn fool."

He spoke softly. His breath fogged the window because the glass had been cooled by the rain. The room behind him was dark, so he was spared having to look at his reflection in the windowpane.

He sipped his drink. "A fool, a coward," he sighed, then added, "a liar."

Every time he saw her, he was lying by not telling her who he was. He knew what he was doing was wrong, but he couldn't bring himself to say, "I'm Smooch. Remember me? The guy your husband wrote to you about. The kind of man you said you detested. Egotistical. Thinks he's God's gift to women. Despoiler of reputations. Smooch." She had ridiculed him in her letters and he had deserved every reproachful word. In his place her beloved husband had died.

Clenching his teeth and closing his eyes, Trevor pressed his forehead against the window. What he was doing was manipulative and downright deceitful. There was no way he could excuse himself.

Actually there was an excuse, but who would believe it? Who would believe that he had fallen in love with a woman he'd never seen merely by reading her letters? He barely believed it himself. Certainly she would never believe it.

Sooner or later he would have to tell her who he was. But when? How? When she found out, what would her reaction be?

Impatiently he turned away from the rain-streaked window and slammed his highball glass down on the tacky table. It came with the drab furnished apartment he hoped he was living in only temporarily.

He knew what her reaction would be when he told her. Fury. Contempt. Hate. Those weren't the emotions he wanted to see burning in her brown eyes when she looked at him.

Going into the bedroom, he stripped. The purple scars that meandered and crisscrossed down his left side were no more than he deserved, he thought with self-loathing. He deserved to be placed on the rack for not having identified himself to her when they had met.

But would he tell her the next time he saw her?

No. What good was making promises in the dark that he knew he wouldn't keep? He wasn't going to tell her. Not yet. Not until...

Lying in bed alone, he watched the rain splatter silver patterns on the windows. He thought about her. About the kiss.

"Oh, God, the kiss," he groaned.

She had such a delectable mouth. Warm and wet and silky. Beyond the restraint she had exercised, he knew there lurked a simmering passion.

You know how I've always loved rain. It's raining today, one of those relentless, steady downpours when it looks like the sun has deserted and forgotten us. I'm not enjoying it. I'm depressed. The raindrops aren't happy, sparkling drops that dance as they splash in puddles. But leaden, ominous things that would weigh me down like chain mail if they fell on me.

I've figured out the difference. Rain is something that must be shared. There's nothing cozier than seeking shelter from the rain with someone you love. But there's nothing lonelier than having to endure it alone.

As Trevor recalled that particular letter, he laid his hand on his body and moaned softly. Still tasting the kiss, he whispered to the shadows, "If you were here with me, Kyla, I'd share the rain with you. I'd share everything."

"But that's crazy!"

"I don't want to discuss it, Babs."

"Because you know you're wrong. Because you know you're just being pigheaded."

"It's not pigheadedness," Kyla averred. "It's common sense."

They were washing the breakfast dishes. Kyla's friend was as transparent as the plastic wrap covering the leftover biscuits. Her early appearance for Sunday morning breakfast was unprecedented. As soon as she had cleared the back door she had begun grilling Kyla about her date with Trevor.

"I can't believe you won't go out with him again."

"Believe it."

"Why won't you?"

"That's my business."

"And you're my best friend, so I'm making it mine."

Kyla draped the dish towel over the rack and turned to face Babs. "Leave it, Babs. Don't you have enough drama in your own life to keep you occupied? Must you meddle in mine?" She left the kitchen and headed for the stairs. Babs was right behind her.

"My love life doesn't need help. Yours is at a crisis point."

Kyla halted on the step and whirled around. "We're not talking about a 'love life.' I don't have one."

"Precisely my point."

"*And*," Kyla stressed, "I don't want one."

"All right. Delete 'love' and insert 'sex.' Let's talk about your sex life."

Kyla resumed her trip upstairs. "That's disgusting."

Babs grabbed her arm to detain her. "Disgusting? *Disgusting*? Since when is a healthy sex life disgusting? You used to have one."

"That's right," Kyla said, yanking her arm free. "With a man I loved, my husband, who loved and respected me. That's as it should be." Tears stung her eyes and she dashed up the remaining stairs before Babs could see them fall.

The Powerses had already left for Sunday school. Kyla was to join them in time for the worship service. They had taken Aaron with them.

When Babs entered Kyla's bedroom, the latter was shrugging off her robe. She took a dress from her closet and stepped into it. Somewhat subdued, Babs sat down on the edge of the bed.

"Ideally that's the way it should be," she acknowledged sulkily. "But we're not all that lucky, Ky. We take what we can get."

"I don't. What I had was perfect. I don't want anything less."

"Well, hell, look at him! Trevor Rule is just about as perfect as you can get."

Just the sound of his name caused Kyla's hand to tremble as she tried to secure an earring in her ear. It wasn't taking much to rattle her today, not after the tearful night she had spent. Seeing Richard's picture on her bedside table had reminded her of her betrayal. She had vowed to keep him alive in her heart. Spending time with Trevor Rule, she had discovered, jeopardized her resolve to hold to that pledge.

To counter Babs's argument she said, "How do I know he's so perfect? I don't know anything about him. I only met him a week ago."

"You know how good he looks. You know that he's considerate, that he drives a nice—if rather boring—car, that he's ambitious, that he's kind to senior citizens and children, that he—"

"All right, I get the point. Besides the fact that he's good-looking, you could be describing thirty other men. I don't want to marry any of them either."

"Who said anything about marriage?" Babs cried. "I'm talking about having fun. Going out." She glanced up at Kyla slyly, "Going to bed."

The kiss, the kiss, the kiss. Damn that intimate and evocative kiss. Why had she permitted it? Why couldn't she forget it? Why had it been so good?

"Don't be silly." Shakily she stuffed tissues into her handbag. Aaron invariably came out of the church nursery with sticky hands. "I don't even think about that anymore."

"Liar." Kyla's head swiveled around. "You might not consciously think about it, dear heart, but you think about it. Ky, you can't just cast off your own sexuality because somebody else dies. You don't dispose of it like a pair of socks that don't fit anymore. It's a part of you and you're going to have to come to terms with it."

"I already have."

"I don't think so."

"What makes you say that?"

"Because you've put on earrings that don't match."

Incredulous, Kyla checked the mirror. Babs was right. Aggravated, she began making the switch. "That doesn't prove anything."

Babs came off the bed and approached her friend. "I know you loved Richard. I'm not trying to talk you into forgetting him."

"I never will."

"I know that," Babs conceded with her kindest tone of the morning. "But he's dead, Ky. You're alive. And being alive is not a sin."

As though refuting her friend's words, Kyla said, "I'm going to be late for church."

At the front door Babs caught up with her. "Will you or not?"

"Will I what?" Kyla asked as she checked her hair one last time in the foyer mirror.

"Go out with him again?"

"No. End of discussion."

Babs pointed her finger at Kyla and glared at her with narrowed eyes. "You had a good time," she accused. "Damn it, I *know* you did."

Too good a time, Kyle thought. "I did him a favor to pay back one. Now we're even. Besides," she added as she pushed open the screen door, "he probably won't even ask me out again."

He did. On Thursday of that week. She hadn't seen or heard from him until the telephone rang in Petal Pushers. Since Babs was busy with a customer, Kyla answered.

"Petal Pushers."

"Kyla? Hi."

"Hello."

"This is Trevor."

As if he needed to identify himself. She had recognized his voice immediately. At the sound of it, a delicious weakness had spilled through her.

"How are you?" she asked, wishing her voice didn't sound so breathless.

"I'm all right. You?"

"Fine. Busy. I've hardly had time to think this week. The days have flown by." She didn't want him to think she had been sitting by the telephone waiting for a call from him. Why she felt it was necessary to play these courtship games, she didn't know.

"How's Aaron?"

"Cranky. I thinks he's cutting another tooth."

A deep rich laugh filled her ear before he said, "Then he has a right to be cranky."

She twisted the telephone cord through nervous fingers. Should she thank him again for Saturday night? No, that would remind him of their date. And of the kiss.

"The reason I'm calling..."

"Yes?"

"It's short notice, I know, but the Haskells... You remember Ted and Lynn?"

"Sure."

"Well they asked me over for dinner tomorrow night. Steaks out on the patio. Would you like to go with me?"

"I don't think I can."

"Lynn suggested it," he rushed to say. "What I mean is, she asked if I'd like to bring someone and when I mentioned your name, she was glad. Seems you two hit it off."

"Yes, we did. I liked her very much. But Friday night is a problem. Aaron—"

"He's invited, too. Lynn said they have a wading pool. She thought all the kids—they have two, you know—could play in the pool." He laughed again and Kyla realized how much she was coming to like that rumbling bass sound. "We know how much Aaron likes water."

"I don't know, Trevor."

"Please."

Kyla gnawed the inside of her jaw in indecision. Should she accept? No. Because she didn't want to give him the wrong impression. On the other hand, how could he jump to the wrong conclusion if her baby was invited along? It didn't sound like an evening that would lend itself to romance. And wouldn't it be ungracious not to accept the Haskells' invitation? She really had liked the friendly couple. One could never cultivate enough friendships with bankers. As a businesswoman, having this contact might prove to be helpful later on. She and Babs might want to expand some day and need a business loan.

Good Lord, whom was she trying to convince?

The fact was that she wanted to go if only to prove that last Saturday night, and especially the kiss, had meant nothing. Trevor was new in town and didn't know many people. He wanted her company. That was all it amounted to.

Blame all her magnified erotic memories of the kiss on Babs, who had recently been taking her to movies redolent with skin, sweat and steam. Blame it on the fact that she hadn't felt the touch of a man's mouth on hers in almost two years.

It hadn't meant *anything*. So why make a big deal of it? Why not just go out and enjoy the Haskells' hospitality?

"That sounds like fun, Trevor. Thank you for inviting me ... us. Aaron and I will be glad to go. What time?"

"Seven o'clock on the dot."

"Actually the digital clock says six fifty-eight, but we're ready."

Kyla stepped aside and Trevor walked through the screened front door. Between the times she saw him, she forgot just how tall he was. Or did he only seem so because he was so muscular? Impressive biceps bunched beneath the short sleeves of his white polo shirt. The casual tan slacks would have elicited a comment about his buns from Babs, had she been there to see him.

"Are your folks around?"

"No. They said to tell you hello. On most Friday nights they meet with friends for catfish and dominoes. They alternate houses."

"Is that the reason you hesitated to accept my invitation tonight?"

One of them, Kyla thought. A minor reason. "Yes. Baby-sitters are hard to come by. By the time they're old enough to trust, they're thinking of nothing but boys."

"Did you?"

"What? Think of boys? Of course," she said, throwing her head back and laughing softly. He liked the way her hair swirled around her shoulders. "With a friend like Babs I had no choice. All through high school we were degenerately boy crazy."

"I see you two degenerates have been working on your tans."

The white sundress showed it off. She had hesitated to wear it because it left her shoulders and most of her back bare, save for a network of straps. After her shower, she had smoothed on a lotion that gave her tanned skin a glowing patina. She had added to the luster by dusting her shoulders with a body powder that had a sheen to it. Her nose and cheekbones had been dabbed with the puff, too. With her sun-lightened hair, she looked summery and golden.

"In the afternoons," she answered, self-consciously aware of Trevor's green gaze moving over her. "There's enough sun left when I get home to get in a half hour's worth."

"It looks great." His voice sounded a bit hoarse. Just the way he had sounded before he kissed her.

She moved away quickly. "Aaron is upstairs."

"Let me help you bring him down."

"Don't bother."

"Four hands are better than two," he said as he followed her up the stairs. "Where Aaron's concerned, I'm not even sure that's enough."

When they came into the nursery, Aaron was standing up in his crib. At his first sight of Trevor, he pointed his index finger, began to bounce up and down against the rails of his baby bed and babbled something that only he could understand.

"I think he recognizes me," Trevor said, pleased. He lifted the boy out of the bed and swung him high over his head. "Hiya, Scout. Have you been a positive terror this week? Eaten any more carnations?"

It was while he was holding the baby over his head that Kyla noticed the scar on Trevor's left arm. It started at his wrist, twisted around his elbow and disappeared into the sleeve of his shirt. When Trevor turned, laughing, to address something to her, he saw where she was looking.

He sobered instantly. "I told you it was ugly."

Her eyes swung up to his face. "You must have suffered terribly."

He shrugged. "Not so much. Ready?"

He carried Aaron while she toted the diaper bag. He had looked at it dubiously when she hoisted it onto her shoulder. "I know. It looks like we're moving," she said, laughing, "but I've learned to go prepared and I'm sure Lynn will understand."

He helped her secure the house. "We'll have to transfer Aaron's car seat from your car to mine," Trevor remarked as they stepped off the porch.

"How far are we going? He can sit in my lap."

"Uh-uh. Let's do this right."

"Will you at least compromise and take my car?"

"Will you let me drive?"

She smiled up at him and dropped the keys into his free hand. "How's the house coming?" she asked him once Aaron had been secured in his car seat and they were driving through the twilit streets.

Trevor had had to push the front seat back to accommodate his long legs. He drove as he had before, with his left wrist draped idly over the steering wheel. Only this time he stretched his right arm across the back of the front seat. His fingers were close to, but not quite touching, her left shoulder.

"Great. Your idea about the dining area in the kitchen was terrific. Even the architect liked it and was miffed that he hadn't thought of it himself."

"It's such a lovely lot. It would be a shame not to enjoy those trees to the utmost."

"That's why I chose to build there."

...*that a house without a tree is nothing. I'd rather live in a tree house like the Swiss Family Robinson, than in a palace that was surrounded by nothing but concrete.*

Ted and Lynn Haskell had equally effervescent personalities. Kyla and Aaron, over whom they made much ado, were welcomed into the noisy chaos of a happy home. Not that their house wasn't lovely. It was. Kyla even felt a mild envy for the gracious rooms that Lynn led her through on the tour that Kyla had requested.

The couple had produced two children as handsome and congenial as themselves. The eldest, a girl of seven, bossily took Aaron under her wing and kept him entertained while the men supervised the grilling of the steaks out on the patio. Lynn was unself-conscious enough to accept Kyla's offer to help in the kitchen.

"Trevor told us that you're a widow."

Kyla's hands paused as she tore at the iceberg lettuce. Had he been talking about her? Apparently Lynn sensed her tension. "I'm no gossip, Kyla. Neither is Trevor. I asked. He told me, but he didn't elaborate. If it makes you uncomfortable, we can talk about something else."

Trevor couldn't have elaborated because he didn't know the facts about Richard's death. Curious, that he had never asked. She glanced at Lynn. "Richard died the day after Aaron was born."

"My God," Lynn said, setting down the bowl of potato salad she'd just taken from the refrigerator. "What happened?"

Kyla related the story. "It hasn't been quite two years yet."

Lynn looked out over the patio where the men were sipping at beers while they tended both the steaks and the children who were splashing in the wading pool. As she watched, Aaron bent at the waist and ducked his head into the water. Apparently he got more than he bargained for. He came up sputtering. Instantly Trevor was kneeling beside the pool, wiping the boy's face with a towel and thumping him on the back. "Trevor and Aaron seemed to have formed quite an attachment. When did you start seeing him?"

"Only a week or so ago. We're only friends. What dressing do you want on the salad?" When Kyla turned around, Lynn was looking at her with an amused expression. "What is it?"

Lynn laughed. "Only that if everything Ted says about Trevor Rule is true, you'd better be careful."

"Why? What does Ted say?"

"That Trevor is ambitious, that he knows no fear, that he's daring in business ventures and that so far they have all paid off. In other words, he usually gets what he goes after." She smiled and sent a wicked grin in Kyla's direction. "If the attention he paid you the other night at the banquet is any indication, I'd say the man's after you. Unless you want to be caught, you'd better run fast." After taking two cans of beer from the refrigerator, she passed one to Kyla. "Come on. I think they can use another."

Trevor had lifted Aaron out of the pool, then had crouched down and placed him between his knees. He was drying the child briskly with a towel, as though it were something he did every day. Kyla popped the top off the beer and handed it down to him.

"I'll take over when you want me to."

Trevor looked up at her with a heart-stopping smile. He sipped the beer and licked the foam off his mustache. "We're doing fine, but thanks for the beer."

"You're welcome." Flustered, she turned away in time to see Ted accepting his fresh beer from his wife. He said, "Thanks, hon," and swatted her bottom. His hand stayed and squeezed her playfully before falling away. Lynn bent down and planted a soft kiss on the crown of Ted's thinning hair.

Kyla felt a loneliness more encompassing than any she had experienced before.

"The house is dark," Trevor commented as he drove Kyla's car into the driveway.

"I guess Mom and Dad are still out." It was odd that they were out this late. Usually the domino parties didn't last much past eleven and it was almost midnight. She strongly suspected that their delay in coming home was calculated.

"Ted and I should have challenged you and Lynn to a rematch."

"Men will never beat women at word games."

"How's that?"

"Women are more intuitive than men."

"Well, my intuition is that Aaron's become deadweight on your shoulder."

"This time your intuition is right."

Aaron, who had fallen asleep on the Haskells' living room sofa, hadn't taken kindly to being roused for the ride home. To prevent a tantrum to rival any recorded in history, Trevor had broken his own safety rule and let him ride in Kyla's lap rather than being strapped into his car seat.

Trevor got out of the car and came around to assist Kyla. "Is your key in your purse?" he asked.

"The side pocket."

He had found the key by the time they reached the front door. Juggling the key, her handbag and the heavy diaper bag, he barely managed to unlock the door and swing it open.

"Thank you, Trevor. I had a good time."

"I'll see you in. I wouldn't let you and Aaron go into an empty house alone this late at night."

There seemed no point in arguing, though it made her distinctly uncomfortable to have him precede her through the dark house and upstairs. He had already switched on the soft lamp on top of the bureau by the time Kyla reached Aaron's room. She lowered the sleeping toddler into the baby bed.

"Can you undress him without waking him up?"

"I think I'll let him sleep in his shirt. I'm afraid if he wakes up fully, he'll think it's time for breakfast."

Trevor chuckled as he set the diaper bag in the rocker near the bed. He watched, fascinated, as her capable fingers moved swiftly to remove Aaron's shoes and socks.

Without waking him, she peeled down his shorts and plastic pants. Automatically she reached for the adhesive tabs that held on his disposable diaper. There her hands stilled.

She became acutely aware of the man standing beside her. The room seemed to shrink, leaving barely enough room for the two of them beside the baby bed. The atmosphere became thick with tension. The air was heavy and uncomfortably warm, almost sultry. The house grew more silent.

It was silly. Ridiculous. Aaron was a baby, sexually undeveloped. But the man standing next to her *was* developed and she was embarrassed to remove Aaron's diaper with Trevor hovering so close. Looking at a naked male child would be an intimacy between them, an intimacy Kyla couldn't engage in.

Apparently he noticed that her deft fingers had suddenly become clumsy and inefficient, because he cleared his throat loudly and moved away.

Faster than she'd ever done it in her life, she changed Aaron's wet diaper. Miraculously, he didn't wake up. Trevor was standing framed in the doorway of the nursery when she turned around after covering Aaron with a light blanket and switching out the light.

"All tucked in?"

"Yes. He had a big night. I think I'll get him one of those wading pools."

She led the way downstairs. There was a tightness in her chest she couldn't account for. Her stomach was fluttering. She felt an insane impulse to talk loudly so that the encroaching silence in the dark house wouldn't smother them.

One of the stairs took Trevor's weight and groaned in protest. He laughed softly and spoke in a hushed tone. "You've got a squeaky step."

"Several, I'm afraid." She sighed as she was reminded of a problem that was never too far from her mind. "It was my parents' dream to sell this house when Dad retired. They wanted to buy one of those fancy motor homes and travel all over the country."

"Why didn't they?"

"Richard was killed." Trevor said nothing, though she sensed a hesitation in his stride before he took the next step down. "I became a liability to them all over again."

"I'm sure they don't see it that way."

"But I do." He had stopped following. She stopped leading and turned around to face him. He was poised several steps above her.

"Why don't they sell it now?"

"They don't want Aaron and me to live alone. Besides, the market for houses in this part of town isn't as good as it once was. Unless the neighborhood is rezoned, I'm afraid they wouldn't make much by selling."

"This worries you, doesn't it? You don't want them to feel responsible for you."

She smiled ruefully. "I'm just sorry they aren't able to realize their dream because of me."

They looked at each other. Silence fell like a final curtain. Even though Trevor had turned on a light in the foyer, the remainder of the house was shadowed and dark.

One side of his face was lit, the right side. She could sense the leashed tension in his body, though they weren't touching. His wavy black hair cast errant shadows over his face. Lean and dark and intense, he looked like the brooding hero of a Gothic novel. He posed no physical threat, but was dangerous just the same. What should have been sinister was scintillating.

He made her tremble.

"I'll let you out," she said hastily, breathlessly, and turned away.

She took only one more step down the stairs before she felt his fingers in her hair, reaching, closing into a fist that caught and captured. A small whimpering sound issued from her throat, but she was helpless. The fist closed tighter around the handful of hair. It rotated once, making his hold more tenacious. Then a steady, unrelenting pull gradually drew her head back, back, until she turned on the step.

With his other arm he lifted her up even as his head descended. He stamped his mouth over hers, hard and unyielding. He didn't step down to bring them together, but hauled her up instead and drew her against him.

Her hands made futile attempts to push him away, but his chest was like a brick wall. Her heart thrummed, echoing loudly in her head. Or was that his heart? She knew nothing but the prickle of his mustache and the firm pressure of his lips against hers.

When he angrily lifted his head, she gasped, "No, Trevor, please."

"Open your mouth."

"No."

"Kiss me."

"I can't."

"Yes you can."

"No, please."

"What are you afraid of?"

"I'm not afraid."

"Then kiss me. You know you want to."

His mouth claimed hers once again. This time it brooked no resistance. It slanted and moved. His lips parted. Hers, obeying a will more powerful then her own, responded.

Then his tongue was there, seeking and finding hers as it had once before. He tasted her thoroughly, until they fell apart gasping for breath.

Hotly, he pressed his open mouth against the arch of her throat.

"No, no," she said, not even recognizing that panting voice as her own.

"I can't believe I'm kissing you."

"Please don't."

"And that you're kissing me back."

"No I'm not."

"Oh, but you are, love."

His mouth brushed the skin of her throat with light airy kisses, pausing to plant heated ones at its sensitive base. "Your skin, oh God, your skin." His hand was caressing her bare back. His fingers slipped between the straps of her dress and pressed her closer to him. Against her stomach she could feel what she told herself was his belt buckle.

Nonetheless she clung to him. At that moment he was the only reality left in the world. Not even remembering how they had gotten there, she discovered her fingers embedded in the thick strands of his hair. Again, her mouth was behaving wantonly beneath his.

"Is it even possible that you could want me?"

"Trevor."

"Because I want you."

Alarmed, she tore her mouth free of his scalding kisses. "No, don't even think—"

He cupped her face between his hands. "Not just sex, Kyla. I want more than sex. I know this is sudden, but I've fallen in love with you."

Huntsville, Alabama

They had bought a house for their fifth wedding anniversary, and it was moving day. The house was a mess. Boxes were stacked everywhere.

"How could we have accumulated so much junk? Did you finish cleaning out the attic?"

When the accountant's wife got no answer to either question, she turned her head to see what had her husband so preoccupied. He was looking through a stack of snapshots, studying each one intently. "What's that, honey?"

"Hmm? Oh, some pictures I took in Cairo."

She shivered and moved toward him. Closing her arms around his shoulders from behind, she leaned down and looked at the pictures over his shoulder. "Every time I think about how close I came to losing you, I shudder. How many days between the time you went on leave and the terrorist bombing?"

"Three," he said grimly.

"Who's that with you?" she asked softly, looking down at the picture he now held. She knew he often thought about the men who had served on guard duty with him at the embassy, especially those who had died.

"The one on the left was Richard Stroud."

"Was?"

"He didn't make it."

"And the other one?"

Her husband smiled. "That handsome devil is Trevor Rule. A Harvard man. Distinguished Philadelphia family. He was a hell-raiser though. We called him Smooch."

She laughed. "No need to ask why. I can see where he might come by his reputation."

"He had a harem a sultan would envy."

"Did he survive?"

"He was rescued, but was severely injured. I don't know if he survived it or not."

"Will you save the picture?"

"Think I should?"

"Was Stroud married?"

"Yes. Why?"

"If the picture isn't that important to you, why don't you send it to his widow? She'd probably like to have it. You all look so happy, like you're having a good time."

"Smooch had just told one of his famous dirty jokes." He leaned back and kissed her. "Good idea. I'll send it to Stroud's widow. If I can track her down."

He tossed the picture into the box of keepsakes they would move to their new house.

Chapter 7

*S*udden?

Sudden? Is that what he had said? "I know this is sudden, but I've fallen in love with you." "Sudden" hardly captured the earth-shattering essence of the statement. The following morning, as Kyla thought back on the scene, she still couldn't believe he had said that.

She had thanked heaven that her parents had walked through the front door only heartbeats later. Having been struck mute and paralyzed by what Trevor had just said, she had made a valiant effort at conversation, explaining that they had just gotten in and put Aaron to bed, and no, her parents weren't interrupting anything.

Trevor, while being polite to her parents, had stared down at her with that single green eye that more than compensated for the lost one. Avoiding his stare as best she could, she had escorted him to the front door and said a perfunctory good-night before Clif and Meg could go upstairs and leave her alone with him again. Even as she closed the door on him, he had stood his ground, staring down at her. It was then that she had vowed never to see him again.

Now, in the light of day, now, with the memory of last night's kiss still burning in her brain, she repeated that promise to herself. "I can't, I won't, see him again."

But it wasn't going to be that easy. He called during breakfast.

"Kyla," he said as soon as she answered the phone, "I'm sorry it's so early, but I have to talk to you. Last night—"

"I can't talk right now, Trevor. I'm in the middle of feeding Aaron his breakfast and he's making a mess of it."

"Will the two of you have lunch with me? You and Aaron?"

"Thank you anyway, but we can't. Dad and I are going to paint my old swing set today."

"When? I'll come by and help."

"No, no, don't do that," she said hastily. "I don't know exactly when we'll be working on it and I can't let you tie up your entire day."

"I don't mind. I want—"

"I've got to go, Trevor. Goodbye."

He came by anyway late that afternoon. She feigned a headache and didn't even come downstairs to say hello. Her parents looked at her disapprovingly once Trevor had left, but they said nothing.

Babs had no such qualms about offering her opinion. Kyla had ignored her less than subtle disparaging looks and grunts. By the end of the week she had become considerably more vocal. The two friends squared off during a lull in business. "The guy has called here several times a day for the past five days."

"That's his problem."

"It's my problem, too. I've run out of excuses as to why you can't come to the telephone."

"With your imagination, Babs, I'm sure you'll invent others. *If* he calls again."

"He will. He's not nearly the coward you are."

Kyla rounded on her. "I am not a coward."

"No? Then why are you going to so much trouble to avoid him? What did he do, something despicable like try to hold your hand?"

"I can do without your sarcasm."

"Want to know what I think?"

"No."

"I think that it was more than hand-holding."

Kyla turned away so that Babs wouldn't see the color flaring in her cheeks. "As I said, you have a vivid imagination."

"Otherwise you wouldn't be running so fast and so hard. If Trevor Rule hadn't gotten to you in some way, you'd be laughing off his attempts to see you."

"They're not funny."

"That's my point. This is damned serious."

"It is not!"

Into that scene, already crackling with tension, stepped the subject of their dispute. The bell over the door of Petal Pushers jangled musically as Trevor came in. Simultaneously the two women turned their heads in that direction. He was looking at only one, the one whose face suddenly lost its high color, the one who nervously ran her tongue over her lower lip, the one who clasped her hands together at her waist in order to keep from flying apart.

"Excuse me," Babs said. She sashayed through the swinging louvered doors into the back room, mumbling something about Mohammed and mountains under her breath.

Kyla stared at the floor that spanned the distance between them. Maybe he had come to order flowers. Maybe he had come to discuss the weather. Maybe he had come for any reason but the one she dreaded most.

His opening line instantly dispelled her hopes.

"Why are you avoiding me?"

All right, he wanted to play rough. She'd be rough. Her head snapped up proudly and she met his gaze. "Why do you think?"

"Because of what I said last Friday night?"

"Good guess."

"Did it offend you?"

"Tossing the word 'love' around like that is offensive."

"I wasn't tossing the word around. I meant it."

"I find that impossible to believe."

"Why?"

She stared at him, aghast. "*Why?* Because we had seen each other exactly four times before you told me you loved me."

"You were keeping count?" Teasingly, his mustache curved above those sparkling white teeth into a lazy smile.

"Only because what you said was so outlandish." Damn his smile and damn his mustache and damn her stomach for doing cartwheels at the sight of them.

"It happens that way sometimes."

"Not to me."

"But to me. I'm in love with you, Kyla."

She turned her back on him and braced herself against the countertop with stiff arms. "Stop saying that. Please."

He moved up behind her. She felt him there even before he placed his hands on her shoulders. His warmth crept over her back the way the sun glides over the beach at dawn.

"What are you afraid of, Kyla?"

"Nothing."

"Me?"

"No."

"Are you afraid of what you're feeling?"

"I'm not feeling anything."

"You're feeling something." He moved her hair aside and trailed his fingers from one side of her nape to the other. "You kissed me back."

Her head fell forward until her chin was almost touching her chest. "It didn't mean anything."

"Didn't it?"

"Only that I hadn't been kissed in a long time."

"And it felt good?"

"Yes... No... Please. I can't talk about this with you."

"It felt good to me, Kyla. So damn good. And right."

She turned to face him, wedging herself between him and the counter. "But it wasn't right, Trevor," she said with emphasis.

"Tell me why."

"Because I love my husband."

"But he's dead!"

"In here he isn't!" she cried angrily, laying a hand over her heart. "He's alive inside me. And I intend to keep him alive."

"That's crazy. It's unnatural."

"And also no business of yours, Mr. Rule!"

She shoved him aside and moved away. When she faced him again, her breasts rose and fell in agitation. Breathing didn't come easily. "I haven't led you on. I've been fair. I told you the second day we met that I wasn't looking for a romance. I had one. A wonderful love affair that will last me the rest of my life. Nothing could top it and I would never settle for anything less."

Impatiently she dashed the tears out of her eyes with the back of her hand. "In spite of my making that clear to you, you came on to me. I'm sorry if you fancy yourself in love with me, but that's something you'll have to come to grips with. I don't want to see you again, Trevor. Now just please leave me alone."

His jaw was rigid. The muscles along it were flexing with anger. Beneath his mustache his lips had narrowed into a tight, thin line. His hands were balled into fists and tapped his thighs. Kyla couldn't tell if he wanted to strike her or kiss her, and didn't know which to fear most.

Finally, he pivoted on his boot heels and strode out the door, letting it slam closed behind him. The bell over the door made a terrible racket.

Kyla slumped against the counter, not realizing until then just how physically taxing the encounter had been. Every muscle in her body felt as though it had been wrung out like a dishcloth. There was a terrible piercing pain between her eyes.

When she had regained a modicum of composure, she pushed herself away from the counter and turned to find Babs standing in the doorway, her arms folded over her breasts, a sour expression on her face.

"Don't say a word," Kyla warned, meaning it.

"I wouldn't think of it," Babs said airly. "You said all that need be said and quite brilliantly, I thought. Any other man would probably turn tail and flee. But not our Mr. Rule. Not by a long shot."

"Damn it!"

His foot punished the brake of his pickup truck as he whipped it off the road onto the gravel shoulder. Rocks sprayed out from beneath the wheels and clouds of dust engulfed the truck before it came to a complete stop. Trevor shoved it into "Park" and folded his arms over the steering wheel. He laid his forehead on his hands.

"Well, what did you expect?"

Had he really thought that he could waltz into her life and, without too much time and effort, have her fall into his arms? Into his bed?

Yes, he admitted now. That's what he had subconsciously expected. Because to George Rule's son things had always come easy.

Sports. Leadership. Studies. Popularity. Women.

To Trevor, life had been a banquet spread out on silver platters. He had even successfully thwarted his father's plans for his life. He was doing what he had always wanted to do. Except for that setback in Cairo, he had led a charmed life. Even then his good fortune had not deserted him. The bombing had left him impaired, but not totally incapacitated as it could have.

Raising his head, Trevor propped his chin on his hands and stared through the dusty windshield. The north Texas plains extended to the horizon in every direction. A barbed wire fence stretched endlessly.

Was that where his life was going? Nowhere?

Kyla's rejection was a bitter pill to swallow. Was this gnawing emptiness inside his gut only the reaction of a spoiled man to whom life had been abundantly sweet until now? Was he to be denied the only thing that was truly important? Were the gods mocking him, laughing at him because he had made one honorable gesture in his life and was to be denied the privilege of carrying it through?

But it was more than that. Honor and duty had little or nothing to do with his behavior toward Kyla now.

He loved the woman.

No longer was she just words written on sheets of inexpensive stationery, words that had filled lonely hours, and alleviated pain, and given him an anchor to hold on to when things had looked their bleakest.

She was a personality. A voice. A scent. A smile.

"And she still loves her husband," he reminded himself grimly.

Richard Stroud had been a terrific guy. Now he was a terrific ghost. And ghosts had a way of making themselves more terrific than the person they had been. One forgot the faults of those departed and remembered only their fine qualities.

But Richard Stroud wasn't his enemy and he mustn't think of him in those terms. Maybe he should give up this whole crazy idea. She loved her husband's memory. She had made her feelings known in plain, understandable English.

Give up while you're ahead, ol' boy. She doesn't want you.

Then he remembered the passion of her kiss, the taste of her mouth, the scent of her hair, the feel of her skin beneath his hands, and knew he wasn't about to give up.

"Not yet." Each precise motion indicated his resolve as he engaged the gears of his pickup and pulled it back onto the country road.

He would give her space, breathing room, time. She was entitled to it.

In the meantime, his days would be busy. He had a lot to do. And at night, in his bed, when his body ached for the appeasement hers promised, he would content himself by reading her letters. They were now like her voice whispering her innermost secrets to him in the dark.

"What's all that, Dad?" Kyla asked as she entered the kitchen.

"This, oh this is nothing," Clif Powers said quickly and began gathering up the papers scattered over the table.

"It's *something*." She hadn't missed her father's haste in removing the documents from her sight, nor the covert glance that passed between her parents. Their expressions were as guilty as Aaron's when she had caught him uprooting her favorite ivy.

Placing her hands on her hips, she said, "All right, you two, confess. What gives?"

"Sit down and have a cold drink, why don't you, dear?" Meg suggested.

"I don't want a cold drink. I want to know what it is the two of you are trying so hard to hide."

Clif sighed. "We might as well tell her, Meg."

Kyla sat down in a chair across the table from her father and folded her arms over the laminated tablecloth. "I'm listening."

"The city council was petitioned for this street to be rezoned as commercial property. We, your mother and I, contested it, but none of the other home owners did. The petition passed in a vote of the council last night."

Kyla assimilated that, for the moment thinking only of what this would mean to her parents' future. "Why did you contest it? Won't that escalate the value of your property?"

"Well, yes, dear, but we don't want to leave this house," Meg said. "Not that they're rushing us. We have a while, but..."

"You don't want to leave because of Aaron and me," Kyla said softly, realizing the reason for their secrecy. "We'll manage. I've always told you that."

"We know, but we never wanted to sell the place out from under you."

"Well it seems that the city council has taken the decision from you. I'm glad. This is what you wanted, to sell the house, buy a motor home and travel."

"But you and Aaron—"

"I'm a grown woman, Mom. Aaron is a well-adjusted child. We'll get a home of our own. It will be good for both of us."

"But we promised you when Richard died that we would never leave you alone," Clif argued.

Kyla reached out to cover his hand. "I appreciate your concern, Dad. You've been wonderful. But you and Mom have your own lives. You've earned these years together. You shouldn't spend your retirement shackled to me." She glanced down at the folded documents. "You've already had an offer to buy the property, haven't you?"

"Well, yes," Clif finally admitted. "But we've got eighteen months to vacate. We don't have to take the first offer that comes along."

"But who knows what will happen in eighteen months?" Kyla said. "Opportunities like this don't come along every day. If this is a fair offer, accept it."

"No," Meg said, shaking her head stubbornly. "We promised you that we wouldn't desert you."

"But, Mom—"

"Until you and Aaron are settled someplace, we won't even think about selling this house. And that's final, young lady." Meg stood up. The discussion was closed. "Do you want that cold drink or not?"

Several hours later Kyla lay in bed and stared at the changing patterns of shadow the moonlight cast on the ceiling of her room.

She was worried about her parents' reluctance to sell the house. The sale would insure them financial security for the rest of their lives. She didn't want them to put it off until they were too old and feeble to enjoy their retirement.

It was for her sake that they hesitated to jump at this chance. Didn't they realize how guilty their sacrifice made her feel? They had already postponed fulfilling their dream for almost two years, as a result of Richard's death. Granted, she would miss them. She would be sad to see the old house razed to make way for office complexes and filling stations. But growing pains always hurt.

It was time she experienced some of her own. Whether her parents sold the house or not, wasn't it time she made a home for Aaron and herself? How to convince Clif and Meg of that was the problem.

With a tired sigh, she forced her eyes to close.

And it happened again.

Trevor Rule's image was projected onto her eyelids. For hours each night, until she finally fell into a frustrated, exhausted sleep, he haunted her. It was as though he were communicating with her on some spiritual plane that she had no understanding of. Her obsession with him was irritating and unnerving.

It had been a month since their showdown in Petal Pushers. She wished she could forget how angry he had looked then. She wished even harder she could forget how he had looked last week when she had accidentally crossed paths with him.

It had been during the heat of the day. She and Babs were making a delivery in downtown Chandler. It had been an order large enough to require both of them, so Clif had volunteered to watch the shop while they were gone.

"Look at that," Babs had said.

"What?" The potted mums had leaked water on Kyla's hands and she was busy shaking them dry.

"Across the street. Yum-*my!*"

Using one damp hand to shade her eyes from the glaring sun, she followed Babs's gaze to the hardware store across the street. Trevor was stepping off the curb into the street where his pickup was parked. He was carrying a bag of concrete mix on his shoulder. As they watched, he swung it down into the bed of the pickup. From that distance, one would never guess he'd been in a terrible accident and had the scars to prove it. He had executed the chore with the strength and grace of an Olympic discus thrower.

Babs smacked her lips. "May the good Lord strike me blind if he's not gorgeous."

"Don't—"

"Hello, Trevor!" Babs sang out.

Gasping in outrage and mortification, Kyla turned her back and opened the car door. She scrambled in and slammed the door behind her. "I'm going to murder you," she hissed to Babs through the open window.

"If you act like an idiot, I'm going to murder *you*," Babs retorted.

Trevor had spotted them instantly and waved. While he was waiting for a car to pass, he took off the slouchy, straw cowboy hat that was shading his head and wiped his perspiring forehead on his rolled-up sleeve. He started toward them before the oncoming car had completely passed, even going so far as to step around its rear. He jogged the remainder of the distance across the street.

"Hi."

God was cruel. No man should have that much sex appeal and be left to run around loose, making a hapless victim of any woman he met.

He combed his fingers through his thick, black hair, pushing back the sweat-waved strands before pulling the cowboy hat back on. With the eye patch, he looked rakish and daring and piratical.

His throat was darkly tanned. At its base lay a rolled and knotted white bandanna. His sleeves had been rolled up so far and so tight that they looked like ropes encircling the teak biceps. The blue work shirt had been left unbuttoned. Kyla envisioned him working shirtless until it was time to drive into town and then pulling on the shirt in haste. Because of the heat, he hadn't felt inclined to button it.

In any event, the long shirttails flapped against his thighs, and his chest was left bare, save for the carpet of dark, damp curly hair that covered it. And covered it beautifully, from the fan-shaped cloud that blanketed the curving muscles of his breasts and swirled around the flat nipples, to that slender, silky line that divided his corrugated stomach and eventually flared around his navel. His chest was magnificent, marred only by an arcing scar that curved under his left breast from beneath his arm.

His jeans had that snug fit and softly faded look that no less than a thousand washings can give them. He wasn't wearing a pair of shiny lizard boots this time, but a pair that had been abused by seas of mud. A pair of worn leather work gloves covered his hands and curled back over his wrist bones.

Most stirring of all was the wide leather carpenter's belt that was strapped across his lean hips. It rested there like a gunslinger's holster and symbolized masculinity just as flagrantly. The building tools dangled against his trim thighs, rubbing against the muscles with every supple movement they made.

He was a living, breathing fantasy, masculinity incarnate.

"What brings you out? It's hot as the dickens."

Babs laughed. "You're even beginning to sound like a Texan. Isn't he, Ky?"

Kyla, inside the sweltering car, sat as rigid and wooden as a mannequin. "Yes, he is."

He braced one forearm on the top of the car. The shirt gaped open wider. Some of the springy hairs on his chest were beaded with sweat. He ducked his head to speak to her directly. "How are you?"

"Fine. You?"

"Fine. Aaron?"

"He's fine, too."

"Good."

"You seem to be working hard, Trevor," Babs said.

Kyla could tell by her strained tone of voice that Babs was irritated with the way the conversation was being conducted. Well, let her be! She was the one who had hailed him over like a streetwalker hollering, "Hey, sailor!" Let her chat with him.

She had thought she would be relieved when he straightened up to talk to Babs. But his doing so had left her with an unrestricted view of his torso. It fascinated her.

She watched a single bead of sweat form on the low curve of his right breast. It gathered itself there until it was a full, liquid pearl. Heavily it detached itself. Slowly it began to roll downward. Kyla's eyes followed its undulating descent over each rib. It could have gotten lost in the soft hair that dappled his stomach, but it had too much impetus now and continued to slide over the bronzed skin. At last, it angled inward toward his navel and funneled straight into that hair-whorled dimple as though it were a chalice fashioned for such a treasure.

"Won't we, Ky?"

Kyla jumped. "What?" Babs had asked her something, but she was helpless to say what.

"I told Trevor that we'd come out to see the house he's building as soon as it was finished."

"Oh, yes, I'd like that," she said vaguely. *Don't look at him anymore. Keep your eyes on the horizon or the parking meter or anything but him.*

Right now her own body was pouring perspiration, and the midsummer heat was only partially responsible. She willed Babs to get in the car and leave.

But it was Trevor who said goodbye first. "I've got to be going. The concrete man is waiting on me. It was great seeing you."

"Bye-bye, Trevor," Babs said.

"Goodbye, Babs. Kyla."

"Bye," she answered in a thin voice.

Only when she knew he had turned his back and was almost at his truck, did she raise her eyes. Then she wished she hadn't. His shirt was plastered to his skin, stuck there by the healthy, virile sweat of a working man. The clinging cloth accentuated the breadth of his shoulders. And the jeans were as flattering to his derriere as they were to his front.

Now, struggling to go to sleep more than a week later, she still saw him that way. His slight limp only accentuated the swaggering walk that never failed to make her mouth go dry.

Sighing resignedly, she turned onto her side and, surrendering to temptation, mentally followed that salty drop of perspiration down his chest again. This time her tongue followed it straight into his navel.

She woke up cranky.

Her mood didn't improve when she reached across the coffeepot on the breakfast table to answer the phone.

"Hi, it's Trevor."

She glanced quickly at her parents. The one time they had ventured to ask why Trevor didn't come around anymore, she had cut them short by saying, "I told you we

were just friends. He's probably found a girlfriend." Unwilling to reveal the identity of the caller now, she simply said, "Hello."

"I got it finished."

"Finished?"

"The house."

"Oh! Congratulations."

"Thanks. Will you come see it?"

Her parents were looking at her curiously. Meg mouthed, "Who is it?" Kyla pretended not to understand the exaggerated pantomime.

"I don't know if I can," she hedged.

"You said you would," he reminded her.

"I know, but I've been awfully busy."

"Before I put it on the market, I'd like your advice on decorating."

"I'm not qualified to give you that kind of advice."

"You're a woman, aren't you?"

Yes, she was a woman. Otherwise her heart wouldn't be throwing itself against her ribs as though looking for a means of escape. Otherwise her thighs wouldn't feel like melting wax and her palms wouldn't be slippery and she wouldn't be thinking about his mouth and her breasts.

"I don't know anything about decorating a house like that."

She saw Meg's eyes slice to Clif, saw Clif's brows bob up once then slowly lower.

"Will you come anyway?"

"When?"

"This afternoon."

"This is my Saturday to work." She and Babs swapped off Saturdays.

"After work. I'll pick you up when the shop closes."

Kyla twirled the telephone cord, wondering if she dare use Aaron as her excuse. Trevor would only tell her to bring him along. And her parents were digesting every word she said right along with their crunchy granola, so

she couldn't use something involving them as a reason not to go.

What did she care how flimsy her excuse was? She had told him in no uncertain terms that she never wanted to see him again. He had a nerve even to call and ask.

But wouldn't it be rude to turn down this particular invitation? She had seen the house under construction. It was obviously important to Trevor to get it just right. His career could be riding on the success of this house. Perhaps he *did* want her opinion on suitable decor and that was the extent of it. He needed a sounding board, someone whose taste he trusted.

"All right. I'll see you at six o'clock."

"Great."

She was busy in the shop all day, but the hours seemed to crawl by. And she stayed hungry. Or was that sinking feeling inside her dread at the thought of seeing him? Or expectancy? She didn't want to know.

At exactly six o'clock, he entered the shop, looking devastating in a sport shirt and slacks. He smelled as though he had recently showered and shaved. His hair was still damp. It curled around his ears and fell over the eye patch with breath-stealing appeal.

"Got any flowers left to sell?"

She laughed, relieved that he was being friendly and treating this date with the lightness it deserved. "A few."

"Ready?"

"Let me get my purse and turn off the lights in back."

In less than a minute she was back. He escorted her out and waited for her to secure the front door. His hand was beneath her elbow as he helped her into his car, but his touch was impersonal. So far, so good.

They made light, inconsequential conversation as he drove through the streets of town, then out into the countryside toward the wooded lot and the new house. He inquired about her parents and she told him they were well. He asked about Aaron and she filled him in on his latest

antics. They didn't speak of the argument that had taken place over a month ago.

"Oh, my heavens!" she exclaimed, when the house came into view. "I can't believe it."

He braked the car in the curved driveway that was lined with boxwoods. "Like it?"

"What's not to like?" Without waiting for him to assist her, she opened her door and stepped out, staring appreciatively at the house. "You didn't tell me it was going to have stained-glass windows on either side of the front door."

"You didn't ask," he replied teasingly. "Come on inside."

It was like stepping into the pages of *Architectural Digest*. The style overall was casual. The house had been designed for comfort and convenience, but no amenity had been spared. The rooms were spacious, but had a feeling of warm coziness about them.

Kyla gave a glad cry when she entered the dining area of the kitchen and saw how well her idea of the sun room had worked. "And look, a boiling water tap in the sink," Trevor said proudly, demonstrating it. "And a built-in refrigerator and freezer."

"It's perfect, perfect," Kyla said, smiling.

"You really like it?"

"It's wonderful!"

"Come outside. I want to show you the backyard."

Redwood decking extended for several yards beyond the house to the lawn, which had already been landscaped. Clusters of azalea bushes encircled the trees, which had been shaped and pruned. Flowers of every variety bloomed in tubs placed strategically on the deck. A fern-bedecked gazebo housed a bubbling spa. In the distance, the creek shone like a silver ribbon threading itself through the leafy trees.

"I can't believe it, Trevor," she said in awe. "You've done wonders. It's beautiful. What decorating you've al-

ready done is perfect. You won't have any trouble selling this house."

He took both her hands in his and turned her to face him. Kyla was surprised. Up until that moment he had hardly touched her. He'd been jocular and funny as he had led her through the rooms of the house, showing it off with the enthusiasm of a ten-year-old with a new bike. Now he was staring at her with an intensity that set her pulse to racing.

"I've stayed away from you, as you asked me to."

"It was for the best."

He shook his head. "I stayed away, but that doesn't mean that I liked it or that I didn't think about you." Kyla swallowed. "Quite the contrary. I think about you all the time."

"Trevor, please, let's not argue."

"I don't intend to."

"Then don't say any more."

"Let me finish." When he saw that she would grant him that, he went on. "You know how I feel about you. Don't you?"

"You . . . You said . . ."

"That I love you. And I meant it, Kyla."

"Please, don't pressure me about it. I can't."

"Can't what?"

"I can't be involved in an affair."

"I know. That's why I'm asking you to marry me."

Chapter 8

May I sit down, please?"

His mustache twitched with a smile. "That shocking, huh?" He led her to an old-fashioned porch swing similar to the one on the Powers's porch. It had been attached to the rafters over the deck.

Kyla was too stunned by his proposal to comment on the swing. She'd always had a fondness for porch swings. Any other time she would have remarked on it. Now she could barely command her limbs to move.

Trevor sat down beside her, but didn't touch her. For a few minutes the only sound between them was the faint squeak of the chain as the swing rocked gently. Crickets chirped from their hideouts. Cicadas had begun their nightly concerts from the dense branches of the trees. Words and phrases flitted through Kyla's head like fireflies, but they blinked and burned out before she could vocalize them.

"I don't know what to say."

"Say yes."

She looked at him through the gathering dusk. "Trevor, where did you get the idea that I wanted to marry you? To marry anybody?"

"I got no such idea. You've made it clear on several occasions that you aren't in the market for a husband."

"Then why did you ask me to marry you?"

"Because I love you and want to be your husband. I want to take care of you and Aaron, be a father to him."

"But that's crazy!"

"Why?"

"Because you know that I don't love you."

He stared down at his hands, turning them over and studying them as though seeing them for the first time. "Yes, I know that," he said finally. "You're still in love with Richard."

She felt compelled to touch him and shyly laid her hand on his knee. "Are you hoping that I'll change, that love will come in time?"

"Will it?"

She removed her hand. "I'll never love any man the way I did Richard."

"I still want you."

"How can you even consider wasting your life that way? Why would you want to marry a woman you know doesn't love you and never will?"

"Let me worry about the whys and wherefores. Will you marry me?"

"You're a very attractive man, Trevor."

He smiled broadly. "Thanks."

Her exasperation showed. "What I mean is, six months from now, or next week, or tomorrow, you might meet another woman, one who loves you."

"I won't be looking."

"But you should be."

"Look," he said patiently, "this fictitious woman could come up and pinch me on the ass, and it wouldn't matter. I've found the woman I want to give my name to."

"But you barely know me."

I know you inside out, he thought. *I know that you love porch swings and sky lights and stained-glass windows and houses surrounded by trees. I know that in the tenth grade you went with a boy named David Taylor and the bastard broke your heart. You have a patch of freckles under your right arm that you consider your birthmark. And you're self-conscious about your breasts because you think they're too small. But I think they're lovely and I can't wait to see them, touch them with my fingertips and tongue, make love to them with my mouth.*

Trevor cleared his throat and shifted uncomfortably on the swing. "I didn't believe in love at first sight either until I saw you in the mall that day. I thought you were beautiful, but you were more than just a pretty woman who caught my eye. I liked the way you talked to Aaron. I liked the way your hands moved as you tended to him." He grinned lopsidedly. "If he hadn't taken a mind to jump in the fountain, I would have devised a way to meet you." He inched closer to her. "Marry me, Kyla. Live with me in this house."

"This house!" she exclaimed softly. "You built this house with the intention of *our* living in it?"

Pleased that he had surprised her, he asked, "Why do you think I paid such close attention to detail?"

Behind her, beyond the walls of glass that opened onto the deck, Kyla could see the well-arranged rooms, rooms that, had she designed them herself, couldn't be more to her liking. "We have an uncanny similarity in taste. It is a lovely house, Trevor, but that hardly constitutes a good reason to marry."

"Right now, it's just a house. I want to make it a home. For Aaron. For you. For us."

She studied him for a moment, shaking her head. "It just doesn't make any sense."

"It makes perfect sense. I want us to be a family. I want to assume responsibility for you and Aaron."

The idea came from nowhere, but struck her with the impact of a speeding freight train. He wanted a wife and child. Now why would a man with Trevor's looks and Trevor's charm, a man who could have any woman he wanted, be proposing marriage to a widow with a child? Unless he couldn't come by them any other way.

Of course! All of Trevor's disabilities weren't visible. Was her main attraction that she didn't and couldn't return his love? Did he need a wife who would make no physical demands on him? To have a child, did he have to marry a woman who already had one? In a quaint fashion, was this to be no more than a marriage of convenience?

"Trevor," she said hesitantly, "your... When you were hurt...?"

"Yes?"

"Did...?"

"Did what?"

"What I mean is... Are you...?"

"Am I...? What?"

She took a deep breath. "Are you capable of intimacy?" She felt small and the world closed in. It had a stranglehold on her throat. Garnering all her courage, she raised her eyes to look at him.

"You've kissed me, haven't you?" he asked in a deep, throbbing voice.

"Yes."

"I've held you."

"Yes."

"Close."

"Yes."

Her eyes fell away and when she didn't say anything for an interminable time he prodded, "Well then?"

She fiddled with the fringed sash at her waist. "I thought maybe since I was a widow with a child, and if... that... had happened to you, then..."

He tilted her head up with his hand beneath her chin. "I'm not only capable of, but eager for intimacy with you." Each word sent a vibrating current through her body that continued to hum, like harp strings long after deft fingers had plucked them. "And just so there's no misunderstanding later, I'll tell you right now that this marriage would carry with it all that the relationship implies. I want to be your husband in every sense of the word. I want you in my bed, Kyla. I want to make love to you. Frequently. Do you understand?"

She nodded her head with no more willpower of her own than one hypnotized. Neither of them ever remembered how his fingers had come to be loosely caging her neck, but both became conscious of it at the same time. They sat very still. His single green eye held hers in thrall as his face moved closer. The instant she felt the brush of his mustache against her lips, her eyelids closed.

What a waste, Kyla thought as his fingers threaded up through her hair to settle against her scalp. What a shame that a kiss like this had to be wasted on a woman who didn't and couldn't love him. How regrettable that the lips that were both fiercely possessive and gently persuasive, enough to cause hers to part as though they were hungry, couldn't be kissing a woman who could return such passion.

Lightly she rested her hands on his shoulders in order to keep from tottering off the rocking swing and the rocking universe.

Trevor's other arm encircled her waist and drew her against his chest. A low masculine growl purred in his throat as his tongue penetrated her lips and tasted her mouth at will.

Kyla had a difficult time restraining her own low moans. The silky lash of his tongue made her think how lamentable it was that this kiss wasn't being bestowed on a woman who could appreciate it.

Then it occurred to her that she was giving every semblance of appreciation. Her back was arched, pressing her breasts against his chest. Her hands had wadded the fabric of his shirt in death grips. Her tongue was responding to the love play of his.

She broke away, experiencing an alarming scarcity of breath. Standing quickly, she wondered what ailment had befallen her knees. They were trembling so badly that they could hardly support her. "I've got to go."

Trevor was having a difficult time breathing too, if that rasping sound filtering through his lips was any indication. "All right," he agreed without argument. It took him a long time to stand up. One swift, forbidden glance down his body made a mockery of her earlier speculation.

Virtually at a run, she went back through the house and waited for him at the front door. Gratefully she sank into the front seat of the car when he held the door for her, not sure when her legs would collapse beneath her.

Trevor didn't attempt conversation as he drove her home. Kyla was relieved. Midsummer madness might have been responsible for his proposal. Maybe he'd only been joking. He could already be regretting that he'd asked her to marry him.

But she knew such was not the case when he cut the car's engine at the curb in front of the Powers's house, turned and laid his arm on the back of the seat and said, "Kyla?" in a blood-stirring tone she couldn't mistake.

It was shocking to discover his taste lingering on her lips when she nervously swept them with her tongue. "I don't think it even warrants further discussion. You can't be serious about this."

"Kyla." He waited until she cautiously turned her head and looked at him. "I'm serious. Do you think I could have kissed you like that if I hadn't been serious?"

"I don't know," she said with a trace of desperation.

He chuckled softly, finding that amusing. "I've kissed many women, but I've never proposed to one. At least I've

never proposed marriage. Rest assured that I'm serious." Taking her hand he raised it to his mouth and kissed the palm. "I know I've taken you by surprise. I didn't expect an answer tonight. But promise me you'll think about it. Think about what our getting married could mean to you and Aaron. To your parents. Sleep on it."

Trevor Rule was a dirty fighter, Kyla thought angrily as she checked the digital read-out on her bedside clock for the umpteenth time. She had charted each hour of the long night, and he was to blame for her sleeplessness.

For one thing her body refused to relax. It was restless, alert to every sensual stimulant. Hadn't her bare legs ever felt bed linens against them before? If so, why were they sliding against the sheets as though that were a new indulgence? And why was this old cotton nightgown irritating her breasts? Why, tonight, were her nipples supersensitive to every brush of the fabric against them? Why did they need soothing? And why, every time she thought of them being soothed, did she imagine Trevor's lips against them?

Repeatedly she swore that these physical manifestations had nothing to do with his kiss. Was she about to have her period? That could be the cause for the achy pressure between her thighs. Could she have gotten into poison ivy? Was that the reason her skin felt itchy and in need of caressing?

"I'm *not* aroused."

Her body argued with her, saying otherwise.

Damn him for using such sneaky tactics. He knew the right button to push. He had subtly suggested that if she didn't marry him, she was being selfish.

All right, she'd play devil's advocate.

It *would* be good for her parents. They would feel free to make their own plans, knowing that she and Aaron would be under Trevor's protection.

And it would be good for Aaron. A growing boy needed a father. Clif Powers had filled that role in Aaron's life so far, but how long could he keep pace with his grandson? Would he be healthy and energetic enough to participate in sports with him in a few years, take him fishing and camping, and do all the myriad, physically taxing things a father does with his son?

But Aaron had a father! Kyla argued. Richard Stroud was Aaron's father. She had sworn to keep Richard alive for his son and she was determined to hold to that vow. It would take more than Trevor's smooth manner and glib tongue to sway her from that.

Besides, a woman didn't commit herself to a marriage because it would be beneficial to the people around her, no matter how attractive the man was. Granted, Trevor Rule was attractive and good husband material. She was aware of the strides he was taking in the community. He was constantly being quoted in the business pages of the newspaper. Obviously he was a man of integrity, honest in his business dealings and respected for his innovative ideas for commercial growth. Physically—

No. It would be better not to think about his physical attributes. Her burst of inspiration that he could have been emasculated as a result of his accident had been disproved only moments later.

No, leave his physical attraction out of this. Thinking about that tended to cloud her mind and color her judgment. The only way to approach this problem was pragmatically.

That was what she did until dawn, when she finally reached a decision. She would find a place for Aaron and herself to live. She would move from this house so that her parents could sell it and carry on with their plans.

Marriage to Trevor wouldn't be necessary. Financially she was holding her own. When he was old enough she would see that Aaron had a close association with other boys his age and their fathers. She didn't need a man in her life.

However, she supposed she should thank Trevor for his proposal and for goading her into making decisions that she had postponed since Richard's death. The sooner she turned him down, the better.

While her parents were dressing for church the next morning, she made the telephone call. He answered in the middle of the first ring. "Hello, Trevor. I hope I didn't wake you."

"Hardly."

"I've come to a decision. I—"

"I'll be right over."

He hung up before she could say another word. Disgruntled, she replaced the receiver. It would have been easier to turn him down over the phone and spare them both the awkwardness of meeting face to face.

Since she and Aaron were already dressed, she carried him and his plastic beach ball outside. If she met Trevor on the front lawn, this could be over and done with before her parents knew about it.

Trevor must have been standing by the telephone with his car keys in his hand because he got there in a matter of minutes. Kyla was surprised to see him emerge from his car wearing a dark suit. His hair gleamed darkly in the sunlight. He gave the large plastic ball a tap with his foot and Aaron toddled off to chase it.

"Good morning," he said.

"Good morning."

She was nervous. This was going to be more difficult than she had thought. While she was trying to concentrate on how ridiculous the idea of marrying him was, her mind ventured onto how good-looking he was. She was remembering the feel of his mustache against the palm of her hand, the way he had of kissing her throat and touching her neck with fingers that seemed to know just the right amount of pressure to apply.

"Trevor," she began, licking her lips quickly and clasping her hands damply together. "I—"

The dog seemed to drop out of the sky. Suddenly it was just there, dancing around Aaron and yapping loudly. The white poodle's movements were frenzied, quick and, to the fifteen-month-old, terrifying. What to the poodle were playful thrusts and parries, to the child must have seemed like vicious attacks.

Aaron screamed, but his screams only seemed to excite the dog more. It bounced around the child like a fluffy white dot, its barking as sharp and rapid as the rat-a-tat of a machine gun.

Aaron took several stumbling steps forward, seeking escape. The dog reared up on its hind legs. Aaron toppled over backward. Then, as agilely as he could, he scrambled to regain his footing and ran blindly toward safety.

Or rather not so blindly. He had a clear choice of whom to run to. But he didn't choose his mother. The child ran toward the large, strong man, who bent down to scoop him up just as Aaron's solid little body barreled into his shins.

The stout little arms wrapped around Trevor's neck. Aaron buried his tear-streaked face in the crook between Trevor's neck and shoulder. Trevor lowered his head over the child's and rubbed his back soothingly. "There now, Scout. It's all right. You're okay. I've got you and I'm not about to let anything hurt you. That puppy just wanted to play with you. Come on now, you're okay."

The animal's owner, a heavyset middle-aged woman, came huffing down the sidewalk. She grabbed up the poodle and swatted him on the rump. "You naughty thing, you. Why did you scare that little boy like that?" Tucking the poodle under her arm, she came rushing toward them. "Is your son all right?" she asked Trevor.

"He's fine. Just frightened." Trevor continued to rub Aaron's back. The boy hadn't moved. His face was still pressed against Trevor, but he had stopped crying.

"I'm sorry. I let go of his leash and he shot off like a rocket. He wouldn't bite. He only wanted to play."

"I think Aaron was overwhelmed." Trevor's large hand covered the back of Aaron's head and held it securely against his neck.

"I'm so sorry." The woman continued on her way down the sidewalk, still admonishing the dog.

Trevor patted Aaron's back. He nuzzled his cheek with his mustache and kissed his temple. "He'll be okay. I think he just—"

His words faltered when he noticed Kyla's face. She was standing close, looking up at him with an expression that arrested his gaze and halted his speech. Tears were standing in her eyes. Her lips were tremulous and slightly parted. She was looking at him as though seeing him, really seeing him, for the first time.

For long moments, they stared at each other, not even aware that the Powerses had rushed out onto the front porch to see what the commotion was about. Meg started down the steps, but Clif caught her arm and held her back.

Trevor, still holding Aaron, reached out his left hand and folded it around Kyla's chin. He made a pass across her lower lip with his thumb. "You were interrupted. What were you about to tell me?"

In that instant, she knew what her answer would be. Aaron needed a father. A living father. Richard's memory would be kept alive, but he wasn't there as a safeguard against the day-to-day terrors of the world, like energetic puppies.

Trevor obviously cared a great deal for her son. Aaron had instinctively sought him out for protection. He was tender and loving and kind and generous. Where else would she find a man willing to take over the responsibilities of rearing another man's child, a man willing to marry her knowing she didn't love him?

"I was about to tell you that I'd be pleased to marry you. If... if you still want me to."

"If I still want you to?" he repeated gruffly. "God, yes, I still want you to."

He closed the space between them and with the arm that wasn't holding her son, embraced her. She didn't know what she had expected. A handshake to seal the bargain? A premarital document to sign? Certainly not the kiss she got. It was a Sunday morning. They were standing in broad daylight, in full view of any neighbor who might venture outside or any motorist who happened to drive by.

But Trevor exercised no decorum in kissing her. He tilted his head to one side, aligned his mouth with hers and kissed her in a greedy, manly way.

Kyla felt a blow to her middle, as though a velvet fist had socked her. It sent ripples of pleasure throughout her body. Vaguely, in the back of her mind, she was disappointed that he was still holding Aaron and therefore unable to pull her against him and complete the circuits of sensation that were popping and sizzling. Everything feminine inside her was craving to be pressed against that hard, virile frame. She wanted to be filled with him.

When he finally raised his mouth from hers, she reeled slightly. His strong arm was there to steady her. It turned her around and guided her toward the house, where she saw her parents hovering on the front porch. Aaron was happily tugging on a fistful of Trevor's black hair. Trevor was smiling broadly and every few steps he laughed out loud.

"Mrs. Powers, Mr. Powers, Kyla has done me the honor of saying yes to my marriage proposal."

Meg immediately burst into tears of gladness. Clif hurried down the steps to pump Trevor's hand. "That's wonderful. We're very happy. We're...well, we're happy. When?" he asked his daughter.

"When?" Trevor echoed.

"I, uh, I don't know." Now that she had made the decision, she felt as if she was being swept along by a tidal wave. "I haven't had time to think about it."

"How about next Saturday?" Trevor suggested. "I came dressed to go to church with you. We can check it out with the minister after the service."

"I think that's a lovely idea," Meg said enthusiastically. "Here at the house, of course."

"Yes, why wait?" Clif added.

Yes, why? Kyla was asking herself. Why did she feel like applying the brakes? Accepting Trevor's marriage proposal had seemed like the thing to do just moments ago, but now she was realizing the enormity of her decision. This was for real. She was about to become Mrs. Trevor Rule. What would everyone think?

Babs left no doubt as to how she took the news. As was her habit she came over for Sunday dinner. Trevor answered the door when she knocked. Clif was cranking the freezer of homemade ice cream Meg had insisted on making for dessert in celebration of the occasion. Kyla was feeding Aaron so he could be put down for his nap before they ate. Meg was spooning up fresh green beans. Trevor was the only one available.

Babs stared at him in wordless awe as he pushed the screen door open and stepped aside. "Come on in. Everyone is in the kitchen."

Kyla hadn't told Babs that she was going to see Trevor. Babs hadn't seen him since that afternoon in town over a week ago when Kyla had acted like such a ninny. Now, where his carpenter's belt had been strapped, a blue and white gingham apron was tied in a bow. He had insisted on helping Meg get lunch ready.

Babs padded into the kitchen behind him. No sooner was she through the door than she demanded of Kyla, "What's going on here?"

Kyla's eyes swept across the other expectant faces, but when no one seemed inclined to answer Babs, the chore fell to her. "Trevor and I are getting married."

Babs's wide china-blue eyes found Trevor. He grinned engagingly. "Surprise!"

"You're getting married!" Babs exclaimed. When he nodded, she clasped his face between her hands and smacked a hearty kiss directly on his mouth. "Since you're marrying my best friend I think I'm entitled to that."

Laughing, Trevor hugged her around the waist and laid another sound kiss on her mouth. When he released her, he said, "I think so, too."

Everyone laughed, including Aaron, who didn't understand anything but the gaiety going on around him. He pounded his spoon on the tray of his high chair.

Lunch was a joyous affair. There was a lot of teasing and talk about the wedding and matrimony in general. Kyla couldn't get accustomed to the idea that in less than a week she would be a bride. Nor could she get accustomed to the affectionate way Trevor treated her.

He sat close. He took advantage of innumerable opportunities to touch her. His arm was often resting across her shoulders. Caresses seemed to come as naturally to his fingertips as kisses came to his lips.

Kyla wasn't annoyed by these demonstrations of affection. Quite the contrary. She found that she was beginning to look forward to them. That anticipation turned to guilt. As far as she was concerned, this marriage *was* a marriage of convenience. Wasn't it?

Trevor spent the afternoon with them. He acquainted them with his background. "I grew up in Philadelphia. Went to prep school, then to Harvard."

"Your mother is dead?" Meg asked him.

"Yes, she died several years ago. I'll notify my father about the wedding, but I doubt he'll be able to make the trip on such short notice."

"He's a lawyer?" Clif asked.

"A very successful one. It was a disappointment to him that I didn't want to follow in his footsteps and make the name of the firm Alexander, Rule and Rule."

"But surely he's proud of your success in your own field," Clif said.

Trevor became reflective. "I hope so."

By that evening everyone in town seemed to know about their forthcoming marriage. "Mrs. Baker has offered to give you a shower."

Horrified, Kyla turned away from the countertop in the kitchen where she was preparing a tray of sandwiches to take out to the men, who were sitting on the porch. "Oh, no, Mom. I don't want any of that folderol. Please thank anyone who calls to offer, but kindly refuse."

"But, Kyla, everyone's so happy for you."

She shook her head adamantly. "I don't want any parties. Nothing. Please. I had all that once and it was lovely. This . . . this marriage isn't like that."

Meg looked at her with undisguised disappointment. "Very well, dear."

Her parents, whose heads were in a cloud of romanticism, would never understand her motives for marrying Trevor. She wasn't certain Trevor understood them either.

She escorted him outside after he had bidden her parents good-night. As soon as they stepped through the screen door and into the deep violet shadows of the porch, he gathered her in his arms and lowered his mouth to hers.

The kiss was intimate and evocative, a mating of their mouths. His tongue stroked hers. His hands slid from her back to the front of her waist. They glided up over her ribs and pressed her breasts. He moaned.

"God, I don't know how I'll make it till Saturday night." His hands fell away. "Do you know how much I want to touch you? But I can't touch you now. If I touch you now, I won't be able to stop until there's no cloth between us and I'm holding you, kissing you, your mouth, breasts, stomach, everywhere."

The last word was sighed into her ear. Then his open mouth slid from just beneath her jaw to the base of her neck. His mustache was a pleasure-giving, conscience-ridding, memory-banishing instrument that left her tin-

gling and warm and moist. If he had strengthened the embrace, she would have allowed it. He didn't.

"Good night, love."

The darkness swallowed him up. Long after she watched the taillights of his car disappear, Kyla stood there on the porch, trembling at the thought of their wedding night. She tried convincing herself that the shivers plaguing her were caused by dread.

But she didn't really think they were.

Everyone's mood the following week was festive. Her parents were more animated than she had seen them since Richard's death. It was plain to see that they adored Trevor and trusted him to make their daughter and grandson happy. Babs's enthusiasm was uncontainable and by midweek was wearing thin.

"But I don't need anything like this," Kyla said of the sexy negligee Babs was holding up to her.

"Every bride needs something like this. Not that they last very long," she said with a naughty wink. The implication made Kyla's stomach feel queasy.

"I've got plenty of nightgowns," Kyla objected in a muffled voice.

"I've seen them. They're wretched. At least for a honeymoon."

"We're not taking a honeymoon. Not right away. We're moving directly into Trevor's house."

"*Your* house and you know what I mean about a honeymoon. You don't have to leave town to have one. Or for that matter, you don't have to leave the bedroom to have one." She laughed gaily. "I've had several myself. So which is it going to be, the peach or the blue?"

"I don't care," Kyla said petulantly, plopping down on the chaise in the boutique's dressing room. "You're the one who insisted I needed a new negligee, you pick it out."

"Boy!" Babs said in exasperation. "What's the matter with you?"

Babs wouldn't believe her if she told her, and she wasn't going to tell her. When you were insane, you rarely went around announcing it to your friends. "Nothing."

"Well, you're sure grouchy. I can't think of a better way to improve your mood than to spend a few days in the sack with Trevor Rule."

She turned to call the salesclerk and missed Kyla's stark expression. She wanted to get caught up in the spirit of the occasion but couldn't allow herself to. Getting excited about the wedding would be disloyal to Richard. No one had mentioned his name in days. It seemed that he had been blotted from everyone's mind but hers.

She clung to his memory more tenaciously than ever, but inevitably it seemed to be slipping from her grasp. She noted these lapses of memory the most when she was with Trevor, who was playing the role of bridegroom to the hilt.

Every evening they went shopping for household items. He wanted her input on everything from blenders to bolsters. He could have read her mind and not picked out furniture she liked better. Their taste in everything coincided. Often she felt like Cinderella having all her wishes granted at once. He spared no expense. As the interior of the house began to take shape, she felt like pinching herself to make sure this wasn't some bizarre dream.

That was how she felt the evening he led her into the master suite to show her the final product of their combined efforts. "They delivered the chairs and bed today," he said, switching on the lamp with the lotus-shaped silk lampshade. "I think everything came together real well."

The room was lovely, out of her dreams. Her eyes surveyed it slowly, and when they came back full circle to the man, he was staring at her intently. Her hair was limned by the lamplight and her body was cast into silhouette through her soft voile dress.

"What is it?" she asked on a soft breath.

"Let's try out the bed."

She reacted with a sudden intake of breath, a lurch of her heart, a blinking of her eyes. He reached for her and within a heartbeat, she found herself lying on the bed with him bending over her. Holding her eyes captive with his gaze, his hand drifted down the side of her neck until it came to rest on her breast and the first button on her bodice. He unbuttoned it. The second. The third.

Still she couldn't move. Not even when he slipped his hand inside her bodice. Her breathing accelerated. Involuntarily her eyes closed.

He wedged his fingers beneath her bra strap and pushed it down over her shoulder. Down, down, until the top curve of her breast swelled over the lacy cup.

"God, you're lovely." He laid his hand on her and rubbed the gentle curve of her breast, then moved lower to graze the responsive crest.

He sighed her name an instant before his mouth claimed hers. His kiss wasn't tempestuous as she had expected. But infinitely sweet and tender and loving. As loving as the hand that continued to fan lightly over her nipple.

He pressed his mouth to her ear. "I want to be inside you, Kyla. I want to feel you coming."

He trapped her gasp behind another deep kiss. His fingertips soothed the flesh that shrank even tighter in response to his bold words.

"Please, love, don't make that sexy sound. Please don't feel this good," he groaned, as his fingers caressed her breast. "Or I won't be able to stop. And I want to be your husband the first time I take you."

Exercising tremendous control, he refrained from other caresses. He restored her clothing and drew her up to stand beside the rumpled bed. She sagged against him weakly.

Smiling into her hair, he returned his hand to cover her heart. "I'll make you happy, Kyla. I swear it."

She buried her face in his neck, not out of passion, but despair. He made her body sing. But she couldn't reciprocate his promise of happiness or love. Because keeping

that one would jeopardize the one she had made long before she ever met Trevor Rule, the one she had made to Richard the day he died.

Chapter 9

Babs filled the house with flowers. Meg laid out a sumptuous buffet. The bakery delivered a multitiered cake. What Kyla had hoped would amount to no more than a small family gathering with their pastor, began to look very much like a wedding.

She fretted over it in her bedroom upstairs. "Everyone is making too much of this." She reached for the buttons on the back of her bodice.

"Everyone should. This is a wedding, for heaven's sake." Babs turned her around to do up the unreachable buttons.

"A *second* wedding."

"So what are you bitching about? Some of us have yet to see one."

Kyla stared at Babs in surprise. "I didn't think you ever wanted to get married."

Babs looked chagrined at having said something she wished she could recall. "Not to anybody I've met so far.

But if one Richard Stroud or Trevor Rule came into my life I'd rope him and drag him to the altar.''

Properly chastised, Kyla stepped into her skirt. "I'm sorry, Babs. I know how lucky I've been.''

"Oh, hell, don't pay any attention to me. I'd hardly call it lucky to have a husband killed by a terrorists' bomb. I'm just jealous because not one wonderful man has loved me and you've had two groveling at your feet."

She laughed at the mental picture Babs's words painted. "I doubt Trevor would ever grovel."

Babs laughed, too. "Come to think of it, so do I." She sighed, "Jeez, Kyla, he's such a stud. But a nice stud and those two qualities rarely go hand in glove."

Kyla didn't want to think about the man who was waiting downstairs for her. Every time she thought of Trevor and the night to come, she began to quake.

"Are you sure this dress is appropriate?" she asked, changing the subject. "I feel like I should wear something simpler."

"It's perfect."

The two-piece silk design had detailed stitching at the shoulders and on the waistband of the dirndl skirt. The pale yellow color and the fabric's icy sheen made it look like lemon sherbet. The only jewelry she wore was a pair of pearl earrings.

"Don't you think you should take that off?"

Kyla followed the direction of Babs's gaze down to her left hand. "My wedding ring." She hadn't even thought of it because it was as much a part of her hand as her fingerprints. Tears welled in her eyes at the thought of removing it. It hadn't been off her hand since the day Richard had slipped it onto her finger with a solemn vow to love her until death.

Slowly, with a twist and a wrenching tug, she removed the ring. Reverently she laid it on the velvet lining of her jewelry box and closed the lid.

"Are you ready?" Babs asked.

"I suppose so," Kyla answered shakily. Parting with the wedding ring had been an emotional upheaval as violent as that of leaving Richard in his grave. All week she had been making light of this occasion. But she couldn't any longer. She was about to marry another man. In a matter of minutes he, not Richard, would be her husband. "Has Dad already taken Aaron downstairs?"

"You're a bride! Stop worrying about Aaron. Surely your parents and I can handle him." Babs reached into a large square box she had carried into the room earlier. "Trevor asked me to give this to you before you came down."

It was a bouquet of white orchids, the Bow Bells that she loved, garnished with white rosebuds and clumps of baby's breath. "My Lord," Kyla breathed, taking the lavish bouquet from Babs's outstretched hands. "There must be—"

"A dozen orchids in all. He was very specific." Her blue eyes were twinkling. "I'm telling you, Kyla, the man is a jewel, and if you make a mess of this marriage, I'll snatch him up without an apology or a smidgen of conscience."

"I'll do my best to make it work," Kyla murmured as she walked dazedly toward the door.

Downstairs, Babs preceded her into the living room. Kyla heard the hushed conversation cease. She took a deep, hopefully steadying, breath. Everyone was looking at her when she entered.

Meg had a damp lace handkerchief pressed to her cheek, but she was smiling. Clif swallowed a lump of emotion that made his Adam's apple slide up and down. Babs was grinning with the romantic mischievousness of a wood nymph. The Haskells, Ted and Lynn, were standing together, unusually solemn.

Finally Kyla looked at Trevor, who was so handsome that she went mushy on the inside. He was wearing the same dark charcoal suit he had worn to the banquet. This time his shirt was ivory. An ivory tie with black pinstripes

matched the silk handkerchief folded into his left breast pocket.

Trevor moved toward her, but Aaron, who could move like a streak of lightning when one least expected him to, darted forward and reached her first. Meg and Babs took simultaneous steps forward to prevent him from tearing her stockings or wrinkling her skirt.

But Trevor reached down and picked the boy up into his arms. "Your mom looks beautiful, doesn't she, Scout?" he asked on a husky whisper when he straightened up.

Aaron babbled something that sounded like "Mama" repeated several times, then stretched forward to smear a rough, wet kiss on Kyla's cheek. He seemed content to remain in Trevor's arms, which was just as well since Kyla didn't know how she could hold her son and the bouquet of orchids at the same time.

"It seems like I'm always thanking you for flowers."

"Do you like them?"

"They're beautiful. Of course, I love them. You were too extravagant."

He shook his head. "This is my wedding day. You are my bride. Today nothing is too good for us, love."

They stared at each other for ponderous moments until Aaron began to wiggle within the grasp of Trevor's arms. Trevor shook himself out of the trance Kyla's appearance had induced and took her arm. Together they moved farther into the room where the others were grouped around the minister.

"Kyla, Trevor, this is a happy day," the minister began.

Though it was the middle of the afternoon and sunshine streamed in through Meg's polished windows, Babs had insisted on having candles. They flickered like winking eyes from every nook and cranny of the room, filling it with the heady scent of vanilla. Someone had thought to put an album of romantic instrumentals on the turntable of the stereo. Surely Babs had depleted the inventory at

Petal Pushers because flowers, not limited to white but covering the spectrum of the rainbow, filled vases and baskets scattered throughout the room.

The service was by necessity informal. During the recitation of vows, Aaron sneezed, spraying Trevor's shoulders. Automatically Kyla reached for her mother's hanky, blotted the damp spots on Trevor's coat and dabbed at Aaron's nose. Trevor smiled on, fondly. Once that housekeeping chore had been attended to, the pastor continued. When he called for the bride's ring, Trevor shifted Aaron in his arm and reached inside his right coat pocket. Kyla stared down at her hand as he slid the circlet of diamonds onto her finger.

Trevor noticed the pale band of skin around the base of her finger and, realizing what had caused it, swiftly lifted his gaze to her face. Her soft look carried with it an apology. An expression she couldn't decipher flashed across his features, but was instantly gone. He pushed the dazzling ring into place on her finger and clasped her hand tightly. The awkward moment passed with only the two of them knowing it had occurred at all.

Several minutes later, the minister said, "Trevor, you may kiss your bride now."

They faced each other. Kyla's eyes came to rest on the knot of his necktie and seemed disinclined to move away. Finally they shyly climbed up his chin, along the sensual mouth beneath the thick brush of his mustache, over the chiseled perfection of his nose to meet that brilliant green gaze. She swallowed timidly.

· Trevor angled his head and lowered his lips to hers. His were parted, damp and warm as they pressed her mouth with a tender, yet possessive kiss. When he withdrew, he smiled down into her face, then kissed Aaron's cheek.

"I love you both." He spoke softly to Kyla's ears alone and she felt a sudden urge to cry.

Before she could, she was spun around and embraced by her parents. Babs made a beeline for Trevor, taking ad-

vantage of the opportunity to kiss him again. Ted and Lynn joined in the exchange of kisses.

To record the day, Clif got out his camera. Kyla smiled for the lens, but she couldn't help but think about the white padded satin album upstairs in her closet that was filled with pictures of another wedding.

As Kyla filled her plate with food from the buffet, Trevor moved up beside her. "If you don't like the ring, I'll get you something else."

"I didn't expect it," she said, looking down at the unfamiliar ring. "But I like it very much." And she did. It was simple and elegant.

"The diamonds are from my mother's wedding ring. Dad sent it to me last week. The mounting was gaudy and didn't look like something you would choose, so I had the stones reset."

"You took your mother's diamonds and had a ring made for me?" she asked, flabbergasted.

"She told me before she died to give her ring to my wife."

"But Trevor, you should have saved it for—" She broke off when she realized that she was about to say, "For a woman who loves you."

"For whom?" The back of his hand made a resting place for her chin and he tilted her head back slightly. "You are my one and *only* wife, Kyla." He bent down and kissed her lightly before dropping his hand.

"I'm sorry I didn't have a ring for you." She couldn't admit to him that it had never occurred to her. Indeed she hadn't thought of wedding rings at all until Babs—God bless her—had reminded her to remove hers only minutes before the ceremony. "I wasn't sure you would want to wear one. Some men don't."

"Well, I've been giving that some thought." He popped an olive into his mouth and chewed it slowly and exaggeratedly as though pondering a tremendously important de-

cision. "I thought I might want something different. Untraditional."

"Like what?"

"Like maybe a gold ring in my ear."

Her mouth fell open and she stared up at him. Then she realized that he was teasing her and she burst out laughing.

"What's the matter?" he asked, pretending to be offended by her laughter. "Don't you think a pierced ear would go well with my eye patch?"

"Yes, I do," she said honestly. "Pierced ears for men is the 'in' thing and I think you would wear an earring with panache."

"Well then, why the levity?"

"I was just wondering what the guys on your construction sites would have to say about it?"

"Hmm, you're right. Maybe I should reconsider."

They laughed together and when it subsided, he said, "That's a start."

"What is?"

"I finally managed to remove that guarded, tense expression from your face and replace it with a genuine, relaxed smile. You actually laughed."

"I laugh all the time."

"Not with me. I want to see you laugh often." He leaned down and added on a whisper, "Except when I take off my clothes."

The thought of that rid her mind of all laughter. "I promise not to laugh then."

She could have kissed her father for interrupting them at that point to take another picture. They were photographed. They ate; they drank numerous glasses of Meg's punch; they said goodbye to the Haskells with a promise to get together soon.

Babs left for a date. "Poor guy," she told Trevor and Kyla at the door. "He doesn't know what he's in for tonight. All this wedding sentiment has put me in a very ro-

mantic mood." With a seductive wink and a jaunty wave, she left.

"Mom, let me help you clean up this mess."

"No, no, no," Meg said, shooing Kyla out of the kitchen. "You and Trevor get on your way."

"But not all of Aaron's things are packed yet. I thought I'd change and—" She fell silent when she realized the other three were staring back at her as though she'd taken leave of her senses. Only Trevor seemed faintly amused. She had come to know that that twitch of his mustache usually heralded a grin. "What's the matter?"

"Well, we, your mother and I, just assumed that you'd leave Aaron here for tonight at least," Clif said uneasily.

Kyla opened her mouth to speak, only to find that she had nothing to say. She closed her mouth without uttering a word.

"Thank you, Clif, Meg," Trevor said to fill an awkward silence. "We appreciate the offer. If Aaron won't be any trouble we'll leave him here tonight. Tomorrow when we come for him we'll bring the pickup. Kyla still has some things to move, don't you, love?"

"Yes," she croaked. "I'll finish packing and get it all out of your way by tomorrow evening."

Since the announcement of her marriage to Trevor, the Powerses had officially sold their house. Kyla knew that the sooner she moved all her possessions out, the sooner the sale could be closed.

However, she wasn't thinking about that now. She was thinking about the night to come when she wouldn't have Aaron to act as a buffer between her and her bridegroom. She dragged out their leave-taking as long as she could without it being obvious.

"Meg knows how to throw a great party," Trevor said once they were alone and on their way home.

"She's always been a gracious hostess."

"I appreciate her efforts."

"She loved doing it."

"I like your dress."

"Thank you."

"Silk?"

"Yes."

"I like the sound it makes when you move."

"Sound?"

"That secretive rustling sound that makes me wonder what your body is doing underneath it."

Her eyes swung quickly to the horizon. "I didn't know it made a sound."

"It does. Each time you move. I find it terribly sexy." He reached across the seat for her hand and laid it high on his thigh. "And exciting."

Her heart slammed against her ribs. Breathing was difficult. She tried to concentrate on how the fabric of his tailored slacks felt against the palm of her hand, but her brain seemed determined to dwell on his excitement, the extent of which she could measure should she move her hand up a scant few inches.

The headlights swept across the front of the house as he braked the car to a stop. "Do you need the bag tonight?" He had carried a small suitcase to the car for her.

"Yes, please. It has makeup and . . . stuff . . . in it."

"Oh, I see. Stuff." His grin did nothing for her heart or her lungs, both of which seemed to have shut down operations for the night. "Well you can't do without your stuff, can you?"

On the porch, he set the suitcase down and unlocked the front door, pushing it wide. Before Kyla could prepare herself, he swept her up into his arms and against his chest. "Welcome home, Kyla."

He carried her inside. As soon as he crossed the threshold, he lowered his head and kissed her. And kissed her again. And again. Until soon it was hard to tell where one kiss stopped and another began.

Both of his hands were occupied. Kyla could have turned her head away and ended the kisses, but she lacked the will

to do so. His mouth was incredibly sweet and warm. She felt an irresistible compulsion to see just how nimble his tongue could be. It thrust again and again into her mouth with a greediness tempered only by tenderness.

He relaxed the arm beneath her knees but kept her anchored to him as she slid down against his body. Finally she was standing toe to toe with him. And still the kiss went on uninterrupted.

With his arms now free, his hands explored. They slid up and down her back. She felt the pressure of his palms on her bottom, urging her closer to his hard middle. Once she was secured there, he made vees of his thumbs and index fingers and bracketed her breasts in the notches. The vees closed and opened rhythmically, gently, causing his thumbs lightly to brush the peaks of her breasts.

She caught her breath. Trevor's hands fell away immediately, but he didn't retreat. He folded his arms around her protectively and pressed her head against his chest.

"I'm about to get carried away," he whispered into her hair. "Making love standing up in the entrance hall isn't the way I planned our wedding night." Chuckling, he put space between them and looked down into her face. "Not without closing the front door first."

When he turned to do that, Kyla moved as far away from him as possible without making it look like an escape. "Are you hungry?" she asked hopefully. "I'll fix you something."

"After that spread Meg had prepared?" he asked incredulously. "One more marinated artichoke and I'd have burst. But I do have some champagne chilling. Would you like to change first?"

First. First. He kept dropping in that one-syllable word that implied so much to Kyla. She knew what was at the culmination of all those "firsts."

"Champagne sounds good." Could he detect the tremors in the corners of her mouth when she tried to smile?

As he walked into the kitchen, he shrugged off his suit jacket and worked at the knot of his necktie. Casually he tossed both of them into one of the chairs at the kitchen dining table as he went by. He unbuttoned the top three buttons of his shirt and, after unclipping his cuff links, rolled the cuffs of his sleeves up to his elbows.

He seemed perfectly at ease. Kyla envied him that nonchalance. She would dearly love to slip out of the new shoes, which had made her toes numb, but she didn't even feel comfortable enough with their privacy to do that.

"Ah, good and cold," he said, swinging the bottle of champagne out of the industrial-size refrigerator. Kyla noticed that the shelves inside it had already been stocked with food, including Aaron's favorites. Didn't Trevor ever forget anything? "Would you get down the wineglasses, sweetheart? They're in that cabinet there," he said nodding toward one. "I put everything up, but you can rearrange it all if something's not convenient for you."

"I'm sure everything is fine," she said woodenly.

She found the champagne glasses and brought him two. She jumped when the cork popped out of the bottle. Laughing, he poured the foaming wine into the glass. Some of it washed over Kyla's hands. She began laughing, too. The icy effervescent wine tingled on her skin as the tiny bubbles burst one by one.

Having set the glasses on the countertop, she was shaking the moisture from her hands when Trevor captured one and lifted it to his mouth. "Allow me."

She watched it. She watched her finger disappear between his mustache and lower lip, but she didn't really believe that it was actually happening until she felt his tongue laving the pad of her finger.

Stunned, Kyla was powerless to do anything but watch as he finished with that finger and sucked the next one into the silky heat of his mouth. He slid his tongue between the next two fingers, gathering up all traces of the spilled wine.

It curled around the beautiful wedding ring he had placed on her finger earlier.

Delicious sensations wound through her. His tongue's deft caresses never ventured beyond her fingertips, but seemed to touch her everywhere, in forbidden places. They coaxed responses from her body she had thought were buried with that flag-draped casket in Kansas.

That melting sensation in her middle. That aching in her breasts that made her want to feel Trevor's tongue there, doing what he was doing to her fingertips. That quickened respiration. That pounding of her heart.

Finally he turned her hand over and kissed the palm, whisking it with his mustache before relinquishing it. She had the impulse to tuck her hand under her arm as one does when one has been stung or has pricked a finger with a pin. Or did she want to hide that hand in shame because it had been guilty of such erotic responses?

"Here's your champagne." Trevor handed her a glass. "To us." He clinked their glasses together and they each took a sip. Then he lowered his head and kissed her softly. "Know what?" he asked while his lips were still resting against hers.

"What?" What cologne does he wear? her mind was asking distractedly. It was as intoxicating as the champagne.

"You taste better than champagne." His tongue swept her lower lip. "In fact you taste better than anything. I could make a glutton of myself on you. I could indulge until I was sated and drunk on you. And I still wouldn't have enough. I'd want...one...more...taste." Between the words, he pecked soft kisses. After the last word, his mouth stayed and he sent his tongue deep into her mouth.

Unmindful of the sloshing, he removed the wineglass from her hand. None too steadily, he set hers and his on the countertop without ever having released her from his kiss.

Slowly he raised her arms to his shoulders. Involuntarily they bent at the elbows to enclose his neck. His hands met at the small of her back. The kiss deepened. He inched forward until she was sandwiched between him and the counter. He rocked his hips from side to side, massaging her softness.

"Oh, God," she sighed when he left her mouth to plant one of those treacherous kisses on her vulnerable throat. Her head fell back. Her eyes drifted open and she gazed at the ceiling hazily as his open mouth touched her skin.

Why was God doing this to her? Why had he sent such a temptation into her life? The marriage itself had been a betrayal of Richard. She didn't love this man, yet she wanted him in a purely carnal way. It was wrong! How could she withstand such an inundation of sexual provocation and not submit to it?

"Would you like some privacy in the bedroom before I join you?" he asked roughly.

Witlessly, she nodded her head and he released her. Like a sleepwalker she turned and wended her way to the other side of the house and into the bedroom. Trevor, having followed her, set her suitcase just inside the door. "I'll be back shortly." The door closed softly behind him.

She carried the suitcase into the bathroom and opened it. As though programmed to do so, she automatically unpacked her cosmetics and toiletries and arranged them on the dressing table. When she chanced to catch her image in the mirror covering the wall, she froze.

Her eyes! What had happened to her eyes? They were aglow, lambent, limpid. They hadn't looked like that since the night she had discovered she was in love with Richard Stroud.

In love! Good Lord, yes. That's what she looked like, a woman in love.

The thought extinguished the light in her eyes immediately, extinguished it so quickly that she could later con-

vince herself that it hadn't been there at all, that it had been a trick of the lighting, a product of her imagination.

In love with Trevor Rule? Impossible. She hadn't known him long enough. She loved Richard. Solely. Exclusively. There was no room in her heart for any other man.

Even if she allowed Trevor the use of her body that night, she wouldn't be betraying Richard. It was, after all, just a body, material and impermanent. Her body had nothing to do with the personality inside it, the heart and soul and mind of Kyla Stroud.

Kyla *Rule*, a malicious imp reminded her.

Kyla *Stroud*, she insisted.

She would sleep with Trevor because she had made a bargain and she intended to uphold her end of it. She would swap him bedroom privileges for the parenting he would extend to Aaron. He would have access to her body, but never, never to her heart. She had promised her heart and love to Richard. Trevor Rule would never be allowed to violate that covenant.

She and Babs had moved her clothes the night before. Her entire wardrobe, all seasons included, filled only a fraction of the closet space Trevor had built into the master bedroom. After a quick shower, she slipped into the negligee she had bought under duress and brushed her teeth and hair. Almost as an afterthought, she applied perfume to the backs of her ears and the base of her throat.

In the bedroom she turned down the bed. She left only one lamp burning. When the soft knock sounded on the door, she whirled around, clasping her hands together. "Come in, Trevor."

He stepped through the door. When the soft lamplight fell on him, Kyla momentarily regretted that she didn't love him. The black pajama bottoms hung low on his hips, held there by a black cord. His chest was most impressive, shadowed by that cloud of dark hair that arrowed down past his navel. She didn't even want to think of what that stripe of hair pointed to. The scar that arced beneath his

left breast intrigued her as it had before. She wanted to touch it, soothe it somehow. His feet were bare. There was a network of scars on his left foot.

Only after she had cataloged his body did she raise her eyes to his face. He was staring at her, a hint of a smile hiking up one corner of his mustache.

"You're beautiful, Kyla." He moved into the room until he was standing an arm's length away.

She couldn't have guessed how appealing she was to him at that moment. This was the woman of the letters, the woman who had spoken to his heart before he even met her. Now, she stood before him, naked, save for a few scraps of peach-colored silk and satin. His most erotic fantasy was close enough to touch. She was breathing, stirring the hair on his chest with each light exhalation.

The golden glow of the lamp enhanced her spectacular coloring. It made her hair shine like copper and her skin take on the richness of old satin. He wanted to wrap himself up in her. Her eyes were velvety dark, unusually wide, incredibly bright.

The nightgown was sheer and curtained her body like a veil. A ribbon was tied beneath her breasts, making their fullness more pronounced. Her nipples were dusky temptations beneath the filmy fabric. Above the brief bodice, the small mounds of her breasts swelled creamy and full.

Her body was cast in shadow against the lamplight. As his eyes moved down it, his manhood grew thick with desire for her. Her waist was incredibly narrow, especially for someone who had carried a child. He was transfixed by the shadowy cleft between her slender thighs, the heart of all that made her a woman. He wanted to honor it, cherish it with his caresses and his mouth.

Unable to stop himself, he extended his hand and cupped it over that soft delta. Shifting the material of her gown so that only one layer was between her and his hand, he pressed. "You're so warm," he whispered fiercely. "Standing here with you like this, I feel weaker than I did

after my accident when I couldn't even move." His hand drifted up over her belly to her breast. "I want you so much it's painful."

His finger moved over her nipple and, when it responded beautifully, he made a hissing sound and crushed her against him. His mouth covered hers and he kissed her with all the fervency burning inside him. He fondled her breast lovingly as his other arm closed around her waist.

Kyla tried to keep herself indifferent. She wanted to step outside herself and observe the embrace from that viewpoint. But it was difficult to remain passive when the heat of his body was seeping into hers, when she throbbed where his fingers had just stroked her. The passion he transmitted delivered with it a lassitude that threatened her resolve not to participate with her mind.

Through the sheer nightgown, she could feel the crisp texture of his chest hair, the erection of his nipples. His thighs were hard and straining against hers. His maleness nestled in the cove her body offered it. He was hard and she wanted him.

Her body and her mind waged war. She struggled to keep her emotions intact. But in doing so, her body unwittingly went as unyielding as her heart.

Suddenly, Trevor withdrew his mouth from hers. The movement was so abrupt that her head snapped back and she fell victim to a cold green gaze.

He gripped her upper arms and shoved her away from him, holding her at the end of stiff, strong arms fully extended. "No thank you, Kyla."

She looked at him fearfully. He was furious and it showed. His dark brows were pulled down low over his eyes. His nostrils flared slightly with each breath.

"No thank you?" she repeated in a thin voice. "I don't understand."

"Let me explain it then." He spoke in a tight voice she knew he must be having a hard time keeping below a

shout. "I don't want a sacrificial lamb beneath me going through the motions of making love."

The hasty lowering of her eyes was as good as a signed confession. "You're my husband. You can demand—"

He laughed harshly. "If only you knew how laughable that was. Demanding isn't quite my style, Kyla. I certainly don't intend to exercise caveman tactics on my wife!"

He released her so abruptly that she reeled against the bedside table. "You may relax," he said scathingly. "You're safe from me. I won't impose my lust on you tonight. Nor will I ever."

Her eyes snapped up. "That's right, Kyla," he said silkily, reading her surprise. "I still love you, but it's not conditional on whether you go to bed with me or not. But I warn you," he said, pointing a finger at her, "that loving you as I do, it will be impossible for you not to love me back."

In a heartbeat, he was towering over her, his left hand knotted in her hair. With his right arm he hauled her high against him and positioned them so there could be no doubt of his readiness to take her if he chose to. He pulled her head back until she was forced to look up into his glowering face.

"I promise you this," he said with soft emphasis, "no one has ever loved you as much as I do. No one has ever made love to you as well as I can. I'll bury myself so deep inside you that when I'm not actually there, you'll feel like a vital part of your body is missing." He lowered his head and branded her breast with his mouth. "Now when you exorcise those ghosts that haunt you, come to me and I'll be more than glad to demonstrate what I'm talking about."

Releasing her, he spun on his heel and stalked to the door. "Sleep well," he tossed over his shoulder, a second before the door slammed behind him.

Chapter 10

Good morning."

It wasn't the tone of voice she had expected, nor that, she secretly admitted, she probably deserved.

Surly, peevish, snide, cruel. Kyla would have expected him to be any of those, but not congenial and seemingly in a good mood.

"Good morning."

She skirted the table where he sat reading the newspaper and made a beeline for the coffee maker on the countertop. There was an empty mug waiting for her. She poured the fragrant, steaming coffee from the pot.

"I hope I didn't make it too strong for you."

She sipped. "It's fine. I like it strong."

"So do I."

She didn't realize he had come up behind her until his breath stirred her hair. She turned around quickly to face him. His arms slid around her waist and pulled her close. Ducking his head, he kissed her surprised mouth. It wasn't

a passionate kiss, but a tender one that was almost as unsettling. "How was your night?" he asked solicitously.

Her night had been wretched. After Trevor had slammed out of the picture-perfect master bedroom suite he had created for his bride, Kyla had collapsed onto the wide bed and wept for what seemed like hours. She longed for familiar surroundings, her own bedroom, Aaron, the comforting presence of her parents. She longed to roll back the clock. She longed for Richard.

And she longed for Trevor.

That particular longing had brought on another wave of weeping.

She had finally fallen asleep shortly before dawn, and had awakened with a dull headache and puffy eyes. When she left the bedroom wrapped in an old robe that she had managed to sneak past Babs's eagle eye, she hadn't known what to expect from her husband of less than twenty-four hours, a husband to whom she had denied a wedding night, if not by deed then by attitude. Sullen fury at best.

She wasn't prepared for the cherishing embrace with which he enfolded her now. Nor for the soft kisses that he employed to trace her hairline. Nor for the gentle, tension-ridding massage his hands were giving her back.

Kyla felt anxiety slowly leaking out of her. She rested her cheek against the muscles of his chest, which were delineated by the tight white T-shirt he was wearing over a pair of ragged cutoffs.

"Can you cook?"

"What?" she mumbled sleepily.

"I asked if you could cook."

She raised her head and took a step backward. "Of course I can cook," she said with some asperity.

His mustache curved over a grin. "Then how about some breakfast?"

"What would you like?"

"What can you cook?"

"Anything," she boasted with a coquettish toss of her reddish-blond hair. "If you'll get out of my way, I'll prove to you what a good cook I am."

He bowed deeply from the waist, sweeping his hand wide. "The kitchen's all yours, milady. I'll just return to my newspaper if that's all right with you."

A few minutes later she set a frosty glass of orange juice in front of him. He tipped the corner of his newspaper down. "Thanks."

She smiled at him. "You're welcome."

"It smells good."

"It's almost ready."

He folded up the scattered newspapers and pushed them aside so she could set the table. Apparently she had found everything where he had had it stored. She laid out place mats and used the casual stoneware and silverware for their place settings. He watched her hands as she expertly folded linen napkins and arranged them in rings in the centers of the plates. Before she could turn away, he reached for her hand and drew it to his mouth. He kissed the back of it.

"It doesn't take long to get spoiled. I think I'm already used to having a wife make such a fuss over me," he said softly.

The way he looked up at her from his chair sent a warm tide of pleasure spilling over her middle. She felt a blush rising out of the unglamorous neckline of her robe.

She tugged on her hand, "I, uh, don't want it to burn."

He released her hand and she scurried toward the range. Moments later, she was bearing a platter of aromatic food to the table. She set it down, then stood by, nervously awaiting his reaction.

"Eggs Benedict!" he exclaimed in delight. The dish had been arranged appetizingly on the platter and garnished with fresh orange slices and sprigs of parsley.

"Do you like them that way? I didn't know."

"I'll eat just about anything that doesn't move off the plate. And rutabagas. Don't ever try to feed me rutabagas."

She laughed. "I think that's the only thing that wasn't stocked in the pantry or refrigerator."

During this exchange she had carried the coffeepot to the table and refilled his mug. As she set it on a trivet, Trevor rose from his chair and pulled hers out for her. She looked up at him in surprise and when she did he pecked a quick kiss on the tip of her nose. "Thanks for breakfast."

"You're welcome." She sank into her chair. Her hands were trembling slightly, but she filled his plate, then her own.

"Delicious!" he pronounced after taking an unabashedly huge first bite. "Where did you learn to cook like this?"

"My mother taught me the basics. And I took a cooking course while—" She stopped abruptly. Trevor's head came up, a question in his expression.

"While?" he prodded.

"While my hus . . . while Richard was overseas."

She had never mentioned the cooking class in her letters. Why, he wondered.

"What did Richard think of your cooking classes?" Had he missed some letters? He was suddenly, unaccountably, furiously jealous of anything she might have written to her husband that he, Trevor, hadn't been privy to. What else had he missed?

"I didn't tell him."

Trevor's grip on his fork relaxed. "Why?"

She took a drink of juice and blotted her mouth with her napkin before answering. "I wanted to surprise him with all kinds of exotic recipes when he came home," she said, cutting into the slice of Canadian bacon. "Babs and I took the class together. It was great fun. Babs was the worst student. She ruined everything she tried, but it wasn't a

total waste of her time because she ended up dating the chef.''

She was chatting now because she was nervous. Trevor could tell because she wouldn't look at him directly, but glanced at a point just off his shoulder. They weren't even at the point where she could mention Richard's name without feeling awkward about it.

''I'll bet you were at the top of the class, because this is great.'' Her head came up and she blessed him with a shy smile that melted his heart and made up for the hellish night he'd spent alone in the guest room. Well, almost. ''I've always ridiculed the former jocks who get married and go to fat. Now I can see how it happens.'' He winked at her.

''Were you a jock?''

''In school.''

''What sports?''

''Hmm, let's see.'' He sipped his coffee. ''Track. Basketball. Rowing.''

''Rowing?''

''I don't think you have it in Texas.''

''That must be what developed your shoulders and thighs.''

When her gaze dropped to his long legs, she noticed the scars. There they were, ugly pink raised seams in his flesh, running the length of his left leg, intersecting and meshing like railroad tracks.

Trevor lowered his fork to his plate and watched her. Bracing his elbows on the table, he folded his hands in front of his mouth and waited for the revulsion he prepared himself to see in her expression. It never came. When she raised her eyes to his face, there was only compassion in her brown eyes.

''I told you it wasn't pretty,'' he said, a definite edge to his voice.

''It's not so bad, Trevor.''

''It's not so great either.''

She looked at his leg again. "It must have been awfully painful."

"It was."

"You've never told me what happened to you."

He shifted uneasily and she attributed that to self-consciousness. "It doesn't matter."

"You once said you were embarrassed to wear shorts. You shouldn't be."

A wry grin slanted his mustache upward. "You don't think all the ladies on the beach would cover their eyes and run in terror?"

"Not at all. You're too attractive."

He sobered instantly. Leaning forward, he speared her with his green gaze. "Do you think so?"

"Yes."

Several moments ticked by while Kyla was held transfixed by the gruff intensity in his voice and the hypnotizing power of his stare.

She willed herself out of the daze and stood up hastily, bumping the table with her thighs hard enough to rattle the glassware. "If you're finished, I'll clean up the dishes."

She spun around, but was brought up short when Trevor dug his fingers beneath the tie belt of her robe at the back of her waist. Giving it a swift tug, her turned her around and pulled her between his wide-spread thighs so that her middle bumped into his chest and his face was on a level with her breasts.

"Thanks for breakfast." The words, spoken in a low, rumbling voice to begin with, were almost completely muffled by the fabric folded over her breasts.

"It was the least I could do."

She lowered her eyes to the top of his head where the dark wavy hair swirled from the crown. It wasn't easy, but she resisted the urge to thread her fingers through the ebony strands to see if they felt as alive as they looked.

Her eyes battled to stay open when he rubbed his hard cheek against her breast, but they lost the contest and

flickered closed. She felt the vibration of the moan that issued up out of his chest as his nose nuzzled her.

"You bathed this morning." It wasn't a question.

"Yes."

"You smell good. Like soap. And powder. And woman."

He made gentle gnawing motions with his mouth that sought and finally found the peak of her breast through the cloth. He didn't actually kiss her. He didn't actually suckle. What he did was rub his open mouth back and forth over her until he felt her flesh respond, then he touched her with his tongue.

"Breakfast was delicious," he whispered. Her skin became damp where his breath filtered through the robe. "Is there any dessert?" He pressed his face deeper into her softly giving flesh. But he pulled back almost immediately and looked up at her. "Hmm?"

When he saw her tremulous expression, he chuckled and stood up, pushing her gently away from him. "Never mind. Let's get dressed and go get that kid of ours before your parents spoil him rotten." He checked the clock on the oven. "By the time we get there, they should be getting home from church. I'd like to take everyone to lunch. The Petroleum Club goes all out on its Sunday buffet."

"We're not members," Kyla found enough voice to say. She was still feeling aftershocks of delight at having Trevor's mouth on her breasts.

"But I am." He tweaked her nose. "I'll clean up the kitchen; you go get ready. I want to show you off." He kissed her swiftly and gave her rump a husbandly pat.

Kyla left the master bathroom twenty minutes later, after having applied her makeup and arranged her hair. That was when she came to the startling realization that she and Trevor might not be sharing a bed, but they were still sharing a bedroom.

She caught him in the act of stepping into a pair of dress slacks. A fleeting impression of light-blue briefs regis-

tered on her brain before she spun around and said, "Excuse me." She almost made it to the bathroom door before his stern voice halted her retreat.

"Kyla."

"What?"

"Turn around."

"Why?"

"Because I want to talk to you."

Slowly she came around, studiously keeping her eyes aimed at a point above his head. Casually he zipped up the trousers and, still shirtless and barefoot, crossed the room toward her. "I showered in the guest bath so I wouldn't disturb you, but my clothes have all been stored in the drawers and closets in here. It will be damned inconvenient to move them."

She wet her lips rapidly. "That's fine, fine. We'll just, uh, try to stay out of each other's way."

"I won't." He laughed, but when he saw her frown he said, "Okay, we'll split the differences. You can get in my way any time you like, and I'll try to stay out of yours. Deal?"

It was too complicated to think through, especially looking at his bare chest as she was. So she merely parroted, "Deal."

"Good." He turned his back—a smooth expanse of darkly tanned skin stretched tautly over rippling muscles—and returned to his closet, where he proceeded to take out a shirt and pull it on with the nonchalance of a person alone.

Kyla forced her feet to move to her own closet. She stood there motionless, working up her courage to take off her robe.

You're behaving like a child, she told herself angrily. The nightgown she had faced him in last night was a thousand times more revealing than the bra and half slip she had on beneath the robe. Swiftly, before she could change her mind, she whipped it off.

"I've been thinking."

At the sound of Trevor's voice, she jumped as though she'd been shot in the back now exposed to him. "About what?"

She willed her fumbling hands to hang the robe on a hanger properly and return it to the metal bar in the closet. It required tremendous concentration because she knew he was probably looking at her back and the slender ivory satin straps of her bra.

"About Aaron."

She hazarded a glance at him over her shoulder. He wasn't looking at her at all. He was tying his necktie, using the mirror he had had mounted over the bureau that was built into his closet. His shirt had been buttoned, but he hadn't tucked in the shirttail yet. The stiff collar had been flipped up against his square jaw. "What about him?" She reached for the dress she had chosen to wear.

"Maybe we should be locating a proper day-care center for him."

"Do you think he's old enough?"

"You're more expert on that than I am. I was just wondering what we'll do with him during the day if Meg and Clif get that motor home and strike out for parts unknown."

That had been a concern of Kyla's, too. "I suppose he should be around other children his age. There's an education in that."

"No doubt. How else will he learn all the dirty words?"

She laughed with him. "But I'd want to investigate the school's reputation."

"Absolutely. It will have to be sterling. We both have to be sold on the facility and faculty before we enroll him. Need any help?"

Before she could formulate an answer, his hands were pushing hers aside. They had been at her waist in back grappling with the lowest button on her dress. How could a man of his size move so silently? She stood ramrod

straight as his fingers negotiated the buttons. After securing the top one, his hands smoothed down her back and settled on her hips.

"No one would ever guess you'd had a baby. Was it a difficult pregnancy?"

"Not at all."

"You're so slender," he said softly, squeezing her hips lightly before his hands fell away. "Can you give me some help here?"

Unwisely she turned to face him. Only a few inches separated them. "Help you? How?"

"Check to see if my collar is turned down properly all the way around. Sometimes I don't bend it down just right and my tie peeks out from underneath."

She gave it a hasty inspection. "It's not quite folded down all the way in back."

"Would you fix it for me, please? It's hard to reach."

"Sure." She spoke with far more carelessness than she felt. Actually she was wondering how she was going to keep her hands out of the black hair that curled beguilingly over his collar if she came that close to touching it.

No sooner were her arms raised and her hands occupied adjusting his collar over his tie than he flipped up his shirttails and unzipped his trousers. Her hands froze. Her eyes sprang up to his. His expression was bland as he casually began stuffing his shirttail into his trousers. Occasionally, too occasionally, his knuckles bumped into her middle.

"Anything wrong?" he asked.

"No, no, nothing," she gasped and quickly folded his collar down. She patted it firmly into place just as the rasp of his zipper reached her ears. Her arms slid from his shoulders. He finished fastening the fly of his pants.

And then they stared at each other while time was held in suspension.

"Thanks," he said after a long, still while.

''Thank you, too.'' His eyebrow quirked with humor. ''For doing up my buttons,'' she added hastily.

''Oh. You're welcome.''

They fell into another staring spell. Kyla was the first to move away, and she did so by turning her back to find her shoes in the closet.

It took the familiar pandemonium that went with cor-ralling Aaron to restore her equilibrium. But even that didn't erase an image in Kyla's mind of light-blue briefs stretched over tight, rounded buttocks.

The Powerses were impressed with the number of peo-ple who greeted their new son-in-law as they ate lunch at the exclusive Petroleum Club. Even Aaron seemed awed by his surroundings. His behavior during the meal was above reproach.

After lunch Trevor drove the Powerses out to the house he had built for Kyla and Aaron. After a tour that left them speechless, Trevor followed them back to their house in his pickup. The remainder of the afternoon was spent packing and loading Kyla's things that still had to be moved.

''He's a tired little rascal tonight,'' Trevor said of Aaron as they tucked him in. He patted the boy on the seat. Aar-on's eyelids were already at half-mast. His stuffed ani-mals were lined up around the slats of the baby bed like sentinels.

''Which is probably just as well,'' Kyla remarked, pull-ing a light blanket over her son. ''The first night in a new place might be traumatic if he weren't so ready to go to sleep.''

''Don't you think he likes the room?''

She heard the anxiety in Trevor's voice and looked up to find that he was genuinely concerned about it. ''What lit-tle boy wouldn't like it?''

She gazed around the bedroom, which had been deco-rated in a railroad motif. The Little Engine That Could was puffing up the hill painted on the wall. A steam-engine-

shaped toy chest, filled to capacity, took up a good portion of another wall. A miniature track had been run around the molding six inches below the ceiling. At the flip of a switch a tiny freight train circled the room at a clicking pace, belching puffs of white smoke every so often and tooting its horn periodically. Aaron had clapped his hands in glee and only frowned in frustration when he realized he couldn't reach it.

Her gaze returned to Trevor. "What I meant was that sometimes when a child sleeps in a strange place it upsets him. Apparently Aaron isn't bothered by it." Aaron was already snoring softly. Kyla covered a huge yawn with her hand as they left the room.

"You're worn out, too." Trevor clasped her shoulders and within seconds his strong fingers were working the knots out of her shoulder muscles. His thumbs magically pressed the tension from the base of her neck. Moving closer and laying his cheek against hers he said, "Want to spend a few minutes in the hot tub? Does that sound good?"

It sounded heavenly. She couldn't think of anything better than being immersed in hot bubbly water.

"I'll meet you out there."

Or anything more dangerous than sharing such a sensual experience with Trevor.

She eased from beneath his massaging hands. "If you don't mind, Trevor, I think I'll just go to bed. This weekend has been so hectic. It's taking its toll."

"All right."

She could tell he was trying not to let his disappointment show. This man had taken her as his wife, knowing she still loved another man. Wasn't she being a rather poor sport? "Unless you really want me to," she added.

He shook his head impatiently. "No. I know you're tired. Good night."

He bracketed her neck with his hands and tilted her head back with both his thumbs beneath her chin. He planted

his lips firmly over hers, parted them, waited for her to accommodate him and, when she did, slipped his tongue into her mouth like a velvet sword.

It was a torching kiss that conveyed all the passion that smoldered within him. His practiced technique ignited her desire until she could swear that tiny tongues of flame were licking at her body.

When he released her at last, she all but sagged against him, so totally had his kiss depleted her. "Good night," she said huskily and moved away toward the bedroom in what she hoped wasn't a staggering walk.

Trevor sat in the dark, idly rocking the porch swing with his heels against the decking.

A terse expletive summed up his mood of the moment. He tossed the remainder of the whiskey he'd been sipping onto the ground. He didn't need alcohol. He didn't need anything to make him any warmer, nothing to increase the heat that simmered in his loins.

He needed Kyla. Naked. Beneath him. Sheathing that part of him that ached with its need for her.

Cursing again, he thumped his head against the thick chain holding up the swing until it hurt badly enough to feel good.

Would she ever love him? Would she ever want him as he wanted her? So far he'd accomplished everything he had set out to. She and Aaron were living under his roof, sharing his life, enjoying his protection.

But she wasn't in his bed yet. Would she ever return his love?

Possibly.

But never if she knew who you were.

He had had every intention of telling her he was the legendary Smooch before they got married, but he had talked himself out of it. Better to be legally bound before breaking the news.

Then he had decided to tell her the morning after their wedding night, after she had had a night of his loving and they were bound not only legally but physically. So much for good intentions.

Well hell, it wasn't his fault that they hadn't had a wedding night, now was it?

But you should have told her by now, his conscience argued.

"Yeah, I know," he answered it out loud.

But how? When? What time was ever going to be right to say, "We didn't meet by accident. I orchestrated everything because I knew before I ever saw you that I was going to marry you and provide a home for you and your son. Why? Well, because I'm responsible for your husband's death and I felt like I owed it both to him and to you. Oh, but I do love you."

He repeated that curt obscenity and pushed himself out of the swing.

Would Kyla believe that he loved her after he told her who he was? Hell, no. *He* wouldn't believe it were the tables to be turned.

Propping his shoulder against the outer wall of the house, he stood at the edge of the deck and stared sightlessly into the near space.

"What the hell am I going to do?" he asked the night.

He knew that with just a little finesse on his part, he could get her to surrender to his sexual advances. He knew enough about women to know that she wanted him, if only she would admit that to herself. But that was the key to it, she had to admit it to herself. When they came together— *Lord, don't let it be too much longer*—she would have to initiate it. He wouldn't be accused later of taking advantage of her that way, too.

You've got to tell her, he was reminded by that relentless conscience.

"But I've got to win her first."

He didn't have to tell her tonight. Or tomorrow. Or even next week. He would take it one day at a time. When she knew he loved her, he would tell her. When the time was right he'd know it.

And if there's never a right time? his conscience taunted him.

But he didn't listen anymore. He began thinking of the woman sleeping in his bed. He envisioned an hourglass with sand the color of her hair sliding through its slender passage. One grain at a time. One kiss at a time. One caress at a time. And her resistance was lessened that much more.

"Your time's running out, Kyla." The hoarse whisper wasn't a threat. It was a promise.

"Sorry, I'm late," Kyla said breathlessly as she sailed through the back door of Petal Pushers. Her arms were full of order blanks and ledgers and catalogs. All were slipping to the floor despite her efforts to keep them secured between her arms and her chest. She piled them on the desk and paused to draw a breath. Her hair had been whipped to a fiery madness by the wind. Aaron had slobbered on her blouse.

"What kept you?" Babs asked sweetly. "Did something come up this morning?"

Kyla pretended not to catch the double entendre. "You can't imagine what a circus it was trying to get the three of us dressed, fed and off for the day." Kyla eased herself down into the chair behind the desk and drew a deep breath.

Babs laughed. "Honeymoonitis?"

"What?" Kyla frowned as Babs hiked a hip over the corner of the desk and leaned forward with an eager expression on her face.

"I know what made you late this morning. Is he as good as he looks?"

Kyla pushed herself out of the chair on the pretext of picking up the papers she had dropped. "Who?"

"Who? For God's sake, Kyla, whom did you just marry? Trevor, of course."

"Oh, Trevor," Kyla said absently, deliberately keeping her back to her perceptive friend. "Good at what?"

"You aren't going to tell me, are you?"

Kyla faced her friend. "About my sex life? No."

"Why?"

"In the first place it's none of your business. And in the second place I can't imagine why you would want to know."

"But I do," Babs said, hopping off the desk and stalking Kyla into the shop. "Every scintillating detail."

"Do we have any orders today?"

"Is he the rowdy, reckless, tempestuous type?"

"Maybe we should change the window displays this week."

"Or the slow, leisurely, languid type?"

"I'm not listening."

"Is he a moaner?"

"Has the mail arrived?"

"Does he talk to you? I'm sure he does. What does he say?"

"Babs!" Kyla shouted to stop the barrage of questions. "We haven't had a conversation this ridiculous since we were in the eighth grade."

"And then you told me everything."

"I've grown up. Why don't you?"

"You even told me what Richard's kisses were like when you first kissed him. Can't you at least tell me that much? What are Trevor's kisses like."

"Indescribable," Kyla said truthfully. "Now can we please change the subject?"

"One more thing."

Sighing, Kyla crossed her arms over her chest and feigned boredom. "What?"

"Is he positively breathtaking naked?"

Kyla swallowed. Then, because she couldn't even imagine what Babs's reaction would be if she told her she didn't know, she simply retorted, "What do you think?"

And from that Babs had to draw her own conclusions.

Chapter 11

They learned to live together. Kyla discovered that her husband existed on very little sleep. He enjoyed staying up late, but he was a jovial, early riser. She had always dreaded getting up in the morning whether she had slept three hours or thirteen. Trevor learned to give her a wide berth in the mornings until she had had at least one cup of coffee.

He was prone to drape clothes over the nearest piece of furniture as he disrobed, and to scatter sections of the newspaper as he finished with them, and to leave empty glasses on end tables. But he was also conscientious about picking up after himself and helping her with household chores without even being asked.

The first week they were married, Kyla wore herself out trying to keep Aaron quiet and well-behaved around Trevor. He wasn't accustomed to having a young child underfoot. She was afraid Aaron's constant activity and incessant racket would disturb him.

But Trevor never showed signs of irritation, not even when Aaron was behaving at his worst. He spent a great deal of what psychologists called "quality time" with the child, doing everything from playing with him on the deck while she prepared dinner, to reading him books, to bathing him when she had both hands full. As for being a good father, Kyla could find no fault with Trevor Rule.

As for his being a good husband, she could find little to complain about either. He was considerate and good-natured. Each night he left her alone in the master suite while he slept in the guest bedroom. He exercised no modesty in changing clothes in front of her. Often one surprised the other in various stages of undress by opening the wrong door at the wrong time. Such scenes never failed to disconcert Kyla, but Trevor seemed to take them in stride.

He was generous with his embraces and kisses, too. Anyone would think they were a happily married couple madly in love with each other. He would frequently slip his arms around her from behind and nuzzle her neck, complimenting her on her hair or her complexion or her figure. He never asked permission for a kiss, but took them as his due. Often his good-night kisses were so tantalizing that as she closed herself up in the bedroom alone, she would curse herself for a fool.

"He's my husband. I owe him conjugal rights. And if being with him would alleviate this jittery feeling inside me, why not?"

Then she would open the drawer in the bedside table where she had placed Richard's picture. (She had had enough sensitivity toward Trevor's feelings not to display it openly.) Gazing down into the beloved face, she would promise him again that he still lived in her heart, that she would never betray his memory by falling in love with another man, and that he would always be her *true* husband.

But her body wasn't so easily convinced. As she lay alone in that wide, empty bed, it wasn't Richard's face that haunted her, but Trevor's. His smile. His hair. His rugged, sun-baked features. His kiss. All vivid.

As the days merged into weeks, that jittery agitation inside her continued to brew until, like all boiling kettles, it had to blow.

It happened after a particularly arduous day in which she had haggled with a wholesaler in Dallas who had billed her for a shipment of roses that Petal Pushers had never received. To top that, she had argued with Babs over her offer to keep Aaron for the weekend while Kyla and Trevor treated themselves to a Dallas hotel's weekend getaway package.

"I think you need the time away. You look like a tightrope walker who has just lost her knack for it," Babs had observed badgeringly. "I keep waiting for you to lose your balance and fall off."

"I'm fine."

"Something is wrong with you, and I intend to find out what it is, if I have to ask Trevor."

"Don't you dare!" Kyla shouted, spinning around to confront her friend. "Stay out of my business, Babs."

She regretted her sharp words the moment they left her mouth and apologized for them. But for the rest of the day, Babs was sulky. Trevor had offered to pick Aaron up at his day-care center, but the job of marketing fell to her. She couldn't find everything she needed because the clerk had rearranged the shelves; the lines were impossibly long and the checkers incredibly slow. Several times she was tempted to leave the groceries in her basket and walk out without them.

By the time she arrived home, she was physically and emotionally exhausted. To save herself a trip back to the car, she tried to carry all three grocery sacks at one time. She was juggling them as she stepped up onto the deck and headed for the back door.

Her turbulent mood wasn't improved by the sight that greeted her. Trevor was lounging in the hot tub, a cold beer near his hand. And Aaron— "Aaron!" she cried angrily. "What in the hell is *this*?"

"This," Trevor said, smiling, as yet unaware of her bad temper, "is pudding painting. The teacher at the school said he loved it, so I decided to try it out at home."

Her child, who was sitting at the small table Trevor had bought for him and placed in the shade on the deck, was covered from head to toe in dark sticky goo that Kyla was monumentally relieved to learn was chocolate pudding.

Thankfully, he was wearing only his diaper. His chubby hands were scooping the pudding out of a bowl and slapping it onto the sheet of butcher paper Trevor had provided for him. He smeared it around, then raised his hand to his face and licked the pudding from between his fingers. Apparently that wasn't the first time his stomach had taken precedence over his artistic endeavors. His face was covered with pudding. He smiled at her through the chocolate mess and chattered something.

"I think he said 'bird,'" Trevor explained. "At least that's what I suggested he paint a picture of."

"He's filthy!" Kyla cried.

She could feel her anger rising as surely as the mercury in a thermometer. Knowing it was unreasonable to get so upset over practically nothing, she nonetheless couldn't control the inevitable eruption of her temper.

"He'll wash," Trevor said pleasantly. But between his arching brows a V had formed and was deepening. "The teacher said it was a very creative exercise for him."

"The teacher doesn't have to clean up the mess," she retorted vituperatively. "And neither do you. I'll be the one who has to. Or didn't you and teacher get around to discussing that in the cozy little chat you no doubt had together?"

She stalked to the sliding glass door and tried to wedge her foot through a crack so she could open it. It wouldn't

budge and with her hands full of the grocery sacks, which were beginning to sag under the slipping contents inside, she was helpless.

Finally, gritting her teeth, she looked at her husband. "I hate to interrupt your bubble bath, Trevor," she said with brittle sweetness, "but I think the least you could is get out of the hot tub and help me."

"Any other time, Kyla, but—"

"Well, never mind then!" she shouted. "I'll do it all myself."

He shot out of the hot tub then, angry and—

Naked.

His feet slapped against the redwood decking, slinging water with each long stride. Kyla stood rooted to the spot, even when he reached her and yanked the grocery sacks from her arms. He secured all three of them in one fist and slid open the glass door with such impetus that it rocked in its track. Heedless of both his nakedness and the water he was dripping everywhere he stormed into the kitchen and virtually slung the sacks of groceries onto the tiled countertop.

Then, with one hand propped on his hip and his right knee slightly bent in an arrogant, belligerent stance, he turned to face her. She read his expression loud and clear. If she could have captioned it, it would have said, "Well, you asked for it, lady."

Furious with herself for making such a scene and furious with him for letting her, she fled into the bedroom and rattled every pane of glass in the house when she slammed the door behind her.

"Am I still in the doghouse?"

Dusk was thick and purple just beyond the plantation shutters on the bedroom windows. Kyla lay on her side, her knees drawn up to her chest. After a long bout of crying, she had showered and put on her nightgown. The sheet was pulled as high as her waist. Her cheek was resting on her hands, which were folded, palms together.

She raised her head slightly. Trevor was at the door, peeking around it as though he might be pelted with flying objects if he dared go any farther into the room.

"No. I'm sorry."

He came in. He was dressed in nothing but a pair of cutoffs and Kyla closed her eyes before returning her head to the pillow. All too well she remembered how his body had looked, soaking wet, the sunlight flickering through the trees and falling onto every silver rivulet that trickled down through that forest of hair on his chest. She recalled the hard, corded muscles of his stomach, the length of his limbs, the impressive sex nestled in a thatch of dark hair.

She had wept hot, bitter tears of regret—regret because she had noticed just how magnificent his nakedness was, regret that in spite of her best intentions she wanted him, and regret that she had denied him to herself for so long.

Now she felt the mattress sink with his weight as he lay down behind her and curved his body around hers. His fingers sifted through her hair, lifting stray curls off her cheek. He arranged the loose strands on the pillow just so. His ministrations were soothing.

"Hard day?" His breath was warm and soft in her ear.

"A bitch."

He chuckled. "Then I guess you weren't ready to see your son looking like something out of a minstrel show, were you?"

I wasn't ready to see you rising out of that hot tub like a male version of Venus, either. "I'm sorry I made such a fuss. It was a combination of things."

He was propped on his right elbow, leaning over her. His index finger swept back and forth over her cheek. "Now you understand why I didn't jump out of the hot tub to help you with your load right away."

"Yes."

"I wasn't expecting you home so early or I would have already been out and had Aaron bathed and ready for supper."

"It wasn't your fault, Trevor. None of it. It was mine." She sighed. "I don't feel well and—"

"What's wrong?" He was instantly alert, his body tensing behind hers.

"Nothing."

"Something. Are you sick? Tell me."

She turned her head up and back and stared at him in a way that conveyed her message.

"Oh," he said in a chagrined voice. "That."

"Yes, that." She turned to her original position.

"When?"

"I discovered it when I came in. I should have known. I was acting like such a viper."

"You're forgiven." He touched her tentatively, laying his hand in the shallow of her waist. "Do you . . . does it hurt?"

"Some."

"Did you take anything?"

"A couple of aspirin."

"Will that help?"

"A little."

"Not much?"

"No. It has to wear off."

"I see."

Moving slowly, he eased down the sheet. The nightgown was short and had narrow straps. It was made out of some thin, white material that reminded him of his most expensive handkerchiefs. There were flowers, white also, embroidered on the hem. Beneath it, he could see the outline of white panties. She looked vulnerable, virginal, and his loins began to ache with desire.

He touched her waist again. She didn't stir. Gradually he slid his hand down and around, giving her time to protest. When she didn't, he pressed his palm warmly over the lower part of her abdomen. "There?"

"Uh-huh."

Moving his hand in slow circles, he massaged her. "Better?"

She nodded.

"Poor baby." He kissed her temple lovingly.

She sighed and her eyes closed sleepily. "Trevor?"

"Hmm?"

"Have you ever lived with a woman?"

His hand paused, but so momentarily that the hesitation was barely discernible. "No, why?"

"Then what do you know about this?"

"Only that I'm glad I don't have to go through it every month."

Without opening her eyes, she smiled. "Typical male answer."

"But honest." He took a love bite out of her bare shoulder.

She didn't actually think about moving her legs. A message to them wasn't consciously transmitted. They just moved, unfolding away from her body, straightening and providing him greater access to her swollen, cramping tummy.

"Did you and Aaron manage dinner without me?"

"Like clockwork."

"What did you do?"

"Well," he said, sliding his legs against hers, catching the backs of her knees with his and filling her insteps with his toes, "first I hosed him down to get all the chocolate pudding off."

She laughed. "By the way, I approve of the idea of pudding painting. He was certainly having a good time. On any other day, I probably would have put on a swimsuit and joined him."

"As we both know by now, you had a right to be out of sorts."

"I shouldn't have yelled at you."

"I liked the part about Aaron's teacher and me having a 'cozy little chat.' The way you said it made me think you

might be jealous." This time his mouth found her ear. His tongue delicately stroked the lobe. "That's so soft. A little fuzzy."

"Go on," she said in a breathy voice.

"I forget where I was."

"You . . . you . . . hmm . . . You, uh, hosed him down."

"Oh, right, yeah, and then I fixed his dinner."

"What did he eat?"

"His favorite."

"Hot dogs?"

"Uh-huh."

"Without the buns?"

"Of course." He kissed her neck and she moaned softly. "Tomorrow morning the birds in our woods will have three hot dog buns for breakfast. I hope they like mustard."

A low laugh issued from her throat and she didn't know whether it was because of his joke or because his mustache was dusting the column of her neck as if it were an object made of rare porcelain. "Did you—"

"I know what you're going to ask and yes, I did. I watched Aaron take every bite and made sure he chewed it."

"Thank you." Her mouth searched for his.

"You're welcome." His lips found hers.

The kiss acted like a spark at the end of two very short fuses. He ground his mouth against hers hungrily and her lips parted for the introduction of his tongue. Her body followed her head around until they were lying face to face.

Her arms locked around his shoulders. The tips of her breasts strained against the front of her nightgown until they touched the furry wall of his chest. He pressed her down, covering a side of her body with his own.

"Kyla, you—"

"Trevor, I—"

"What?"

"Trevor?"

From the bed came sounds. Gratified groans. The silky shifting of linens. Soughing breaths. Incoherent whispers. Whimpers of pleasure. The music of mating.

His hands moved with restless greed. He touched her thighs; for a fleeting second her calf filled his palm. He ran his fingers along her fragile collarbone. He cupped her breast.

"Ahh." Her back arched and she tore her mouth free of his kiss.

"What's the matter?"

"It's tender."

"Oh. I didn't . . . it is?"

"Yes."

"I'm sorry."

"No, it . . . actually it felt good."

"It did?"

"Oh, yes," she sighed as he gently caressed her again.

"Like that?"

"Hmm."

"And the nipples?"

"Yes, yes."

"Tell me, if—"

But he never finished the sentence, because her fingers wove themselves through his hair and drew his head down for another avaricious kiss.

When it ended, he lowered his head. It moved from side to side ardently pressing hot, random kisses into her breasts. His hands formed a brace for her ribs. He shifted her beneath him. His knee separated hers. The nightgown was pushed to her waist. She tucked his hard thigh high between hers. She moved against it. Rotating. Rubbing. Reaching.

"Damn!"

He lay atop her, his breath thrashing like a strong wind in her ear. She could feel the rapid thudding of his heart where his chest crushed hers. Between his powerful hands,

he was holding her head immobile. His fevered face was buried in her hair.

"Don't move, sweetheart."

"What is it?"

"Please don't move, my love," he groaned. "Be still for just a minute."

She did as he asked. Several moments later, he slowly raised his head. His face was infinitely sweet and his expression compassionate. One corner of his mustache crawled up to form a rueful grin. "Wouldn't you know it? I get you just where I want you and it's the wrong night."

Embarrassed, her eyes fell away from his face. He kissed her cheek and moved away, coming off the bed completely. Bending at the waist, he laid his palm against her flushed cheek. "Are you all right?"

She wasn't in pain, except for the lower part of her body, which was aching abominably, and not with the miseries of menstruation. "I feel better," she said inanely.

He straightened and uncomfortably shifted his weight from one foot to the other. His fingers raked strands of ebony hair off his forehead. "You skipped supper. Are you hungry?"

"No. Did you eat?"

"I nibbled. I'm fine." They looked at each other briefly, then away, realizing at the same time how banal this conversation was after the passion that had seethed between them only moments ago. "Well, I'll leave you alone now. Good night."

He turned and headed for the door. The muscles of his back rippled beneath the smooth skin. The cutoffs gloved his buttocks.

"Trevor?"

He spun around. "What?"

"You . . ." *Don't stop now. You've gone this far.* She swallowed her pride and her better judgment. "You don't have to go."

Trevor looked at his wife. She was propped up on her elbows. The nightgown's embroidered hem was riding her upper thighs. Her tousled hair was tumbling over her shoulders like spun pink gold. His kisses had left her lips wet and berry-colored. The fabric of her nightgown was damp where his mouth had been. It clung to her breasts, transparently molding to the tips, which were making rosy inverted dimples against the soft white fabric.

He grimaced and rubbed his moist palms down the legs of his cutoffs. "Yeah, I do. I have to go. If I stay..."

If he touched her again there would be no stopping him from consummating his marriage and quenching his raging desire. Hell, he wasn't fastidious. But the first time they made love, he didn't want her to feel embarrassed or uncomfortable or to regret it for any reason.

"But hold the thought," he added on a husky whisper seconds before he left the room.

Aaron was already in his high chair and Trevor was turning strips of bacon in a sizzling skillet when Kyla warily approached the kitchen the following morning.

"Good morning, baby." She leaned down to kiss Aaron. He affectionately bopped her on the nose with a soggy piece of bacon. "Thanks a lot," she muttered.

"It was either get him up or let him jump in his bed until all the springs broke," Trevor said, taking the skillet off the burner and moving toward her.

"Thank you for seeing to him."

"My pleasure."

He clasped her waist lightly and drew her forward. He gave her one of those morning kisses that smelled like after-shave and tasted like teeth recently brushed. Kyla wouldn't have minded if it had lasted longer, but after smacking another quick kiss on her mouth, he said, "Sit down. You must be starving."

She glanced worriedly at the clock. "I've got to hurry. I overslept."

"Take your time. I called Babs and told her not to expect you on time this morning. Aaron's school isn't expecting him until around ten."

He set a platter of bacon and homemade waffles in front of her and sent her salivary glands into delirium. "I am starving."

"How are you otherwise?" He bent down and slid his hand past her waist. "Tummy still hurt?"

"It's much better."

"And here?" He palmed her breast and gently rolled her nipple between his thumb and finger.

She could barely breathe and gasped out, "Fine...much fine... I mean much better."

"That's good." He kissed the top of her head and sat down across from her. While she fumbled with her napkin and tried to remember how to use a fork, he buttered a waffle for Aaron and slid the plate onto the high chair's tray. "Here, Scout. Attack."

They laughed at the child's atrocious table manners and Kyla remarked, "We've got to start doing something about that." When she realized she had included Trevor in that statement, making the "we" sound so permanent, she glanced up at him. His expression was warm and flooded her body with a golden heat.

"How did you sleep?" he asked.

She noticed that his fingers were so long and strong that they barely fitted in the crook of the coffee mug's handle. Yet they could be so gentle when they touched her body, as they had been only moments ago. Getting a bite of waffle past her thickening throat was no small task, but when she did she answered, "Fairly well."

She had dreamed of him and awakened perspiring, with her heart pounding and her breath coming in short, rapid bursts. At least she could now satisfy Babs's curiosity and tell her without any exaggeration that Trevor was breathtaking naked.

"I didn't sleep too well last night," he said.

"I'm sorry. What was wrong?" He had certainly taken her breath when he came out of that hot tub. His chest and thighs and—

"It was too hard."

Kyla's fork clattered to her plate and when she reached for it, she knocked over her orange juice.

Aaron pointed and said, "Uh-oh! Uh-oh!"

Trevor scraped back his chair and lunged for a dish towel. He blotted it against the spreading puddle of juice. "I was referring to the bed in the guest room."

"What?" Kyla's head swiveled around. His mustache was twitching with his need to laugh.

"The *bed* was too hard."

Her cheeks were bathed with hot color. Thankfully she was spared further embarrassment when the telephone rang. Trevor answered it.

"Dad!" he exclaimed.

Kyla lifted Aaron, who had polished off his waffle in record time, onto her lap. He reached for the food left on her plate and between her kisses, he ate that as well. She glanced at Trevor, who was smiling broadly into the receiver.

"Sure, no problem. What time...? For how long...? Is that all...? Well, that's better than nothing.... Okay, we'll be there. Bye." He hung up.

"Your father?"

"He's flying down today to spend the night with us. That's all right with you, isn't it?"

"Certainly. I know you were disappointed that he couldn't come down for the wedding."

"I want him to meet you and Aaron. He can only stay one night and then he has to make a trip to L.A. for some case he's working on." He popped a piece of bacon into his mouth and chewed vigorously. "I want to drive him around town and show him some of my buildings. You know we— Say, I'm sorry. I didn't mean to get carried away."

Actually she was enjoying his enthusiasm. "Go on," she urged. "What were you about to say?"

"We didn't get along very well. Not until after my accident."

"He wanted you to be a lawyer?"

"And I had other ideas. But while I was in the hospital, we came to an understanding and now everything's great between us."

Her smile was genuine. "Are you driving to Dallas to pick him up?"

"If you don't mind. He gave me his flight number. I thought we'd all have dinner in the city."

"Aaron included?" she asked worriedly.

"Of course, Aaron included. He's part of this family." He scooped the child out of her arms and held him high over his head. Aaron squealed in delight. "Dad loves to eat Italian." He named a famous Dallas restaurant. "Should I call and make reservations?"

She hated to dampen his excitement, but apparently he didn't realize what a risk it was to take a fifteen-month-old child to a sedate restaurant for a leisurely meal. "I don't know if that's a good idea, Trevor. I'm not sure they welcome children there."

"Hey, if they don't want our kid in their restaurant, we'll take our business elsewhere."

From the maître d' to the lowliest dishwasher, everyone in the family establishment was charmed by the three men, George Rule, Trevor and Aaron. Kyla's anxiety was all for naught because Trevor had spoken with the maître d' personally when making the reservation and the staff was prepared for Aaron before the party arrived.

Her initial meeting with Trevor's father, amidst the confusion at the airport, had gone more smoothly than Kyla had had any right to expect. At first Aaron was shy with the tall, white-haired man with the authoritative voice. But no more so than George was with the child.

Deliberately Trevor seated them in the back seat of the car together and by the time they reached the restaurant, located in Dallas's prestigious Turtle Creek area, the two were fast friends. In fact it was George who carried Aaron inside and showed him off to everyone as his grandson.

"Trevor tells me I'll miss meeting your parents," George said on the drive back to Chandler.

"We got a postcard from them yesterday from Yellowstone," Kyla said. "They're having the time of their lives."

She explained to George that the Powerses had sold their house within days of her marriage to Trevor. What furnishings Kyla didn't want, they had sold at auction. Trevor had helped Clif pick out the motor home that best suited their needs. Meg had furnished it with the giddy excitement of a little girl with a new dollhouse. Two weeks later they had left.

"She gets homesick for them," Trevor said teasingly, reaching across the front seat to tug on a lock of Kyla's hair. "They spoiled her rotten."

"So do you."

His head swung around. She had been as surprised as he to hear herself make that statement, but she realized after vocalizing it that it was the truth. Trevor glanced out the windshield to make sure he wasn't endangering them, then looked at Kyla again.

"I'm glad. That's what I want to do."

They continued staring at one another until George coughed loudly and said, "I don't know about you, Aaron, but I'm beginning to feel like a fifth wheel."

There was enough daylight left when they reached Chandler for Trevor to walk George through some of the building projects he was working on. Kyla remained in the car, watching their silhouettes move against the darkening sky. Trevor had hefted Aaron to his shoulders where the boy rode, his legs straddling Trevor's neck. They made a poignant picture.

"But that should be Richard," Kyla whispered, fighting the tears that blurred her eyes.

She wept because she couldn't convince herself of it. If the man should be Richard, why did it look so right for her son's fat fists to be trustingly clenching handfuls of Trevor's black hair? Why did it touch her heart so achingly to see Trevor swing Aaron down carefully and unabashedly give him a hearty hug? And why did she want to feel those same strong arms holding her?

George was justifiably impressed with the house and heaped unqualified praise on his son. Kyla carried Aaron off to bed and after a brief visit with George, excused herself to give Trevor and his father some time alone.

"I've got a bruise on my shin the size of a fifty-cent piece," George said. "Any particular reason why you kicked me under the table when I mentioned your stint in the Marines?"

Trevor had been glad Kyla was involved wiping spaghetti sauce off Aaron's mouth and had missed his father's inopportune comment at dinner. "I'd rather Kyla not know about that. She doesn't know how I got hurt."

"Any of it?"

"No."

"Hmm."

Trevor knew his father well enough to know that even a "Hmm" was never casually spoken. "You certainly fell in love and married quickly, didn't you?"

"Is that so odd?"

"For you it is." His son looked at him sharply and George smiled. "Your reputation with women reached even your ol' dad's ears, Trevor. This sudden romance is out of character."

They were sitting out on the deck in the comfortable chaise lounges. George was puffing on a cigar, which his doctor had advised him to give up. Trevor was glad the darkness covered his uneasiness. He didn't like the direction the conversation had taken. "I love her, Dad."

"I don't doubt that now that I've seen you with her. It's just strange that 'Smooch,' as your buddies used to call you, fell so hard and so fast."

"I've been in love with her for a long time," Trevor said, almost beneath his breath.

George rolled the cigar between his fingers, studying its glowing tip. "She wouldn't have anything to do with those letters you pored over and wouldn't let out of your sight while you were in the hospital, would she?"

Trevor should have known better. Nothing, not the most trivial scrap of evidence, slipped past the shrewd George Rule. To him nothing was insignificant. Trevor got out of his chair and walked to the edge of the deck. He propped his shoulder against the wall and stared out at the darkness as he had done weeks before while ruminating on how to tell Kyla who he was. "Dad, I'm going to tell you a story you're going to find hard to believe."

When he concluded his tale, several ponderous moments of silence followed. Finally George said, "I promised never to interfere in your life again, Trevor, but you're playing with fire."

"I know," Trevor admitted, turning around to face his father.

"How do you think this young woman is going to react when she learns the truth?"

Trevor hung his head and slid his hands into his trouser pockets. "I hate to think about it."

"Well, you'd better think about it," the older man warned, "because she *will* find out." He pulled himself to his feet and ground out his cigar in the ashtray Trevor had provided for him. Laying a hand on Trevor's shoulder, he said, "But who knows? It might work out. If you love her enough."

"I do."

"Does she love you?"

Trevor hesitated, his eyes slicing toward the darkened master bedroom windows. "I think she might be coming

to. Or maybe she's just getting used to having me around. Hell, I don't know.''

George smiled. Then his fond gaze rested on the eye patch and he was reminded once again of how valuable his son was to him and how close he had come to losing him. Moisture gathered in his eyes and he pulled Trevor forward for a fiercely emotional, if short-lived, embrace. ''After what you went through, son, you deserve to be happy.''

''No, Dad,'' Trevor said roughly over his father's shoulder, ''after what she's been through, she deserves to be happy.''

Soon afterward they said their good-nights and George ambled toward the guest room where Trevor had placed his suitcase.

Trevor approached the door to the master suite with the dawdling, shuffling footsteps of a boy who had been sent to the principal's office. His stomach was doing handsprings. His heart was thudding.

Just what the hell was wrong with him? Was he excited at the thought of her welcoming him into bed? Or frightened at the thought of her rejection?

Frightened? Of a woman weighing no more than one hundred and ten pounds? Don't be ridiculous.

Then why are you standing out here like a moron, staring at this door with your stomach in knots and your heart pounding and your palms sweating and your groin . . .

Oh, God, no, don't think about your groin.

Were his knees really shaking? Why, for God's sake?

He was a grown man, not a schoolboy. This was his house. He had built it. He had financed it. He had a right to sleep in any damn room he pleased.

She was his wife, wasn't she? And yeah, he *had* been spoiling her for the past few weeks. He'd walked around on eggshells, doing and saying everything he could to please her and nothing that might upset her.

Hadn't she been pleased when he installed her old re-painted swing set in the backyard for Aaron? Hadn't she been pleased when he built that sandbox? And hadn't she laughed when he engaged her in a tickling match as soon as they had filled it with soft, cool sand? And hadn't she returned the kiss that wrestling match had resulted in?

Hell, yes she had! His nickname hadn't been Smooch for nothing, you know.

But he hadn't carried that or any other kiss further than he thought she wanted it to go. He had been acting like a lackey to win her approval. He'd slunk around with his tail between his legs until it was getting damned uncomfortable. Well, it was high time he started letting her know that he was the man in the family and that as such, by God, he had some rights!

The door burst open under his hand and he closed it with a resounding slam. Kyla bolted upright in bed and clutched the sheet to her breasts. "Trevor? What's happened? What's wrong?"

"Nothing's wrong. All right, I'll tell you what's wrong," he snarled as he stalked into the room, armed to the teeth with righteous indignation. "My dad is sleeping in the guest room. So for tonight, Mrs. Rule, we share this bed."

Chapter 12

All right."

Her softly spoken concession effectively disarmed him. His inflated wrath went as flat as a fallen soufflé. He rolled his shoulders to collect himself. "Well, good," he said tersely. "I'm glad you see it like that."

For some reason, her obliging conciliation only served to make him madder. He didn't need her to patronize him. No, sir!

He tore off his clothes with jerky, angry pulls and pokes and punches. One by one the garments were slung away from him. They were left wherever they happened to fall. When he was down to his briefs, he yanked back the covers and thrust his feet between the sheets. After brutalizing the pillow with his fist, he ground his head down into it.

"Good night."

"Good night, Trevor."

He turned his back to her, rocking the entire bed while he adjusted himself into a comfortable position with all the querulousness of a fairy-tale giant.

There! Guess I showed her.

If that were the case, why was it *his* body that was stiff and burning with lust? Why was it *his* heart that ached with love denied release?

Kyla awakened to find him watching her. He lay on his side facing her, his tousled dark head pillowed on a bent elbow. Silent and still, the only part of him that moved was that single green eye that wandered over her face and hair as though cataloging every detail.

She didn't realize she had lifted her hand until she saw it move into her range of vision. Lightly she touched the black eye patch. "You never take it off."

"I don't want you to see it."

"Why?"

"It's so ugly."

"It wouldn't matter to me."

"Curious?"

"No. Sad. I was just thinking how pretty your eye is and what a shame it is that the other one was lost."

"I'm grateful that one was spared."

"That goes without saying."

"If for no other reason than for this moment. I wouldn't trade looking at your face right now for anything in the world." His voice was rough with emotion.

Kyla's throat ached with the need to cry. Her hand moved from his eye patch down to his mustache. Her fingers coasted over it lightly. Then she touched his upper lip.

Trevor's breath hit the back of his throat. Heat filled his sex.

She had never touched his face. Now she engaged in an orgy of touching. The bones in his lean, dark face were pronounced. His brow bone jutted over his eyesockets. The wing-shaped brows were sleek and thick. A bristly

beard stubble covered the lower half of his face. His mustache, which her fingers couldn't leave alone, was amazingly soft. With her fingernail, she languidly traced the shape of his lower lip.

"Be careful, Kyla."

She withdrew her finger a fraction. "Why?"

"Because for almost seven hours I have been lying here wanting you. Do you understand?" She nodded. "I don't think it's too smart of you to touch me now. Unless..."

He left the condition unspoken, but they both knew what it was.

Outside, bright sunlight was already filtering through the leafy branches of the trees and casting wavering patterns against the closed shutters. Birds were chirping happily. Squirrels chased each other through the upper branches. Butterflies flitted from flower to flower. Redbirds and bluejays looked like brightly feathered arrows as they darted among the trees.

The activity in the bedroom was considerably less obvious, but no less energetic. Emotions seethed between them like huge swells in the Atlantic. Longing was so thick it was palpable, desire so potent it could be breathed. If auras could be seen, the air around them would have shimmered with a red glow of mounting passion.

Her body didn't demonstrate its longing as blatantly as his, but she suffered from the same affliction. At that moment, Kyla thought of nothing more than satisfying her need to be cosseted, caressed, covered, completed.

She touched his lower lip again.

In one fluid motion, he brought them together, positioned her beneath him and captured her mouth in a hot, hungry kiss. Hard and bold, his manhood sought the heart of her femininity. Found it. Favored it with urgent caresses.

"God, I want you." He frantically groped for the hem of her nightgown. Her hands plucked at the elastic waist-

band of his briefs. One hand slipped inside and touched the taut curve of his buttock.

Groaning, his mouth found her nipple and closed around it while he enjoyed the silky smoothness of her panties and the contours they confined. She sighed his name and raised her knees. His fingers slipped into the waistband of her panties.

The bedroom door flew open and with the impetus of a miniature cyclone, Aaron came bounding into the room. He was chattering as raucously as were the bluejay and squirrel outside.

The breath leaked out of Trevor's body in a slow steady hiss, relieving the tension in his chest. He pressed his forehead against Kyla's and wished he could relieve the pressure in his loins as easily. A laugh began deep inside him and left his lips on an expulsion of air against Kyla's mouth. "Remind me to throttle him later."

Kyla, too, was feeling the agony of forcibly subduing passion. Sighing, she pressed her face into the warmth of Trevor's neck. "If I don't get to him first."

Trevor rolled off her, but kept her locked in the security of his arms. Together they turned their attention to Aaron.

"He must have talked his indulgent grandfather into releasing him from his crib," Trevor observed.

Attuned to the adoration of his audience, Aaron took center stage and performed some of his cutest tricks. Their laughter only encouraged him. Wearing a sappy grin, he started turning in slow circles. Heedless of their warnings that he was going to get dizzy, he circled faster until, drunk, he reached out to break his fall.

What his hand grasped was the decorative pull of the bedside table drawer. Gravity tugged at Aaron and he was too dizzy to counteract it. His bottom landed solidly on the carpeted floor and the drawer came out of its mooring to drop into his lap.

He wasn't hurt, but the two adults reflexively sat up when they saw that the inevitable was about to happen.

Aaron stared at them in stunned surprise, then glanced down at the drawer lying in his lap.

The framed eight-by-ten picture of the Marine in full dress uniform was the only thing in the drawer. Aaron slapped the nonglare glass with his hands and said, "Da. Dadadada." He smiled up at his spectators, fully expecting an ovation for his brilliant performance.

The arms still holding Kyla in a loose, affectionate embrace went as hard as steel. Gradually they released her. She felt their warmth being taken from her by slow degrees. Then, with one violent motion, Trevor came off the bed on the far side and swept up the trousers he had left lying on the floor the night before. He shoved his legs into them and zipped them with a vicious tug as he strode toward the door.

"Trevor, please!"

He spun around, bare-chested, barefoot and furious. His jaw was bunched with rage and there was a cold glint in his eye as it took a bead on the woman now sitting up in the bed, her hair a mess, her face pale, her lips tremulous, her eyes pleading.

"I won't be a stand-in," he growled. "As long as there's another man living inside your skin, madam, there's no room for this." He crudely cupped himself. His chin bobbed once for emphasis before he stormed out.

"It's Lynn Haskell," Kyla reported, holding her hand over the mouthpiece of the telephone receiver. "She's invited us to a picnic at the lake on Labor Day. Do you want to go?"

It had been a week since George Rule's visit. The most miserable week of Kyla's life. The tension in the house crackled like old paper and was just as flammable. The suspense of not knowing what would touch off the inevitable conflagration was nerve-racking in the extreme.

Trevor never lost his temper, never raised his voice. Kyla would have welcomed it if he had. He was rather like a

brooding, dark thunderstorm that refused to break. It lurked overhead, ominous and threatening.

He treated her no less politely than he ever had, but there had been a noticeable suspension of his demonstrations of affection. He rarely touched her, and then only out of necessity. With Aaron he behaved in the same loving way. With her, he was remote and mechanical.

Which was the way I wanted it in the first place, she rushed to remind herself every time she had a yearning for his brilliant smile...or a meaningful glance...or a touch...or a kiss.

Now, in response to her inquiry, he shrugged noncommittally. "I'll leave that up to you, Kyla. Whatever you want to do."

She shot him a withering look. He ignored it and bent back over the wooden puzzle with the oversize pieces that he was patiently working with Aaron for about the tenth time that evening.

She couldn't keep Lynn on the phone indefinitely. She had to tell her something. But what? The Haskells were Trevor's friends. Whether he said so or not, she was certain he wanted to go. Lynn was too astute to see through a lame excuse. Getting outside and spending a day at the lake would probably be good for all of them. Hopefully it would relieve some of the tension.

"Lynn, we'd be delighted to join you." From the corner of her eye, she saw Trevor glance up at her, but he immediately returned his attention to Aaron. "What can I bring? No, no, I insist."

Invariably, the first Monday in September in Texas was cloudless and blisteringly hot. This Labor Day proved to be no different from its predecessors.

"Kyla, they're here," Trevor called from the front porch where he had hauled their gear and stood waiting with Aaron. The Haskells had suggested that they all travel to

the lake in their van since it would hold both families and the picnic paraphernalia as well.

"Coming." She went through the house checking to see that doors were locked and that she hadn't forgotten anything vital. When she reached the front porch, Trevor and Ted were loading the back of the van and Lynn was giving Aaron a "pony ride" on her knees.

"Hi. Climb aboard while there's still room for you," Lynn said, her holiday spirit showing.

During the drive to the lake Ted teased Kyla about her packing. "If I'd known you were going to bring along that much stuff, I'd have rented a trailer."

She wondered if the other couple noticed that she and Trevor could banter and joke with them, but that they had little to say to each other.

He had dressed in faded cutoffs, jogging shoes in sore need of retirement and a gray sweatshirt with the sleeves cut out. He had also enlarged the neck so that the crisp, dark pelt on his chest filled the jagged, uneven V.

Kyla had pulled her hair back into a ponytail. She had worn a pair of old shorts over her bikini trunks and had tied the tails of a matching shirt at her waist. It gapped open to reveal the bikini bra underneath. She was glad she hadn't tried to look nice. By the time they reached the lake, she had been mauled by Aaron, who had caught the infectious holiday mood from the rambunctious Haskell children.

They reached the lake, found a spot they all agreed was perfect and began the chore of unloading the van. When they were finished, Trevor celebrated by taking a can of beer from the cooler and gulping it down in three swallows.

He drank another to squelch the flames of desire that licked his belly when Kyla stripped down to her bikini after Lynn suggested that they work on their tans.

They trekked to the water's edge with the children. Aaron splashed about happily and wasn't satisfied until his

mother had been showered with the cool lake water. When her nipples pouted against the cold, Trevor grumbled a feeble excuse and went back to their picnic spot for another beer.

He carried it down to the lake and offered Kyla a drink. When she accepted it, she accidentally touched his hand. And when her head tilted back, he wanted nothing more than to open his mouth over her exposed throat.

While he and Ted stayed in the shallow water with the children, Lynn and Kyla swam out to the dock that was buoyed in deeper water. Trevor watched every graceful arc her arms made through the water. His gaze was trained on her when she pulled herself up the ladder. Standing up to wave to Aaron, her slender body was silhouetted against the summer sky. Water sheeted on her thighs and coursed down her flat tummy.

"I'll be right back," Trevor muttered.

"Where are you going this time?" Ted asked him, shading his eyes against the sun and looking up at Trevor.

"I, uh, I think Aaron wants a cookie."

He picked up Aaron, who was perfectly content piling lake mud onto his knees, and carried him up to the van. Aaron got a cookie and Trevor drank another beer.

After a lunch that would have fed a caravan of gypsies, the children napped in the shade. When they woke up, everyone walked to the baseball diamond. The annual citywide "Skins and Shirts" game was a tradition among young businessmen. Anybody who wanted to play was to bring his equipment and meet at the diamond where they were divided into teams.

Trevor had just one eye and he walked with a limp, but months of physical therapy and a daily exercise program that he kept to religiously had put him in far better physical shape than the pencil pushers who had thirty or more pounds of sedentary living to lose.

Kyla gnawed on the knuckle of her index finger when he stepped to the plate in the ninth inning. The Skins, the

team both he and Ted were playing for, were behind by three. The bases were loaded. There were already two outs. It all depended on Trevor. He rose to the occasion, knocking in a grand slam home run.

Kyla, like everyone else rooting for the Skins, went wild. Trevor received the hearty congratulations of his teammates. Then he and Ted came jogging toward their families.

"You were great!" Lynn said enthusiastically to Trevor.

"Hey, what about me?" Ted asked, affecting hurt pride.

"You were great, too." Lynn wound her arms around her husband's neck and kissed him soundly.

"I was holding my breath," Kyla said, laughing excitedly. As she smiled up at Trevor, her face was bathed with sunlight and her eyes were squinting against the glare. Behind a thick screen of curling lashes, he could see that they were shining. Her hands were pressed against her chest as though she were trying to contain her jubilance.

"It was a lucky shot," he said modestly.

They took hesitant steps toward each other. Paused. Then Kyla flung herself against him and, coming up on tiptoe, pressed her mouth against his for a kiss befitting the hero of the day.

Trevor, reacting instinctively, wrapped his arms around her waist. The taste of her delicious mouth for the first time in over a week sent a shaft of pleasure spearing through him. It exploded like a fireball in the bottom of his belly. Lost in her taste, drowning in it, his tongue thrust deep. Heedless of the daylight, the crowd, everything, his hands slid to her derriere and lifted her against his swelling manhood.

Something, possibly Ted tapping him on the seat with his baseball glove, but something, reminded him of where they were. He raised his head and, looking down at Kyla, laughed shakily.

Kyla gazed up at him, a bewildered expression on her face. Her eyes were smoky. Her breasts were rising and falling rapidly with each breath. Her lips were red and wet and slightly roughened by his mustache. Lifting three fingers to them, she touched them tentatively, as though they'd been scorched.

"Ready to get back?" Ted was standing with Lynn, their arms linked loosely around each other's waists. Each had a child by the hand and Aaron was terrorizing a doodlebug at their feet. "How 'bout a beer, Trevor?"

"Yeah, sure, a beer."

He drank that one in two swallows, swam to rinse off the sweat and grime of the game, then chased his swim with another beer.

They nibbled on leftovers for supper and gradually a healthy tiredness settled in. Trevor was mellow and feeling no pain by the time the van was loaded and they started the drive home. Traffic was congested. He was happy to relinquish the responsibility of coping with it to Ted.

In fact, he relinquished every responsibility except that of finding a resting place for his head against Kyla's shoulder. He leaned against her heavily and let his arm slide down her side until his elbow nestled in the valley between her thigh and lap. His hand curled around the inside of her thigh. He stroked the smooth skin with a lazy thumb and found that it felt good to move his arm slightly so that the hairs dusting it dragged against her smooth flesh.

Once he thought he turned his head and kissed her neck, but he wasn't certain if he actually carried out the intention or just thought about it so hard that he imagined he did.

When they reached home, he concentrated on not appearing tipsy—as he had a sneaking suspicion he was—in front of their hosts. He soberly thanked the Haskells for a great time and bade them good-night.

He realized just how rubbery his arms and legs were as he tried to carry their picnic gear up to the porch. After taking a few staggering steps and dropping the picnic basket twice, he mumbled, "Think I'll wait till tomorrow to put all this stuff up," and dropped it all onto the ground.

"That's fine," Kyla said, pressing her lips together to keep from laughing. "But could you please unlock the front door?" Aaron, who was asleep in her arms, was becoming heavy.

"Sure, sure."

Stupidly, he just stood there looking at her while the seconds ticked by.

"You have the key, Trevor."

"Oh! Of course I do." He went on an uncoordinated search through his pockets until he produced the key. Holding it up inches in front of her nose he said, "Ta-da! See, I told you I had it."

She suppressed another laugh, but he seemed not to notice as he wrestled with the lock.

"Someone has changed the lock!" His exclamation was spoken just as Edison must have said of the first light bulb, "It works!"

"Turn the key so the teeth are up."

He did as Kyla instructed. When the lock clicked open and the door swung wide, he gazed down at her and said, "You're wonderful. Did you know that? Wonderful."

She rolled her eyes with a long-suffering expression and pushed her way past him, going straight to Aaron's room and putting him to bed with dispatch. Minutes later when she came back through the living room, Trevor was sprawled on the sofa, one arm and leg dangling. She checked to make certain he had relocked the front door, then moved toward the couch and bent over him.

He was asleep. She brushed back a strand of wavy black hair that had fallen over his forehead. He awoke. "Kyla?"

"Hmm?"

"You're sweet."

"Thank you."

"So sweet and beautiful."

"Oh, yes, I know."

He missed the wry inflection in her tone. He had no idea he was being humored. All he knew for certain was that the pale moonlight, spilling through the glass doors, looked beautiful on the face of the woman he loved.

He hooked her behind the neck and pulled her head down for a kiss. Kyla, not prepared for this sudden move, much less the passion behind the kiss, lost her balance and feel atop him. Trevor struggled to right the situation but only succeeded in rolling them both to the floor.

For several moments, he didn't comprehend that the soft pillow his head was lying heavily on was Kyla's breasts. Not until he lifted his head and gazed down at her. Then he lowered his face and nudged aside the shirt she had retied at her waist before the trip home. He touched her with his lips.

"You smell like sunshine." His nose rooted in the valley between her breasts. "I love the smell of sunshine."

He shifted so that his thighs came to be settled between hers in a snug fit. If it registered with him that her arms were lying listlessly at her sides and that her hands were turned up in an attitude of surrender, he didn't comment. He merely rearranged them so that they rested above her head, then with his index finger traced the inside of her arm from palm to armpit as though drawing a path for her veins to follow.

"If sunshine had a taste, it would taske like you, too." His mouth moved over her breasts, lips opening and closing as though taking bites. He got caught up in what he was doing and made a savage attempt to untie her shirt-tails. When they finally came undone, he cast them aside and attacked the front fastener of her bikini.

When she lay bare beneath him, he whispered huskily, "God above, you're beautiful."

He touched her reverently, his fingertips brushing back and forth across the soft flesh. He took his time. He made no apology. Because he was convinced she was just another dream. One of many about Kyla. But God, this one seemed real!

He cupped a breast in each hand and reshaped them with kneading motions of his fingers. Lightly he pinched her nipple between his thumb and finger, then lowered his mouth and entrapped it.

The sounds he made were those of a starving man who had just found sustenance. He suckled both breasts. He rubbed his mustachioed lip over the nipples now made glossy by his kisses. He made a sharp point of his tongue and played with them, tempting them to shrink, to become harder. And they complied.

Vaguely he became aware of the writhing movements beneath him, speaking to his body in a language it understood even if he wasn't translating too clearly.

He levered himself up and unfastened her shorts. Unerringly his hand wedged itself past them and into the damp bikini trunks. He cupped the delta that fitted his palm to perfection. He rubbed it, pressing, luxuriating in the soft fleece that covered it. His fingers curved down into the sweet mystery below.

His groan started in the bottom of his soul and rumbled through his entire body. "You're wet for me."

Passionately he kissed the throat from which a sobbing sound emanated and introduced his fingers into the fount of that seductive wet heat.

His breath rushed in and out of his body. Or was it Kyla's? He wasn't sure. He solved the riddle by clamping his mouth over hers and kissing her until neither of them could breathe at all. His tongue reached for her throat.

Her shorts came off easily. The trunks required considerably more patience and skill, both of which had deserted him by the time he whipped them from her ankles.

Frustrated and clumsy, he freed himself from his clothing.

God, her skin was cool.

And he was so damn hot.

Her body accepted him. He sank into her silky wet femininity and shuddered with the pleasure. He was enveloped by warm, creamy womanhood, and it was the best it had ever been.

His mouth settled against her ear. "I've waited for this for so long. I've wanted... But it's much better... You're... my love...."

With his hands beneath her hips, he lifted her higher against him and moved with swift, sure thrusts. Her body began to quicken around his. The breasts beneath his mouth trembled and the nipple against his tongue pearled into a hard round button.

And just as he felt the sweet rush of her release pouring over him, he came in a torrent.

Huntsville, Alabama

"I'll never move again. We're living here for the rest of our lives."

"Fine with me," the man said tiredly. "Helluva way to spend Labor Day. Laboring!"

"But we got everything put away. Finally. Everything except that box with all your Marine junk in it."

"It might be junk to you, but some of it means a lot to me."

She patted his hand. "I know. I was only kidding. Come to think of it, did you ever send that picture to that guy's widow? Stroud, wasn't it?"

"Yes, and no, I never did. I'll do that tomorrow." His brow wrinkled. "But I don't know how to find her."

"Why don't you send it to the Marine Corps? I'm sure they could forward it to her."

"Good idea." He stood up and offered his hand to help her up. "Let's go to bed. I'm exhausted. But don't let me forget to fish that picture out and send it off tomorrow," he added as he switched out the light.

Chapter 13

It took her a moment to remember why she was sleeping on the floor. Without pillow or blanket or anything to alleviate the discomfort, she had slept a dreamless sleep for the first time in weeks.

Moving nothing but her eyes, she looked through the glass doors and saw that it was still very early. Hesitantly she stretched her cramped legs and tried to sit up. His fingers were snared in her hair.

It took some gentle tugging, but at last she was free. She picked up her discarded shorts and tiptoed toward the hall. On the way to Aaron's room, she refastened her bikini bra, the cups of which had passed the night bunched up under her arms.

Aaron was still asleep and showed no signs of waking up any time soon. He had had a strenuous day yesterday and it was taking its toll. Kyla was thankful. Right now, she had to think and needed no distractions.

She pulled on her shorts and crept back through the house. Trevor hadn't stirred from his place on the floor in

front of the living-room sofa. He wasn't snoring, but his breathing was deep and steady. Kyla slipped outside without awakening him.

She took a towel from the stack they kept in the closet near the hot tub and walked through the woods toward the creek. The morning was still. The new sun hadn't yet penetrated the dense branches of the trees. The undergrowth was cool and damp against her bare feet.

The creek flowed lackadaisically. Heavy rain turned its current into a series of rushing swirls. Otherwise it was calm and provided a great breeding ground for crawdads. Aaron had clapped his hands in delight over one when Trevor—

Trevor.

His name echoed through her mind, eradicating all other thought. Sighing, Kyla spread her towel on the deep grass near the creek bank and sat down. Raising her knees to her chest, she propped her chin on them.

It had happened.

She closed her eyes as tremors of pleasure shimmied through her at the memory. Pressing her forehead against her knees she tried not to recall the splendor of his lovemaking, but her efforts were to no avail. Her brain might not want to remember, but her body was relishing every sweet recollection.

Why hadn't she resisted? She could have. He'd had too much to drink. When he collapsed on top of her, she could have shoved him away from her and he probably wouldn't have known the difference. Why hadn't she?

Because I wanted to make love with him.

There. She had admitted it.

She raised her head and stared at the creek as though expecting it to debate with her. It continued on its unconcerned trickling course toward lower ground.

Kyla had wanted him to make love to her since the kiss following the baseball game. That kiss had been a turning point. Even now, she could remember exactly how he'd

looked as he came jogging toward her, limping more than usual after the exertion of the game.

His grin had been a wide, white swath beneath his mustache. Pointed clumps of black hair, wet with perspiration, had striped his forehead. The waistband of his cutoffs had been damp with sweat, stretched and slightly curled away from his navel. His legs, even the scarred left one, rippled and bunched with sinewy muscles as he came toward her.

Never had she seen a man so rawly masculine. Trevor epitomized the male animal and everything inside her that was woman gravitated toward it as surely as the creek flowed toward the lake.

The kiss he had pressed onto her mouth had been salty, gritty. The sweat that had plastered down his chest hair also plastered her to his chest. When she felt his hands, powerful and manly, anchoring her against his aroused manhood, she had known then that she wanted him, and that she would have him, by her own design, if not by his.

Later, when he had started kissing her breasts, she wished with all her might that nothing would interrupt this time.

Call it wicked.

Call it unfaithfulness to Richard.

Call it what you like, but she had wanted to feel Trevor Rule inside her.

"Kyla?"

She jumped and whipped her head around. Trevor was standing behind her wearing only his cutoffs, the shadow of a beard and a wary expression.

"Hi."

"Are you all right?"

She returned her gaze to the creek, finding it difficult to look at him after last night. Her chest hurt with the effort to breathe. "Yes, I'm fine. I woke up early and the morning was so pretty.... Is Aaron awake?"

"He wasn't when I left."

"I guess yesterday wore him out."

"I guess so."

He crouched down beside and slightly behind her. Idly he plucked bunches of grass, examined them, then scattered the blades back onto the ground. "What time are you going to work this morning?"

"I'm not. Babs and I traded off, last Saturday for today. That's why I was in no hurry to get Aaron up."

He acknowledged the information with a brief nod and stood up again. He was restless. Neither was talking about what was most on their minds.

From the corner of her eye Kyla saw him wander toward a tree. He stopped. He turned and looked back at her. When he finally got to the tree, he raised his arms and propped them on one of the lowest branches slightly above him. He draped his wrists over the rough bark and hung his head to stare at the ground.

She laid her head back on her knees and prayed for something to break the silence.

"Did last night really happen, Kyla?"

Just as she had always thought, God had a sense of humor. Be careful what you pray for.

She glanced in Trevor's direction. He was now pinching pieces of bark off the oak and flicking them into the water. "Don't you remember?"

"I remember either an incredibly erotic dream—" he took a deep breath "—or the best thing that's ever happened to me." Her head came around quickly, swinging her hair like a red-gold cloak around her shoulders. He saw the tears standing in her eyes. A spasm of monumental regret twisted his features. "God, I'm sorry."

"It's all right."

"The hell it is."

"No, really."

"I was drunk."

"You were relaxed".

"Did I hurt you?"

"No."

"Force you?"

"No."

"Was I abusive?"

"No."

"Because I could never forgive—"

"Trevor, I wanted to!"

The hundred and one apologies he had cataloged in his mind, died on his lips. "You did?"

"Yes." She drew a shuddering breath and started plucking at the same grass he had deserted. "I've been doing some thinking."

"About what?"

"That you might . . . might want other children, other than Aaron, I mean. Some, at least one, of your own. It would have been unfair of me to . . . to withhold—"

Her lips were stopped by a long, tanned finger being laid against them. No longer could she avoid that piercing green eye. It beamed straight into her soul. "I would like to have at least one child of my own. And I appreciate your willingness to accommodate me. But is that the real reason you wanted to make love to me?"

"No," she whispered, shaking her head. "I just didn't know what else to say."

"Why did you want to make love with me, drunken and stupid as I know I must have been?"

She turned her cheek into the palm that had provided a resting place for it. Her eyes closed and two of the tears that had collected in her eyes rolled down her cheek. But when she opened her eyes, she was smiling. "You weren't drunken and stupid."

"Could've fooled me."

Laughing, she reached up and touched his hair affectionately. "You were as you've been since I first met you."

"Which is?"

"Kind, generous, fun to be around."

"Please, no more. I don't want to get a swelled head. But are you describing me or Santa Claus?" He assumed the wheedling expression of a little boy asking for one more piece of candy. "Don't I have any attributes of a more romantic nature?"

Her laughter was as sparkling as the creek water in the sunlight. "Need your ego stroked?"

"For starters," he drawled.

She shot him a shy look, but continued playing the game. "All right. What do you want to hear? That you're dashing and as handsome as the devil? That my best friend thinks you're a hunk and a stud, but a nice stud and that's rare?"

"Your best friend? How she'd get in here? I want to know what you think."

"All of the above," Kyla confessed in a raspy voice.

"Is there more?" His nose got lost in the loose curls above her ear.

"Should I go so far as to say that the mere sight of your body sets my blood on fire?"

"Sounds good to me."

Her head fell back when his lips found her throat. "You're incredibly good looking and sexy and—" She clamped her lower lip with her teeth.

"And?" he prodded, bringing her head up to meet his gaze.

"And," she added slowly, "I'm very glad I'm married to you."

He called upon a deity, whether in prayer or vain, Kyla was never sure. He applied the lightest pressure to her shoulder and she lay down on the towel. He followed her down, partially covering her body with his.

"I love you, Kyla Rule."

Her arms folded across his back. Their bare legs entwined. What their bodies had done only hours before, their mouths now reenacted.

"You're taking the day off?" he asked gruffly several moments later.

"Uh-huh."

"Then so am I. But let's get Aaron up, feed him and take him to the day-care center anyway."

"Why?"

Her husband grinned down into her face with a roguish gleam that made her heart flutter and her thighs liquefy. "Because I want to spend all day in bed tumbling my wife."

" ... Yes, yes ... "

"Like that?"

"Yes!"

"I'm afraid when I press so deep, I'm hurting you."

"No ... It ... ah ... Trevor ... yes ... "

"Sweetheart ... Kyla ... I can't ... How much longer do you think? ... "

"Not yet. I want it to last forever."

"So do I, but ... "

"Now, now, now ... "

"You're so beautiful."

"You make me feel beautiful. And naughty."

"Naughty?"

"I've never been set in front of a mirror to be admired. It's decadent, isn't it?"

"Purely. But this way I can see all of you at once. Lift your arms."

"How? Like this?"

"Perfect. Did you breast-feed Aaron?"

"For a while. Why?"

"Just wondering. Your breasts are so pretty. Did I say something wrong?"

"No, it's just—"

"What?"

"Some of the things you say embarrass me."

"Don't be embarrassed. I love you. Does it bother you for me to touch you like this?"

"Bother me? Hardly, I ... ah ..."

"Oh, God, look at you. I barely touch you and ..."

"You know just how to touch me ... how to ..."

"You taste like milk."

"Use your mustache—"

"Sweet, sweet milk."

"And your tongue—"

"You taste like Kyla."

"So don't say it's ugly."

"Every man should have a left side with a racetrack carved into it."

"Do the scars ever hurt?"

"No."

"Never?"

"Well, sometimes."

"Why does this one curve all the way from your spine to your sternum?"

"Right now I'm glad it's there."

"Glad?"

"Yes. Because your lips feel so good against my chest."

"I'd kiss it even without the scar."

"Would you, love?"

"Yes. I've wanted to kiss your chest for a long time."

"That's not my chest any longer. That's my navel."

"Close enough."

"Speaking of close ... hmm, hon ..."

"You got me off the subject. Why did they cut you like that?"

"I was bleeding internally from several organs."

"Oh, Lord."

"It's all right. Just keep doing what you're doing and I don't even remember it."

"Like this?"

"Oh, baby, that feels good. Kyla... Kyla... Oh, sweet-heart, oh... That's the first time you've touched me."

"The first time I saw you—"

"Yes?"

"When you got out of the hot tub—"

"Yes?"

"You were breathtaking."

"No, this is breathtaking.... The way you're touching me now... that's breathtaking."

"...but I told Babs there was no way I would sneak onto the bus with the football team."

"You were a good girl."

"I was a coward, always afraid of getting into trouble. So I rode home with the band where we belonged."

"And Babs?"

"How did you find that little patch of freckles?"

"Just lucky, I guess."

"That's my birthmark."

"Yes. Now tell me about Babs."

"Well, when we got back to the school, she came off the bus with this guy she had previously called an 'ugly moose.' She was wearing a... I don't know... a *look*, and I knew what had happened. That's also when I knew that she and I were different. I couldn't just have sex for the sake of sex."

"Damn! Sure about that?"

"Trevor, stop it now. I thought we were going to talk."

"Then stop lying there looking so delectable. All right, I'm sorry. Let's talk."

"I forgot what we were talking about."

"Were you a virgin when you got married?"

"The first or second time?"

"Very funny. Answer the question."

"That's not what we were talking about."

"You're right. Sorry I asked. It isn't any of my business."

"Yes, I was a virgin."

"You almost sound ashamed of it."

"I'm afraid you'll be turned off by my lack of experience."

"Would I be doing this if I were turned off?"

"I don't know which I like best. What you're doing or the expression on your face while you're doing it."

"Look at the way it curls around my fingers. It's such a pretty color. And soft. And so is this."

"Trevor...what?..."

"Relax."

"But what...No!"

"I want to."

"No, I..."

"Please, Kyla, let me love you."

"But...oh, my God...Trevor?..."

"Yes, love, yes. You're infinitely sweet."

"No more, please. I can't stand it. My sides are hurting."

"One more. This one's about a man who goes into a pet store to buy a parrot."

"Trevor, I mean it now, no more of your dirty jokes."

"You're laughing."

"That's my point. I shouldn't be. I'm a lady."

"How can you pretend to be a lady while you're straddling my lap and I'm making lunch out of your nipples?"

"Trevor!"

"Ouch, hon. Be still or you'll cripple me more than I already am. On the other hand, go ahead and squirm. They look damn cute when they jiggle."

"You're outrageous."

"Wait till you hear the joke."

"There's no stopping you?"

"No. Now be a good wife and listen. The guy goes into the pet store and... Kyla, I thought I told you to be still. This guy goes into the pet store and the owner says, 'I've

got this terrific parrot.' 'Can he talk?' the man asks. Kyla, you're asking for big trouble. Now stop that. 'Sure he can talk,' the pet store owner says, 'but there's one problem.' Kyla, I'm warning you. 'What's the problem?' the guy asks. 'The parrot can talk, but he hasn't got any feet.' Kyla . . . So the guy says, 'Then how does he stay on his perch?' And the pet store owner says . . . Oh, to hell with it.''

"That's the joke?"

"No, but I just thought of a better punch line."

"That was the hardest part to accept. There was nothing the Marines could send me. No mementos. Nothing. It was as though he had never existed. That broke my heart. There wasn't even enough of him to fill the casket.''

"Don't, don't, sweetheart."

"He deserved a better death. And dealing with the military was frustrating. They couldn't or wouldn't tell us anything for security reasons. The details were so sketchy.''

"For instance?"

"Richard wasn't even in his own bunk that morning. Why? Why didn't a single thing belonging to him survive the blast? I wanted something tangible, something of his that I could hold in my hand. A razor. A wristwatch. Anything.''

"Shh, shh. If it's going to upset you, don't talk about it anymore."

"It's not as painful as it sounds. In fact it feels good to talk about it. And you're a dear to listen.''

"I love you, Kyla. We've needed to talk about Richard. I wanted both of us to have the freedom of speaking his name out loud.''

"I loved him, Trevor."

"I know."

"And do you know that I love you? I didn't think I could ever love another man, but I love you. I just realized it. I love you! Trevor, are you crying?"

"I love you so much, Kyla."

"You won't ever leave me, will you?"

"Not a chance."

"Swear it."

"Never."

"I can't believe it's raining."

"Just an afternoon thundershower. It'll be over soon. Then we'll dress and go get Aaron."

"But not yet. Let's enjoy the rain."

"Rain is no fun unless it can be shared."

"How do you do that?"

"What?"

"Read my mind."

"Do I?"

"From the very beginning, you seemed to know what I was thinking. How?"

"Because I love you."

"Yes, but—"

"Turn around, Kyla."

"I don't understand how you—"

"Are we going to make love one more time before we go get Aaron or not?"

"Hmm, Trevor, not fair. You know when you touch me there I melt."

"Where? Here?"

"Yes, yes."

"And when I kiss you there?"

"I die a little."

"Then kiss me at the same time and we'll die a little together."

Huntsville, Alabama
A letter was mailed.

Humming, Kyla checked the pot roast. Even Meg Powers would have been proud of it. Kyla replaced the lid on the roaster and turned off the heat in the oven. It would keep warm until Trevor and Aaron returned. Trevor had taken the child with him to run an errand, leaving Kyla at home to prepare dinner, a task she now took pleasure in.

In fact she was finding pleasure in just about everything she did these days. For the past three weeks, since Labor Day and the night following, she had lived in a bubble of happiness.

"A few days off has certainly done wonders for you!" Babs had exclaimed the day Kyla went back to work after the holiday. "You're shining like a new penny. And I'd be willing to bet that Trevor is the one who polished you to that glow."

Kyla's laugh at the ribaldry had been lusty. "You're right, I'm in love."

"Well it's catching, because Trevor has already called twice to see if you'd arrived yet, and he said to give you a kiss for him when you did, which I refused to do. What's happened to the two of you?"

"Nothing," Kyla lied airily, as she reached for the telephone to return Trevor's call. It had been all of half an hour since she had seen him.

"I'll bet you've been renting X-rated movies for the home VCR."

"Nope."

"You ordered that kit of marital aids I showed you in *Playgirl*? What did Trevor think of the edible panties?"

"Will you hush!" Kyla had said, laughing. "I did no such thing." Then into the telephone she said, "Hi, darling. You called?"

"You're taking ginseng tablets?" Babs had persisted. "Feeding him oysters on the half shell every night?"

"No! I'm sorry, Trevor. Babs just wanted to know if I was feeding you oysters on the half shell every night....
What?... No, I can't tell her that.... No... Oh, all right. Babs, Trevor said to tell you that if he were eating oysters on the half shell every night, we'd have to buy a new mattress. Now be quiet, please. I told you I'm in love and I want to talk to my husband.''

And I am in love, Kyla thought happily, as she went through the living room, picking up the toys Aaron had left in his wake. Noticing the unopened mail lying on the hall table, she took it into the kitchen on her return trip and sat at the bar on a high stool to sort through it while waiting for her men to come home.

One envelope in particular caught her eye. It was from the Marine Corps. Slashing it open, she found another envelope inside with *Please forward* stamped on it. The name printed in the upper left-hand corner sparked her memory, but she didn't recall why until she noticed the return address. Huntsville, Alabama. Hadn't one of Richard's friends been from Huntsville, Alabama? Curious, she slit open that second envelope and took out the single sheet of plain white stationery. A photograph dropped to the bar.

The letter was brief. It introduced the sender, who expressed sympathy over Richard's death. It explained that the sender had recently found the photograph and thought that Kyla might like to have it. It ended with a heartfelt wish for her future happiness.

Laying aside the letter, she picked up the snapshot. Smiling at her from the center of a trio of Marines was Richard Stroud. He looked just as she last remembered him. He had a military haircut, high over his ears and short on top. He was in his full dress uniform, but there was a jocular smile on his face, as though someone had said something exceptionally funny just before the shutter was snapped. The lens had captured Richard's sweet, spontaneous smile.

He was standing between two other Marines. Their arms were companionably resting on each other's shoulders. The sender of the picture had considerately captioned it for Kyla. He had identified himself as the man on Richard's right. He had an open, down-home face, a toothy grin and big ears. One wouldn't hesitate to buy a used car from a man with a face that honest.

Kyla's eyes slid to the other side of the picture. "Smooch" had been neatly printed under the man on Richard's left. One would be wise to exercise caution before buying a used car from him.

Could anyone that good-looking be trustworthy? He had the grin of a hungry alligator, a brilliant white smile that slashed across his darkly tanned face. Mischievous green eyes viewed the world through spiky black lashes. He looked ready to wink, and Kyla got the distinct impression that he had made the funny remark that the other two men were laughing at. Smooch's smile was smug, unapologetically arrogant, indubitably conceited.

And familiar.

It was her husband's smile.

There could be no mistake. Even with the skinhead haircut of a Marine, without the eye patch, without the curving mustache, there was no mistaking that smile.

Kyla dropped the photograph as though it had burned her fingers. She stared down at it where it lay on the bar, but couldn't bring herself to touch it again.

There had to be a logical explanation. Richard and Trevor arm in arm? Trevor a Marine? How had a picture of Trevor come to be captioned "Smooch," a nickname she remembered well from Richard's letters to her from Egypt?

Smooch was the womanizer. The shameless playboy. The friend of Richard's she knew she couldn't stomach should they ever meet.

And she was married to him.

The implications associated with that rushed at her like a swarm of killer bees. She covered her head. She bit her lower lip to catch the sob that rose out of her chest. She forced down the scalding bile that suddenly filled the back of her throat.

There had to be some explanation. Of course there was. Trevor would come in and see the picture and say something like, "Gee, that's spooky. Can you believe that guy looks so much like me?" Or, "They say everyone in the world has a twin. Guess this Smooch is mine." Or, "It's amazing what they can do with trick photography these days."

It had to be a mistake.

But there was no mistake and she knew it.

She heard his pickup pull into the driveway. Her insides were roiling, her blood was churning, her head was thundering, but on the outside, she looked as immovable as a wood carving.

"Before you get mad," Trevor began the moment he stepped through the door, "Aaron and I took a vote and decided unanimously that it wasn't too close to dinner for him to have a cookie. So we broke open the package on the way home. That's why his shirt—What's the matter?" He had chanced to glance up and noticed her condemning expression. Cookie-smeared hands didn't warrant the intensity of it. "Kyla?"

He moved toward her and when he reached the bar, he saw the picture. He muttered an obscenity and spun around. Reciting a dictionary of curses, he went to stand in front of the windows. Shoulders hunched, he slid his hands, palms out, into the back pockets of his jeans.

"Come here, Aaron." With much more composure than she felt, Kyla picked up her son. She felt like screaming until she couldn't draw another breath, like bashing her head against the wall, like bashing Trevor's against it.

Lifting Aaron to the sink, she washed his face and hands, then set him on the kitchen floor and surrounded

him with brightly colored plastic measuring cups, which were among his favorite playthings.

Finally she returned to the bar, picked up the snapshot and studied it for a moment before she said, "You take a good picture."

Trevor came around slowly, pivoting on the heels of his western boots, which Kyla knew now were as false and phony and affected as everything else about him.

"So now you know."

"Yes, I know," she snapped. "It's true what they say, isn't it? Clichés always have an element of truth to them. The wife is always the last to know."

"I would have told you."

"When, Trevor? When? When we're old and gray? When I was too feeble to hate you with every fiber of my being as I do now?"

"Me or what I've done?"

"Both! I can't stand the sight of you. *Smooch*!"

She uttered the name as though it were the most loathsome epithet. He winced. "I knew how you felt about Smooch. That's why I never came right out and introduced myself to you."

She laughed, a bit hysterically. "Smooch. I'm married to Smooch, a man known for his sexual conquests. A man who would tumble anything in skirts because all cats are gray in the dark."

"Kyla—"

"Didn't you tell Richard that once?"

"Yes, but that was before—"

"I don't want to hear it," she shouted, slicing the air with her hands. "I don't want any explanations from you except one. Why did you do this? What purpose did it serve? What sick, sick game have you been playing?"

"It isn't a game." His reasonable tone contrasted jarringly with her shrill one. "It was never a game. Not from the beginning."

She reined in her temper and drew in several restorative breaths. "And just when was that? I assume our meeting wasn't accidental."

"No."

"Then when did this start?"

"When I woke up in a hospital in West Germany and discovered I was alive. Missing an eye, injured almost beyond repair, but alive."

"What did that have to do with me?"

He took a step toward her. "You wanted to know why Richard wasn't sleeping in his bunk." She nodded, though no question had actually been asked. "I came in drunk the night before the attack on the embassy. Richard helped me get undressed. I barely remember it, but I do remember falling into his bunk. He was sleeping in mine when that bomb went off."

One hand flew to her mouth, the other gripped her stomach. Tears sprang to her eyes.

"My sentiments exactly," Trevor said grimly. "When I realized that Richard had been killed in my place I didn't care if I lived or died." He looked away, reliving all the pain, literally feeling it rack his body again, reducing him, making him less than a man. "But I lived. With the help of an orderly who befriended me I found out about you and Aaron. When I was well enough to leave the hospital, I came looking for you."

Kyla folded her arms across her stomach. She paced the length of the bar, rocking slightly forward and back from the waist, as though excruciating pains were tearing her insides to shreds.

When she rounded on him, she cried, "In my opinion you have carried your military duty too far. You went above and beyond the call. I don't want a husband who married me out of a sense of obligation, thank you very much!"

Her voice was so loud and vitriolic that Aaron stopped tapping the cups against the floor and looked up at her. His bottom lip began to quiver. "Ma-ma."

Wrested from a pit of humiliation by the tremulous sound of her child's voice, Kyla knelt down beside him and smoothed her hand over his head. "It's all right, darling. Play with your cups. See? Oopsy-daisy. They fell over. Stack them back up for Mommy."

Temporarily mollified, Aaron went back to his play. Kyla faced Trevor again. His face was almost as stony as hers. His lips barely moved. "It isn't like that."

"Then tell me what it's like," she sneered. "Tell me what motivated you to move here and seduce me into—"

"*Marriage*, Kyla," he said with angry emphasis. "What's so dishonorable about that?"

"Because it was all a setup. I can't believe I was gullible enough to fall for it, to fall for you. Your manners, your concern for Aaron, your instant attraction to me, your...your everything. Your damn conservative car! You stepped straight out of the Widow's Guide for A Dream Second Husband, didn't you? Why did you go to so much trouble? What made you do it?"

"I love you."

She stretched her arms out in front of her as though warding him off. "Don't...don't you dare play word games with me." She virtually spat out the words because she didn't want to alarm Aaron with her loud voice again.

"I'm not, Kyla. I was and am in love with you."

"That's impossible."

He shook his head adamantly. "There's one essential part of this story that you don't know yet."

"Then pray tell me what it is."

"Your letters."

She fell silent, dumbfounded by what he'd just said. "My letters?"

"Your letters to Richard."

She sank onto the stool as she stared up at the man who had reverted from a loving husband into a stranger again. It had happened so quickly. Seeing the picture of him had ripped the rug out from under her. Now she felt as though the floor had just dropped away. When would she hit bottom?

"You read them?" she asked with an inflection that clearly indicated she thought that was the most heinous crime he had committed so far.

"They were sent to me by mistake when I was in the hospital." He told her about the metal box and of his granting Richard the favor of using it. "When they sent me my belongings, that box was among them. I opened it and, yes, Kyla, I read your love letters to your husband."

He reached across the bar and covered her hands with his own. "I don't expect you to understand, but I swear to you, I credit those letters with keeping me alive. Every precious word did me more good than any medicine, any surgery, any therapy. They made me want to live again, so that I could meet the woman who wrote them. I memorized each one of them. I could recite them word for word to you now. They're engraved on my mind more deeply than the Pledge of Allegiance or the Lord's Prayer. They—"

"Oh, please. Save it for your next victim." She snatched her hands from beneath his. "I don't want to hear it. Do you think I'd ever believe another word you said after the way you've tricked me?"

"I didn't think of it as tricking you, Kyla."

"No? The orchids, the house." Coming off the stool she began to pace again. "Everything. It all falls into place now. The way you seemed to read my mind. And all the time you *knew*. You knew because you had read my letters."

"And responded to what they said."

"No wonder you could manipulate me so effortlessly."

"I was giving you what was in my power to give."

"Courting me and being so nice to my parents and—"
Suddenly, her body yanked to attention. Her brown eyes
narrowed as she glared at him. "My parents. *You* managed to get their property rezoned at such a propitious
time, didn't you?"

He closed the space between them in three long steps and
laid his hands on her shoulders. "Now, Kyla, before—"

She flung off his hands. "Didn't you?"

"All right, yes!" he shouted back.

"And the sale of their house? The sale that we all mar-
veled over because it commanded such a premium price.
The sale that went through in record time without a hitch
just in time for our wedding. You arranged all that, too,
didn't you?"

His face was closed and hard and as guilty as sin.

"I see," she said on a soft laugh. "Well it's no wonder
you felt like you could marry me and take Aaron to raise.
You had bought and paid for us, hadn't you?" Her hands
were running up and down her arms vigorously, as though
washing away a feeling of uncleanliness.

"Stop that. Damn it, I've told you that I love you."

"I can't tell you what a comfort that is coming from a
man known to his cronies as Smooch."

"Those days are over."

"No doubt they are. But you went out with a bang,
didn't you? You made certain that your final conquest was
a woman most unlikely to refuse you, a poor lonely widow
lady with a child to raise. Come on, Trevor, confess. Didn't
you think, in that manipulative, conniving, devious mind
of yours, that I might accept you when other women
would scorn you now that you aren't quite so handsome?
Widows are more desperate for a man, aren't they?
Wouldn't poor little Kyla Stroud be so anxious for a man
to take care of her that she would overlook an eye patch
and a limping, scarred body?"

She wouldn't let herself feel ashamed for the flicker of
emotion that crossed his face.

"That's not true."

"Isn't it? When you were once again sure of your sex appeal, how did you plan to dispose of Aaron and me? Or did you plan to? Was I to be so grateful for what you did to me in our bed, that I'd overlook what you did in others'?"

His head dropped forward. "What do you want from me, Kyla?"

"I want you to leave me alone." She picked Aaron off the floor, protectively hugged him to her chest and stormed to the back door. "You've done so much for me, Trevor. You've lied and manipulated my future. You married me out of pity and because you were afraid that I was the only woman who would have you now. But there's one more thing you can do for me, Mr. Rule. You can get the hell out of my life."

Chapter 14

You're just plain stupid, you know that?"

Babs had sat enthralled while Kyla poured out the entire ugly story. She had arrived on Babs's doorstep an hour earlier. To say she was upset was putting it mildly. Aaron had been fed a grilled cheese sandwich, bathed, dressed in one of Babs's T-shirts and diapered from a supply that Babs kept for his visits. He was sold on the idea that it would be great fun to sleep in Aunt Babs's bed, and that was where he was.

In the living room of the small apartment, Babs sat on the floor, legs crossed, while Kyla occupied a corner of the short sofa. Two glasses of white wine stood on the coffee table.

Kyla had fully expected Babs to share her outrage over Trevor's treachery, taking up arms if necessary to railroad him out of town. "Stupid?" she repeated, thinking she'd heard Babs wrong.

"Stupid. Dumb. A real... Oh, never mind," Babs said irritably, getting to her feet. "I'm going to bed."

"Wait a minute," Kyla exclaimed. "Haven't you listened to a single word I've said?"

"Every self-pitying syllable."

"And that's all you can say about it?"

"That's all I'm going to say about it. If you expect me to sit here with you and hash over what a louse Trevor Rule is, then you're in for a disappointment."

"But he is! Didn't I just tell you—"

"Yeah, yeah, you told me all about it. About how he woke up in a military hospital on foreign soil, half-blind, half-paralyzed, not knowing if he was going to live or die, and if he did live, if he'd be able to crawl, much less walk, much less make love or anything else a normal man has the privilege of doing. He woke up to find out that his friends had been blown to kingdom come by a bunch of fanatics, but miraculously his life had been spared. But to an insensitive cad like our Trevor, I doubt that bothered him much."

Scorn dripped from her voice like the water from the wineglass she had just rinsed out in the kitchen sink.

Stung by Babs's sarcasm, Kyla said, "All right, I'll concede that physically he had a difficult time."

"Now don't go exaggerating things, Kyla."

"It was *hellish*, okay? But what about the letters? Reading them, memorizing them like some pervert."

"The creep! How could he do something like that? Even Van Johnson never did anything that sentimental in his movies. Imagine Trevor doing something that horrible. Imagine him having the nerve to rearrange his future just so he could be near the woman who composed those letters. Imagine him, a man who could have had any woman he wanted with a crook of his finger and a come-hither look, going to all that trouble to meet you, his soul mate. And he didn't even have the decency to lure you into his bed first. No, he had to go and marry you!"

"Only out of pity," Kyla tightly reminded her unsympathetic friend. "Only to pay me back for Richard's death because he felt responsible."

"Right, so he'd be considered a martyr. Any other man would have come to see you, paid you his respects, humbly apologized for being alive when your husband was dead, offered you his help, probably his money, and when you refused he would have gone away with his conscience salved. But not Trevor. Oh, no. No doubt he wanted the world to think he was a do-gooder. So he hung around and got to know you, married you, took your son under his wing and built you a house a Rockefeller wouldn't be ashamed to claim." She made a tsking sound and shook her head. "What a creepy, sneaky heel. What a rat."

"You don't think it was sneaky the way he manipulated the rezoning of my parents' property?" Kyla exploded angrily. "You don't think it was underhanded the way he helped push the sale of their house through?"

"What a dastardly deed," Babs cried, shielding her eyes with her arms and feigning horror. "He handled all the dirty work so they wouldn't be bothered with it. He exacted a top price for their property, closed the sale and got them on their way to doing what they'd been wanting to do for years. The man has no heart. And the way he treats Aaron is positively sickening. Doesn't he know that most fathers don't treat their natural children that well? If he wanted to be a real father to the boy he should throw in a few harsh words, a little neglect, a lot of impatience."

"Enough, Babs. Soon I'll have to roll up my pant leg." Kyla rubbed her throbbing temples. "I might have known you'd take up for him."

"Take up for a louse like that? No way. If I were doing that, I'd probably tell you straight out what a selfish bitch you are."

"Selfish?"

"You wouldn't know something good if it came up to you on the street and bit you in the butt. If I were taking

Trevor's side, I'd point out that some people prefer martyrdom to happiness."

"Stop it!"

"It's safer. There's no risk involved. When you don't love, you don't risk losing."

"You've got stars in your eyes for him. That's what this sermonizing is about. You've had a crush on him from the beginning."

"Granted. I've always had a weak spot for hunks with a sentimental streak."

"Well, the two of you would get along great. You both think with your genitals."

Babs sucked in her breath and held it for a long time. Gradually she let it go, but her body remained rigid. "Before I smack you, which is something I've miraculously restrained myself from doing so far tonight, I'm going to bed. Aaron, whose mature company I much prefer over yours, can sleep with me. You, my friend, can fend for yourself."

"Come back here. You can't just walk away from a fight."

"Watch me."

"I'm sorry for what I said. That was dreadful and I didn't mean it. Babs, please, tell me what to do."

Babs spun around and confronted her. "All right, you asked for it, here it is. You're not fighting with me, Kyla, you're fighting with yourself. And it's not me you're angry with. You're not even angry with Trevor. You're mad at yourself."

"What do you mean?"

"You were the Honor Society student. You figure it out. Now, good night."

Babs went down the hall and closed the bedroom door behind her. Tears smarted in Kyla's eyes as she returned to the living room. She prowled it aimlessly, nursing her indignation with self-pity.

So much for friendship. She felt betrayed. Murky waters could be closing over her head for the third time while she waved frantically at the shore where Babs stood mocking her, and she wouldn't feel more forsaken.

She had counted on Babs's unqualified allegiance. She had expected Babs to rally to her side and chant like a cheerleader, "That's a girl, that's telling him. Way to go. Right on." Instead Babs's sympathy had lain solely with Trevor.

Kyla flopped down on the couch and took a hefty draft of wine. "No wonder," she mumbled. Babs was female. She had fallen under *Smooch*'s spell. She, like hundreds before her, had been dazzled. That was it. Babs had become a traitor over a pair of muscular biceps and a dark curving mustache. What was loyalty to a friend when weighed against the way Smooch filled out his jeans?

Scoffing, Kyla took another sip of wine.

And what had she meant by the crack about Kyla being mad at herself?

Nothing. Absolutely nothing. Babs loved to drop little half-finished, underdeveloped tidbits of thought like that into conversations like spoonfuls of cookie dough onto a baking sheet. And that's what they were, half-baked.

But if that were so, why did she keep dwelling on it?

Why was she giving any thought to the possibility that she *was* angry with herself? What did she have to be mad at herself for?

For falling in love with Trevor.

She slammed the glass of wine onto the coffee table and stamped to the window. Pulling viciously on the cord of the blinds, she raised them to peer out. She saw nothing but her own image reflected in the glass. Face to face with herself, she was forced to argue.

Admittedly she was smitten by him. She wasn't immune to a nice pair of biceps either. And what about his generosity? And his constant kindness? And his lovemaking?

To stifle a sob, she crammed her fist against her lips. She didn't want any reminders of the way she had gloried in his tender loving. Guilt had a brassy taste. Somewhere along the way, living with and loving Trevor had become more important than keeping Richard alive in her heart. She had let the signal fire go out and that was an unpardonable offense.

Babs was right. She was angry with herself for loving him despite it all.

She couldn't hold it against him that he'd been in Richard's bunk the morning the embassy was bombed. That had been a quirk of fate. He hadn't used her letters to exploit her, but to grant her her heart's desire. He was an exemplary parent to Aaron. He was ambitious and successful, but not one of those men enslaved to his work for the sake of making a buck.

True, he had lied by not telling her that he had known Richard. Yet if he had introduced himself as Smooch, she would have run just as hard and fast as she could, and forever been without him. If he had married her out of a sense of duty, then he was an actor of Olivier's caliber.

Love like that which Trevor had given her couldn't be faked, nor could it be summoned on command. It had to come from the heart.

If a love was that strong, what could be wrong with it?

She fled Babs's apartment. Once in the car, a thousand possibilities flickered through her mind like insects caught in a headlight's beam. What if he had already left? What if she had lost her love for the second time? The first time, she had had no control over the loss. But this time she would have thrown it away.

As Babs had said, she was just plain stupid.

She released her pent-up breath on a wave of relief when she saw both his car and his pickup still parked in the driveway of the house. Entering through the front door, she saw that there was a feeble light on in the bedroom and rushed toward it.

Trevor was sitting on the edge of the bed, his head bent over a sheet of paper, which had been folded so many times that the creases were worn thin. She recognized it as one of her letters. Others were untidily stacked at his side. The light she had seen came from the fireplace where an unseasonable fire was burning. He was reading by firelight.

He glanced up when he heard her come in. His inquiring gaze held hers until she reached him, then she looked down at the frayed letter. Taking it from his hand, she read it. When she came to the line that said, "He sounds like the kind of man I detest," her eyes clouded with tears.

Moving quickly, she snatched up the scattered letters one by one, envelopes included, until she had them all. Crossing the room, she moved aside the brass fire screen and threw them onto the dying fire.

"Kyla, no!"

The paper caught, crackled and curled, making a pastel pyre atop the logs. The flames were short-lived. Within moments the letters burned themselves out, shooting sparks up the chimney.

Kyla's face was streaked with tears when she turned to face him. "You don't need another man's leftovers, Trevor. If you want to know what I think, what I feel, ask me. Let me open my heart to you. Richard..." She paused and drew a deep, rattling breath. Her nails bit into her palms. It was the most painful thing she had ever had to say, but she finally voiced the truth that she had ignored for so long. "Richard is dead. I loved him. We created another human being through that love. I'll always be grateful that Aaron is a living testimony to it. But Richard is gone. I love you."

"Kyla." His voice broke on her name.

She threw herself into his arms. They wrapped around her, drawing her small frame against his. He buried his face in her neck. "I love you, Trevor. To know it, all you have to do is look at me. Read it in my eyes."

"No, don't leave me," she protested. With amazing strength, she clasped his thighs between hers.

"Aren't I getting heavy?"

"I like it."

"You're weird." He raised his head from the pillow to smile down at her.

"*I'm* weird? You're the one who fell in love with a woman through her letters to another man." She angled her head back to see him better. "What if I'd been a troll?"

"If you'd been a troll, if you'd been anything except exactly what you are, I would have introduced myself, offered my condolences, offered my financial assistance and bade you farewell."

"That's what Babs said."

"She did?"

"When she was still speaking to me, that is."

"Have I missed something?"

"I'll tell you all about it in the morning. Right now I'm busy." She allowed her tongue the unbridled pleasure of investigating his ear.

"I presume our son is safe," Trevor murmured around the tip of her breast, which responded beautifully.

"He's sleeping with Babs."

"You consider that safe?"

They laughed and when they did, Trevor grimaced. "Does that hurt?" she asked.

His lips tilted into that hungry alligator grin. "Laugh some more."

Instead they kissed. When she felt his body filling with renewed desire for her, she clasped his head with both hands and raised it above hers. "Forgive me. I said some terrible things to you. About your scars."

"I knew you didn't mean them."

"And about your eye patch." She touched his cheek lovingly. "I think I know why you chose that over a prosthesis."

"Why?"

"You wear it out of defiance of the disability it represents. It would have been easy for you to wear a glass eye, to cover your scars. But you never take the easy way, do you, Trevor?"

"Not anymore. I used to. Before this happened to me, I didn't take anything seriously. I thought life was a series of parties held in honor of me. I found out the hard way it just ain't so." He pondered his next thought as he let strands of her hair slide through his fingers. "Or maybe I used the patch as a shield. Beneath it is the ugliest scar of all. Maybe I was afraid that if you saw that, you'd see the ugliest part of me, which was my deception."

"No more secrets between us, Trevor."

"None. Never. All my defenses are down."

His fingers got lost in her hair and his voice turned soft and raspy. "You were justifiably furious, Kyla. I *did* trick you into marrying me. But after I saw you, and you were even more beautiful than the things you had written, I simply had to have you, by fair means or foul. It was never my intention to replace Richard in your heart, but to create a place there for myself."

"I guess your biggest transgression was impatience."

"How's that?"

"If you had introduced yourself as Smooch—"

"You would have hated me on sight."

"Initially, maybe. But not after I got to know you. What I'm trying to say is that I feel like this was inevitable."

"You mean that no matter how it came about, we would be married, lying here, doing this?" He moved inside her.

"Yes," she gasped softly. "Remember when you said that as long as there was someone else living inside me there was no room for you?"

Chagrined, he smiled lopsidedly. "Very crudely put, if my memory serves me."

"Crudely, but accurately." She touched his mouth with hers and left it there against his mustache. "You fill me completely, Trevor. Body, mind, and soul."

Then very gently, and with no interference from him, she threaded her fingers up through his hair and removed the eye patch.

Yes...Get 4 Silhouette Intimate Moments novels (a $10.00 value) and a Tote Bag FREE!

SLIP AWAY FOR AWHILE... Let Silhouette Intimate Moments novels draw you into a world of love and romance as it is experienced by real men and women. You'll find it's easy to close the door on the cares and concerns of everyday life as you lose yourself in the timeless drama of love, played out in exotic locations the world over.

EVERY BOOK AN ORIGINAL... Every Silhouette Intimate Moments novel is a full-length story, never before in print, superbly written to give you more of what you want from romance. Start with 4 new Silhouette Intimate Moments novels—a $10.00 gift from us to you—along with a free Tote Bag, with no obligation to buy another book now or ever.

YOUR FAVORITE AUTHORS... Let your favorite authors—such as Elizabeth Lowell, Maura Seger, Heather Graham Pozzessere, Erin St. Clair, Mary Lynn Baxter, and others—take you to a whole other world.

ROMANCE-FILLED READING... Each month you'll receive novels created especially for you—a woman who wants a more intense, passionate reading experience. Every book offers you romantic fantasy...dynamic, contemporary characters...involving stories...and stirring passion.

NO OBLIGATION ... Each month we'll send you 4 new Silhouette Intimate Moments novels as soon as they are published, without obligation. If not enchanted, simply return them within 15 days and owe nothing. Or keep them, and pay just $9.00 for all four books. And there's never an additional charge for shipping or handling.

SPECIAL EXTRAS FOR HOME SUBSCRIBERS ONLY ... When you take advantage of this offer and become a home subscriber, we'll also send you the Silhouette Books Newsletter FREE with each book shipment. Every informative issue features news about upcoming titles, interviews with your favorite authors, even their favorite recipes.

So send in the postage-paid card today, and take your fantasies further than they've ever been. The trip will do you good!

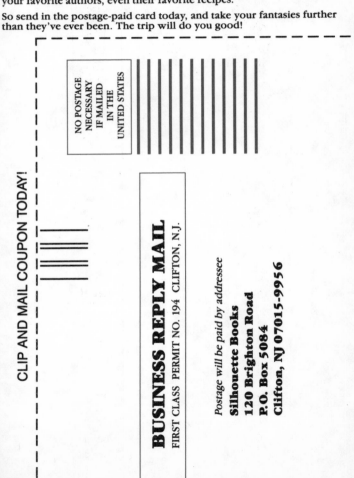

CLIP AND MAIL COUPON TODAY!

NO POSTAGE
NECESSARY
IF MAILED
IN THE
UNITED STATES

BUSINESS REPLY MAIL
FIRST CLASS PERMIT NO. 194 CLIFTON, N.J.

Postage will be paid by addressee

Silhouette Books
120 Brighton Road
P.O. Box 5084
Clifton, NJ 07015-9956